# dedication

To my daughters, Julia and Leah. May you always be confident and secure in your beautiful, remarkable, inspiring individuality. Never let anyone make you feel less than the perfection you are. And if by chance someone does, I'll kick their ass.

# chapter

## one

BIG BONED. PLUS-SIZED. JUNK IN the trunk. Muffin top. Thunder thighs. Chubster. *Fat.* I've heard it all over the course of my life because, unfortunately, that's what I am. There's no two ways around it or my frumpy, jiggly body. I am *not* the ideal. While the majority of Americans are tipping the scale these days, I'm still not considered the image of flawless beauty and sleek perfection most men desire. How do I know this, you ask? Well, because I'm single. Alone, unloved, unwanted. Twenty-five and on the road to spinsterhood. Heartbreaking, I know. But don't dwell on it. I don't. I mean, I guess that's what I'm doing right now, but that's only because the bitch in my chair just rudely pointed out the obvious.

"You have such a pretty face." I force an unenthusiastic smile, assuming she'll leave it at that, letting the unspoken words "if you only lost weight" dangle awkwardly between us. But nope. Not this time . . .

The Barbie doll-looking wench actually takes the liberty to

continue. "I bet you could be a model. You know, like for Lane Bryant or, *oh!!!* What about *Hips and Curves?* With your cheek bones and trendy style you could . . ." She rambles on and on about my finest qualities, all while sticking it to me about my unavoidable plumpness.

Nodding and yessing her to death, I go on with my work. Painting her face is effortless. I have a great canvas. Smooth ivory skin, neatly groomed brows, and lips that collagen freaks would pay insane amounts of money for. This chick is everything I wish I was. Blonde, blue-eyed, spunky, beautiful, and most importantly, *thin.*

As I brush her lids with a shimmery pink shadow, I allow my insecurities to get the best of me. Thousands of recurring promises to restart a diet, rejoin the gym, and revamp my life jog through my discouraged mind. I've been here before. A beautiful girl sits in my chair to be dolled up for a date or a wedding or *whatever* and I swear to myself I'll do everything in my power to look more like her.

But it never works. I don't have solid motivation. My parents love me as I am—they're great parents. Great, *overweight* parents. I'm perfect to them even if I can't squeeze my ass into a pencil skirt the way I long to. My best friend, Tatum, is the most non-judgmental person in the entire world. She has friends of all races, creeds, and sizes. Her last birthday get-together looked like a meeting between the United Nations and Ringling Brothers. No joke.

And then there's me. Don't get me wrong, I love so many things about my life. My job, my apartment, my family, my friends. Oh, and I have great hair—even if it's not the color of Goldilocks' here in my chair. Yes, thank you God for gracing me with a long flowing mane of hazelnut locks, but did you have to give me Mom's ass and Dad's sausage fingers? I mean, what do you have against me?

It's not God's fault I'm five foot six and over two hundred

and twenty pounds. And I should love myself no matter what. Be proud of my accomplishments and happy for what I do have. Unfortunately, I'm my own worst enemy. Positivity has never been my strong point. And goddamn it, sue me for loving food. I'm Italian. We eat. *A lot.* It's a lifestyle. And no amount of burpees or crunches can burn away the nine hundred course meal Mom makes every Sunday without fail. *Meatballs, pasta, prosciutto bread. Yum!*

"Hello?" The girl interrupts my drooling. "I think you're putting on a little too much liner."

I have a heavy hand but I know what I'm doing. Her eyes look sick. She should thank me for making the turquoise hue pop even brighter. I step back to appraise what looks like a makeup masterpiece. I'm usually all for what the client wants, but she looks gorgeous and I'd hate to erase what I've already done. "Would you mind letting me finish first? I think you'll really wind up li—"

"No! I said it's too much. Tristan *hates* too much. It's his birthday and I want to make sure he likes how I look." She fingers her hair and purses her lips.

I stop myself from rolling my eyes but try to convince her one more time. "I *promise* it won't be too much. In fact, I think your boyfriend will—"

Miss Prissy Pants releases a haughty laugh, snort and all. "Oh yeah? How would you know? You're a pretty girl but I don't see how someone like *you* would care about impressing anyone else."

*Whoa.* Did she just—? Yeah, she totally went there. I'd love to smack the MAC right off her face, but instead I take a cleansing breath and let it roll off my too-wide shoulders. *Kill her with kindness, Leni. The customer's always right.* "Of course. I'm sorry. Let me just grab some remover." I ignore the vein throbbing at my temple, telling me to get the tweezers and pluck this girl's brows to smithereens.

When I return to bitchface she's staring at herself in the vanity mirror, admiring my work. She likes it. I can tell. Usually when a client is unhappy they avoid the mirror after the first glance. She's turning her head to see her makeup at every angle. I might not look like her but that doesn't mean I'm not good at what I do.

"Um, you sure you don't want to keep it? If *you* like it, that's what matters. Don't settle for less just to impress your man." I don't know what's come over me or why I'm being so persistent but it has to have something to do with the irony of the situation. She's drop dead gorgeous, with or without makeup, and yet here she is worried about looking the way her boyfriend prefers. If she's not secure in her own skin, how can someone like me ever be?

She takes one more look, focusing her attention on the beautiful mixture of colors I've applied to her eyes. I expect her to storm out of my chair and demand a refund or another makeup artist, but to my surprise, she smiles and says, "You know what? You're right. It does look pretty awesome, if you ask me. Continue. I'm sorry I was such a bitch."

And with that, my faith in humanity is restored. It's not every day someone who looks like her is as nice on the inside as they are on the eyes. I smile back and keep on with my bad self and my mad cosmetology skills.

"MOM, DAD, LENI? YOU GUYS here?" My brother, Reynold, bursts through my parents' house, bellowing like, well, like Reynold. He's always making an entrance, no matter what the event. Today just happens to be any other ordinary Sunday dinner, but in true Reynold style he stumbles in like Cosmo Kramer and steals the attention of everyone around him.

"My baby boy!" Mom runs over to him and squeezes his

cheeks. They're covered in dark, prickly scruff. He's been grow-ing out his beard and taking the whole men-with-hair-do-it-bet-ter movement by the balls. I can't blame him; it totally suits him. He's really good looking and, geez, does he know it.

"Smells good, Ma. What time's dinner?" He beelines it to the stove and lifts the lid off the big pot to take a peek.

Mom scurries over and slaps his hand. "Leave it! And don't touch the bread. Your sister already ate half a loaf. Save some for dinner."

"Leni, I thought you were doing the no carb thing. What happened, babe?" Reynold sits next to me at the kitchen table, kissing my round cheek and punching me in the arm.

"I tried but carbs make me happy. Sorry not sorry."

"No, Leni! Carbs are the enemy. I gave you the list of the good ones. Come on! We've been over this a million times. Cut them out and you'll see a huge difference."

Leave it to my younger, in shape, muscular brother, to try to school me in the weight loss department. I know he means well and he has a point, but I'm not in the mood. "Can we not today? Please? For once? I just want to enjoy my pasta and my loaf of bread and be left alone." I had a rough morning—as in I ripped a pair of my favorite leggings pulling them up over my bubble butt—and I'm in desperate need of food therapy. Believe me, I know how ridiculous that sounds, but fuck off.

"Suit yourself, but you'll want to up your game *soon*," he sings, wiggling in his chair like he used to when he was a kid with an entertaining story to tell.

"And why's that?" I prod, wondering what the hell he's up to.

"Where's Dad? I wanted to wait for dinner to tell you guys, but I'm too excited."

"In the living room watching the game. *Dad!* Come in here, the Golden Child has news!" I holler in the direction of the den, envisioning Dad's huff as he hauls himself off the couch.

My father enters the kitchen, rubbing his beer belly. "This better be good. The Jets are finally coming back. Josie, can you grab me another cold one?"

My mom does as asked—good Italian wife that she is—and then joins us at the table to pet and adore her wonderful son. "So, what's up, Rey?"

"Yeah, what does any of your news have to do with me abandoning my beloved carbs?" I ask, curiosity eating away at me. *I wish it would eat away ten pounds while it's at it.*

"This!" Reynold pulls a black, velvet box from his pocket and slams it down on the table. He opens the square with a tiny squeak and a two-carat, princess cut diamond ring glistens under the light of Mom's Tiffany chandelier like a Baby-Jesus-in-the-manger miracle.

Mom gasps. "Oh, my baby boy! How wonderful! When? How? What can I cook?"

I shake my head. Now do you see why my life revolves around food? My mother's had a menu set in her head for everything from our baptisms to the day I got my first period.

"Calm your buns, Ma. I haven't figured out how I'm going to ask her yet, but I'll probably do it tonight. I can't hold on to this thing knowing it's not on her finger." My brother's face beams with happiness. Reynold's been dating his girlfriend, Ashley, for three years now. I'm certain she was designed with my brother in mind. Not only are they perfect for each other, but she fits in with our family, too. We all love her. She's a doll—like a real, live, blow up doll. Not the slutty kind, the flawless from head to toe kind. No, Ashley's gorgeous, sexy, smart, refined. I want to hate her for it, but I can't because she's the sister I never had. Besides Tatum, of course.

I jump up and throw my arms around my brother. "Wow, Rey! This is amazing! I'm so happy for you!" I truly am. I don't have one jealous bone in my body. I mean, it's completely normal for your younger brother to tie the knot before you do. It's absolutely acceptable for your parents to dote on him and his soon-to-be fiancé as if the sun rises and sets in their beauty. It's positively okay that I'll be forced to jam my ass into a couture bridesmaid gown.

Reality sets in. That jealousy I swore I didn't feel creeps up on me, too. "Hey, Ma. No pasta for me today, okay?"

Reynold nudges me with his burly shoulder and chuckles. "That's my girl! I'm proud of you!"

And just like that, I start my one millionth crash diet, praying that this time something will keep me going and magically melt the pounds away.

# chapter

## Two

HAVE I TOLD YOU ABOUT the many excruciating weight loss journeys of Madeline Moore? No? Oh boy! Pull up a chair. This is gonna be fun.

When I was twelve, my parents sent me to Fat Camp. Yes. It exists. Lake Wanna-Losa-Poundsa. Okay, I'm joking about the name, but not about the torture I endured. Drill sergeant-like camp counselors who count calories and track your cardio minutes. Mean girls taunting you even though their triple chins far surpass your double chin. Horny, pre-pubescent boys eager to get their hands on chubby titties and jiggly asses. It. Was. A. Nightmare. I still hold a grudge against my parents for sending me, even if it was just one summer. That one summer scarred me for life. This one time, at Fat Camp . . .

Yeah, I survived and lived to laugh about it, but that was the year I realized that my size was an issue. Up until that point, I'd been okay with being the bigger girl. Tatum was a string bean and I was a . . . *potato*. There was nothing wrong with that. In fact, string bean and red potato salad is scrumptious with some olive oil and balsamic vinegar. However, it was the year when the great divide happened. The pretty girls vs. the not pretty girls. Tatum fell effortlessly into the first category; curly blond hair, dainty turned-up nose, chestnut colored eyes, and a tiny, perky body. Because of my portliness, I settled in comfortably on the *other* side of the tracks.

It wasn't blatant. The boys hung around me because I was good at sports and had a funny sense of humor, and although they always called me cute, I *was* chubby. That alone landed me in the reject pile. Along with Caroline Hartnett and her mouth full of braces and Helen Chaney who was notorious for showering once a month, when it came time for spin the bottle, the boys prayed they didn't get stuck with me. Whatever. I was a late bloomer. I couldn't care less about how boys felt or didn't feel about me. Then. But once I was home from Fat Camp . . . let's just say, I'd seen the light.

Years after that fiasco, in high school, I tried out for the part of Juliet in our school's performance of, yup, you guessed it, Romeo and Juliet. I was more than fit for the part. A true Shakespeare nerd at her finest, I could recite that poetic work of art like it was nobody's business. Our chorus director had written a few original songs to bring the play up to date, and my angelic singing voice—to quote Mrs. Lopez, herself—was practically tailored to every note in every song.

After my own stellar audition, Anthony Ricciardelli, the tenth grade stud, aced his tryout and was chosen as Romeo on the spot. He was a shoe-in; it wasn't a surprise. Every teacher in the school knew him, loved him, and treated him like an Adonis. In turn, every girl in the school did the same. So when Anthony became our Romeo, it was common knowledge that he would have first pick of his Juliet. The obvious choice should have been me. As I said before, my audition rocked. But, in true fat-girl-loses-every-time fashion, he chose Rebecca Grady—tall, blonde, skinny, and with as much talent as a cardboard box. I later heard locker room gossip that Anthony refused to work alongside the fat chick with the pretty voice.

It was heartbreaking, like everything at that age is. I wanted to crawl under a rock and die. *After* I devoured a box of Twinkies. Anthony Ricciardelli thought I was fat so that meant the whole school would agree like sheep following a teenage boy's herd.

I remember staring in the mirror in my bedroom, crying. With a package of Yodels in one hand and the garbage pail in the other, I vowed to myself that I would try. I was pretty. I was talented. I had plenty of friends. The only thing stopping me was my weight. The very next day, I went to the corner drug store and grabbed the first diet pills I could find off the shelf. The young clerk sold them to me without question. I assumed he agreed with my decision. *Fat girl needs to lose weight. Fine by me.*

But it wasn't fine. At all. The pills curbed my hunger, but made my heart race. I lost ten pounds in a week and the same day I got on the scale to relish in my achievement, I passed out in gym class because I was dehydrated and starving. Talk about drama. My mother almost killed me after they brought me back to life, and my brother was mortified. Only a year younger than me, we shared the same school and similar cliques. Word spread that Reynold's sister had overdosed on Sibutramine, and while most couldn't even pronounce the word, it was gossip. *Negative* gossip. My own brother refused to be seen with me for the rest of his entire freshman year. Yeah, good times.

And that leads me to my adult years. I never scored in high school. While Tatum was having the time of her life banging guys from the football, lacrosse, and baseball teams—not all at once—and Reynold had his pick of every cutie from here to kingdom come, I flew solo to every single milestoneish event there was. Prom—alone. Graduation parties—alone. College frat parties—alone. By the time I was nineteen, I had grown comfortable in my skin. Okay, maybe not *comfortable*, but I learned to accept it. A Size 2 would never be in my future, but I did long for a man as part of it.

Sick and tired of feeling sorry for myself, I started working out at the campus gym. In accordance to a strict regimen from Reynold, I followed a clean diet and stuck to an hour of cardio five times a week. It was working. My normal, scale-tipping 220 melted to just shy of 170. It was my lowest weight ever. I was on top of the world. Ready to try my luck at dating and putting myself out there. I could fit in trendy clothes and smile without worrying about scrutiny. I knew I'd risen above my negative aura when someone at the gym made a snarky remark; something along the lines of how *The Biggest Loser* was one of her favorite shows. I shrugged it off, because I was no longer a loser. I was a winner. That was my new attitude.

Until Alex fucked that all up.

At my leanest, I "snagged" the *it* guy. Alex Cruz. God, was he hot. I still get a warm and fuzzy feeling when I think about how it felt to be near that douche. I loved everything about him. Especially the way other girls looked at me when he escorted me around campus. He'd never called me his girlfriend, but we were close, like *really* close friends. With benefits. He was my first kiss. First guy to cop a feel under my shirt. The first guy I ever slept with. I can't say I didn't enjoy it, but what I *didn't* fancy was the non-exclusivity of our arrangement. A few times I brought it up to him and he shut me up with a mesmerizing kiss. I didn't know any better, so I went along with it because I liked the attention and the companionship. I was a fat girl trapped inside a body smaller than the one I was used to. Confidence was hard to come by, no matter what the mirror told me to believe. So I let him do what I would disown my own future daughter for *ever* doing. I allowed him to use me and I turned a blind eye to it the entire time.

After three months of hooking up, I discovered Alex had been dared to be with me. Yup—*dared*. It was part of some twisted fraternity initiation that had later been banned. Later meant shit to me. *Later* was too *late*. Alex swore on everything good and holy that even though it had started out as a joke, he'd *kind of* fallen for me. At that point of humiliation, it didn't matter. I'd been duped, had, done for. I felt like shit and needed to run away from everything that reminded me of that pitiful feeling.

I dropped out of school and gained back all my weight, plus some. It was a lonely go of it for a while. I shut everyone out until something appealed to me. *The mask of makeup.* A few subscriptions to Glamour and a trip to Sephora in the city led me to my calling. Cosmetology school gave me a confidence I never knew—something to hide behind. Painting *my* face made me feel pretty, regardless of the rolls that bulged out of my jeans. Making other people happy with my hands made me feel worthy. I had a gift and no matter how big or small I was, people liked me for how I made them look.

Win-win, right? Well, technically, I don't feel like I'm winning today. I've spent the last half hour browsing through bridesmaid dresses with Ashley and I'm two seconds away from jumping in front of the subway that runs beneath the shop.

"Ash, I love you, but I'm not even gonna pretend I want to try that on."

Ashley's holding up a pale pink, strapless mermaid gown. Doesn't she know that attempting to get my portly body into that dress would be like trying to fit someone's big toe inside a keyhole? Ain't happening.

In true Ashley sweetness, my soon-to-be sister-in-law shushes me with a soft caress on my arm. "Leni, you don't give yourself enough credit. Besides, Reynold told me how good you've been and I can see it myself." Ashley holds my hand and appraises me at arm's length. Her hazel eyes peruse my entire body with a genuine smile.

The fact she notices the ten pounds I've shed puts an extra *umph* in my frump. "I did lose a little, but it's still not enough to stuff myself into something that form fitting, babe. Forget a mermaid, I'll look like a beached whale and you know it."

That lands me a smack in the ass. "Shut your trap. How 'bout I make you a deal?" Ashley returns the dress to its rightful rack behind her and spins around with a devilish grin.

*Oh boy.* I *totally* don't like the looks of this. "What are you up to, oh sneaky one? Your eyes are scaring me. They're doing that freaky, whirly thing they do when you're concocting a diabolical plan."

"Oh, please. And how many times have you been around for my so called *concoctions*?"

Is she joking? "One word—" I start.

"Shit! *Vegas*." Took the words right outta my mouth. "Okay, you got me there."

"Yeah! So, before you get any crazy ideas, let's not forget that shit show." My brother's loving girlfriend planned his entire twenty-first birthday surprise. Her intentions were forthright, and most of the trip went swimmingly. Until Reynold wound up drunk *and* naked in the fountains of the Bellagio—during show time. Long story short, he was arrested for indecent exposure and disorderly conduct and we almost missed our flight back home the next morning waiting around for the police to release him from custody. Insanity doesn't come close to describing what went down during that trip. I can guarantee Reynold won't be opting for a bachelor party in the City of Sin. I know this much is true.

Ignoring the million and one reasons I am not agreeing to one of her plans, Ashley ushers me toward another section while skimming through more gowns. There's no denying she's afraid to tell me, but rather than play the curiosity killed the cat game, I nudge her to get on with it. "Go on. You were saying? I know you're dying to get it out."

The giddy bride-to-be nearly levitates off the ground as she rubs her hands together. *This is gonna be a doozy, isn't it?* "Just hear me out before you say no, okay?"

I nod, unconvincingly, but ready to see what she's cooked up.

"Okay. So, my friend Jane and her wife Mandy just got their personal trainer licenses. They need clients and they're willing to take on a few newly referred people for half the cost of what they're set to charge. I'm already on board to start up with Jane on Monday so I can get myself in tip top shape for the wedding."

"Because you're not *already* runway ready? Come on." I scoff. She's perfect from the roots of her highlighted hair to the French manicure on her toes.

Rolling her eyes, she defends her cause. "Oh, hush. I want to tone up a little, but this isn't about me. What if—and please don't take this the wrong way because you know I love you just the way you are, Leni, but—what if we did this together? By the time the wedding rolls around next year we'll both be svelte and slim and—"

Time to burst her happy bubble. "You know how much I hate working out, don't you? I mean, like I despise it. I'd rather chew off my left arm than do a push up."

"Yeah, I know. You don't need to remind me, but—" Her expression turns serious, a glint of sadness in her colorful eyes. This girl is like a sister to me and heart-to-hearts are our thing. I've come to recognize when one's about to go down and the sitting room of Always a Bridesmaid Boutique is about to become the venue for our next intimate chat.

Ashley leans in so we're toe to toe and grips my shoulders. Her sympathetic expression says it all. "Babe, you're not happy and I know it. You're doing a great job with whatever you're doing right now, but for as long as I've known you, you've practically been *dying* to be thin. Let me help you. Please, Leni. Let's get you where you wanna be for once and for all."

I pull in a long, shaky breath. I should be pissed or hurt or embarrassed, but I'm not. Ashley's one hundred percent right. I have never learned to embrace my curves. I'm not happy. I'm doing what little I've committed to for now, but I'm one fast food temptation away from fucking it all up and binging like there's no tomorrow. I want to be thinner for this wedding. I want to be skinnier for *me*. I'm ready to change and I just don't know how, but I have every reason to get my act together right in front of me.

In a little over a year, there will be an event which my entire gossipy family will attend. I'd love to give them something positive to talk about this time, rather than be on the receiving end of their inquisitions about why I'm still single.

Then, there's the problem of eternalizing the way I look *now* with photographs that will wind up in my brother's wedding album. As Ashley's maid of honor and the only sister of the groom, I'll be in too many pictures to count. And let's face it, no one wants to look back at pictures years from now and be filled with regret.

And lastly—the main reason I'm considering taking Ashley up on her offer—I finally have someone willing to do this *with* me. Reynold's good at coming up with a meal plan and a list of daily exercises, but he's no gym partner. The fact Ashley is willing to join me along this journey means the world to me. The struggle is real and she totally gets it. As much as I want to say no, I'm honestly not sure I can.

But I still have to give her a hard time. It's what I do. So before I give in—even though I'm already sold—I scrunch my face and throw my hands to my hips. "And what's in it for you?"

Her eyes flash with bright specks of hope as a smile creeps across her glossed lips. "When you get to where you want to be—which you so *will* because you'll have me in your corner this time—you're going to wear the dress *I* choose."

"Oh, no. Not that. Anything but that." I told you she was

diabolical.

She crisscrosses her arms over her chest and tilts her head up, nose and chin pointing toward the ceiling. "It's non-negotiable, Madeline Moore. You have your work cut out for you and that means I do too because I'll be dealing with your whiny ass for the duration of this training. I want more than anything to help you be the woman you want to be, but you can bet your left tit I'm gonna want some kind of reward after this. I pick the dress. Take it or leave it."

Just as I'm about to spit out "leave it" and run out of the store, a gaggle of young girls enters through the front door with a ringing of a bell. There has to be twelve of them, all giggly and excited, and rail fucking thin, of course. I instantly spot the bride—the center of the clan, a thick wedding organizer in her hands. Her bridesmaids gather around her, smiling while they look over her shoulder at the swatches she's arranged neatly in her planner. I can only imagine how easy this process will be for them. They can pick any dress off any of these racks and have not a single concern about which piece of flesh will hang out, bulge out, or pop out.

My heart aches to be able to go through life with that kind of ease. I think about Ashley and how she has to settle for a frumpy maid of honor rather than be accompanied down the aisle on the happiest day of her life with one of the beautiful bombshells in this other wedding party. I hate the idea of what's ahead. I shudder at the mere thought of what this personal trainer will put me through. And I'm not comfortable in the least with having no say in a dress that has to go on *my* body. But I love Ashley and I want to do this for her. Hell, I want to do this for me and every plump bridesmaid that ever felt inferior to the chicks who can slide right into a Size 2, off-the-rack sample.

I steal my attention from the group of girls happily sifting through gowns and turn back to Ashley. My decision is easy. It's everything else I'm afraid of. "I'll do it," I say, and feel as if a heavy weight—pun totally intended—has been lifted off my shoulders.

Ashley jumps up and down and claps her hands together. "Yay! Thank you! I promise I won't let you down and you'll love the dress I choose. You won't be sorry, Leni!"

I shake my head, shooing away all the negative thoughts. Deep down, underneath all the blubber, the cellulite, and the extra baggage, I know this is the right thing to do and surprisingly enough, I'm up for the challenge. I think.

# chapter

# three

ASHLEY NEVER MENTIONED THAT JANE was *the* G.I. Jane. Holy Mother of God, I've never seen a woman with so many muscles. It's scary, and crazy, and kind of freaking hot. "Ash, I want to look like her when this is all over."

Ashley giggles, no words necessary. Her thoughts mirror mine—*fat chance in hell.* "You never know, babe. Crazier things have happened."

"Yeah, like me being carried out on a stretcher after three minutes with this chick. You do know I won't last a whole hour with her, right?"

"Leave your negativity at the door," she smarts and points at the plaque right beside the entrance to the gym. Sure enough, it says the exact same thing. *Clever.* However, if I had a choice it would say something like *welcome to hell.* But that's considered negative so I'm already losing this battle.

"Hey, girls!" Mandy bypasses Jane who's been on a call at the front desk for the last few minutes. If I thought Jane's physique was flawless then this woman's body was carved out of stone. It can't be natural. She's got to be an alien, or a robot. No human I know is this naturally proportioned and athletically enhanced.

Ashley is first to greet the Gym Goddess with a warm smile and a hug. "So nice to finally meet you! Jane can't stop talking about you. She's head over heels for you, girl."

"She better be," Mandy quips, winking my way. The whole interaction totally intimidates me. I am by no means uncomfortable with same sex marriage, dating, you name it, but the "she better be" throws me off. Is she implying that she'll nunchuck her chick into submission? *Who am I kidding? She'll use her bare hands.*

"You must be Madeline," Mandy extends a strong hand to me and I shyly reciprocate.

"Leni, please. And it's nice to meet you, too."

"Then why do you look like you just crapped yourself? I won't bite, Leni, I promise."

Ashley and Mandy share a laugh as my stomach inverts into my abdomen and nearly falls out my rectum. Am I that transparent? The mixture of embarrassment and fear must be written all over my face.

"Leni here is a gym hater."

Mandy gasps and every occupant of the gym turns their head to see what's going on. *Way to ease away the discomfort, girls. Real good.*

"There'll be none of that. By the time you're done with us you'll hate the gym so much you'll fucking love it." Mandy's face is painted with pleasure as she says the meaningful phrase. I get it. I've heard this before—people learn to crave the pain, love the burn, and embrace the after-workout-soreness. I want more than anything to be that type of person, but I've been here before and I just can't get comfortable with having to ask for help to sit on the toilet after leg day. That ain't cool, no matter how much my rocking ass with thank me for it later.

I take a deep breath and decide to go with it. If you can't beat 'em, join 'em, and I am obviously ill equipped to give these two any kind of beating. "I'm ready. You've got my word. I might whine and bitch, but it'll all be worth it in the end, right?"

"Exactly!" Mandy shouts.

"Yay, Leni! I'm so proud of you!" Ashley beams.

I wish I could be that excited about the torment ahead.

AN HOUR LATER, I SWEAR to Jesus Christ and every saint, martyr, and Apostle that I'm going to die. Death by lunges wasn't what I imagined in my obituary, but they better call the morgue because I'm done for.

"Fuck!" I scream, keeling over and collapsing on the rubber mat.

"Let it out, babe. Yell all you want, but you did it and lived to tell about it." Jane kneels beside me on the floor, handing me a sweat rag and my water bottle.

"Barely," I manage to breathe, realizing that I did in fact live to tell the tale of the Lunge Monster and her evil queen, Squat Beast. "But—would you look at that? I still have a pulse."

"That you do. I'm proud of you, Leni. I wasn't sure you had it in you."

"I was," Ashley's quick to interrupt Mandy at my defense. "You got this. I told you! And the first day is always the hardest, but tomorrow you'll get back on the horse and—"

"Tomorrow?" I nearly cry. Like full on, sobbing, weeping, throwing a tantrum *cry*.

The three mocking bitches laugh, clearly ignoring the seriousness of this ludicrous situation.

"Yes, tomorrow. And the day after that, and the day after that, babes. After you're done down there on the floor, you're going to come into our office and we're setting you up with a weekly diet and exercise plan. This won't be easy, Leni, but nothing worth it ever is. You game?"

Can I say no? I want to say no. I really, really want to fucking say no. But I can't. She's right. It's time to grab life by the balls—if I had any, I would have squatted them off today—and do this shit wholeheartedly. "Yeah, I'm game," I whisper.

"Say what?" Jane barks. "I didn't hear you." She cups her ear and leans down, waiting for my response.

"Yes! I'm game! You happy?"

"Yes!" they all shout in unison.

"And you should be, too," Ashley reminds me.

And I am. I truly am so proud of myself for getting through this without giving up. It's an accomplishment and while I'm certain this'll be an uphill battle . . . I think I can, I think I can, I think I can.

OKAY, SO SCREW THE GYM, *this* is the hardest part of the whole shebang. *Willpower.* I have none. And while I emptied my fridge and cabinets of anything unhealthy and fattening, I have no problem getting in the elevator in the hallway, taking it down to the lobby, and walking (exercise!!!) the three blocks to Mc-Donald's to feed my late night craving. But I digress.

When I watch TV I like to snack, and I don't care who you are but carrots and hummus are not considered an acceptable *Late Nate with Jimmy Fallon* accompaniment. I want chips, dip, popcorn, something with crunch that isn't a raw vegetable! But I refuse to undo what I did today with Ashley, Jane, and Mandy. Forget about disappointing myself—I've learned to live with self inflicted guilt—I can't let *them* down. They put their faith in me and I want to deliver. So, instead of laughing it up with my man Jimmy, I decide to call it a night before the temptation of food, alcohol or anything with a caloric intake over five comes knocking on my door.

Tomorrow is a new day. I'll be in pain, I'll want to eat things I shouldn't, I have to start my daily walking regimen under Jane's instruction, and I'm not looking forward to any of it, but if I learned anything today, it's that Ashley was right in that dress store the other day. I don't give myself enough credit. I can do this. I will do this. G.I. Jane and Mandy, beware—you'll make a gym lover outta me yet.

# chapter

# four

MY TUNE IS MUCH DIFFERENT this morning. Less a song, more a battle cry. "Ouch! Ooo. Eee. Ahhh." I can't even get my legs over the mattress without wincing. How the hell will I ever get them to *walk* again? The sore-beyond-belief lumps of dead weight that seem to have replaced my legs, protest everything my brain is telling them to do. And, you know what? I don't blame them. The shit I made these poor, flaccid, underworked muscles do yesterday—"I'm so sorry," I cry, rubbing my legs in hopes they'll sympathize with me and get to doing what they were designed to do.

But I can't wait for them to move of their own accord so I force myself to roll off the bed—yes, roll—and land on the floor with a loud thud. "Jesus!" I whimper, soothing my elbow where I banged it against the bed frame. I'm a walking—well, not really—disaster. This can't be good and there are no excuses. *Be stronger than your excuses, Leni.* If I can get through this pain and go on with the workout plan, I can do anything. I'm sure of it. However, I've gotten pretty comfortable here on the plush, cream carpet and I've just spotted a giant bag of Kit Kats hidden under the bed! *Oh my God! Mecca!*

I almost reach out for the bag of wonderfulness but force my nose in the air in disgust, remembering that nowhere on the "what to eat" list from Jane and Mandy are Kit Kats or their equally yummy counterparts Twix (the backup plan buried deep inside my closet). *Willpower, I apologize to you, too. Just like my leg muscles, you'll be tested in ways you've never imagined possible.*

I hate that I forgot that stash because it's just another obstacle to zig zag through, but just like the gym, I'll face this head on. Tossing every smidge of leftover candy in the trash moves straight to the top of my to-do list. Which also includes crawling to the bathroom so I can wash up, stuffing my junk in the cute pair of yoga pants and running shoes Tatum helped picked out on our shopping spree at the athletic store, and setting my feet to the pavement at Central Park. I hope my body cooperates because it actually sounds like a great start to my day. A new start I hope to implement into my daily routine and one that Jane and Mandy suggested since my options stretch far beyond the gym. *"You don't have to sequester yourself to the four walls of this torture chamber, as you like to call it, Leni. You can work out—aka a nice, brisk, break-a-sweat walk—anywhere. Your home, the park, the mall. Just make sure you incorporate an hour of cardio at least five times a week, and you'll keep me—and your scale—very happy, babes."*

Jane's lecture rings loud and clear through my thoughts as I drag myself to the bathroom. I consider texting Tatum to see if she wants to put her new sports bra to use, but decide against it because I want to do this for the first time on my own. There's something empowering about being able to face your fears without an entourage of people holding your hand. I know I'll need all the support I can get in the coming months, but doing this solo just seems right.

I almost yank the pedestal sink out of the wall hoisting my

ass off the tile floor, but once I'm in an upright position I take a deep, soothing breath, and smile at myself in the mirror. Time for the daily pep talk. Ashley told me about these books she reads by Joel Osteen. I'm not exactly a fan of preachers shoving the praises of The Lord down my throat, but Ashley's advice—and her daily Instagram posts—resonate. Now, while I would totally prefer the Cliffs Notes version of said books, I'm happy to let Ashley pump me up with the key lessons she took away from preacher man's sermon.

Today's message: *you may think there is a lot wrong with you, but there is also a lot right with you,* is where I start. I look long and hard, focusing on all the things I actually like about myself. My long, wavy, umber locks, swirling with natural golden highlights. Chestnut-colored eyes that sparkle with amber flecks. Unblemished ivory skin with the tiniest of freckles peppering an upturned nose. And heart-shaped lips with a pale pink hue. I'm not a horrible sight—in fact, I think I'm kinda pretty—but I doubt Osteen's message is skin deep. He wants us to look further, dig deeper, see the big picture. So I do. I look past the extra layer of plump skin that serves as a double chin and ignore the bit of flab hanging over my pajama pants. My weight is something I've always considered a negative, but there are so many positives that will help me get through this and once I've shed some of the negativity, the world will be my oyster. Well, I hate oysters, so let's call the world my triple decker bacon burger with mushrooms and cheddar. Yeah, that sounds much better.

OKAY. SO LET'S ADD WALKING through Central Park to the list of things I hate besides oysters. *Hate. Check. Done.* Well, not really done because it's barely been twenty minutes and I have to clock sixty, but if I'm being honest, I wanted to be done after ten.

My first eager steps onto the dirt loop were super awesome. I had a kick to my step and a happy sway to my ultra curvy hips. My new pants and sneakers gave me that *dress for the part* confidence I would have lacked if I'd thrown on a pair of ratty old sweats and the only rubber-soled shoes I own—my Chucks. But, *looks* aren't everything, remember? Except that they are because I don't know if it's just me or what, but Central Park is flooded with the hottest of the hot and I simply do not belong here.

On the Reservoir Loop alone, I ran into a woman whose shorts were so skimpy I could see what she ate for breakfast, a dazzling young man with washboard abs and the brilliant decency *not* to wear a shirt while his sweat glistened in the sunlight, and a gaggle of middle aged women that I could swear I saw on an episode of *New York Housewives* once. The terms *you're out of your league, you're fooling yourself,* and *you're better off running in the dark where no one can see you,* jog through my mind at a faster pace than my feet can hit the pavement.

I can't help thinking that I look like some wanna-be trying to fit in with the cool kids. I try to push the negative thoughts aside and overcome the pessimism—the way Ashley and Joel would pray for me to—but this has been my struggle for so long it's almost a part of who I am. When you grow up being made fun of for your flub and eventually learn to accept that you're not getting the hot date because you chose Oreos over the treadmill, it kinda sinks in that *this is it. This* is *me,* and even though I've tried to lose the weight many, many times before, the truth remains the same. I'm chubby. I'll never be a twig, but that doesn't mean I don't deserve happiness in the form of— holy shit—of *that!*

A gorgeous guy in expensive looking running shoes, a sweat-soaked V-neck T-shirt, and the sexiest manbun I have *ever* seen, zooms past me. He winks and smiles as he whooshes by in a mix of sweat and man and some kind of delicious body wash. *Dayum!* A wink for me? *Nice!* I would walk five *hundred* miles (and I would walk five hundred more) just to see that guy once a day! I crane my neck and slow my pace to get a better look, but he's gone, disappearing behind a dip in the track, before I can ogle any longer.

Just like that, the torture of getting into shape has its visual advantages and plenty of pros to outweigh the cons. Pros: I'm here, I'm moving, I've got a blood-pumping, feel-good attitude, *and* manbun dude gave me a wink. Cons: this sucks, I'm hungry, I'm tired, and I'd rather be reading than walking. Luckily, my warped mind is smart enough to focus on the pros list. So I dismiss everything that could possibly weigh me down, turn up the volume on my iPod, and lip sync the words to *Fallen* by Imagine Dragons while I jog it out. It's a beautiful day, I'm rocking new kicks, one of my favorite bands is blasting motivational lyrics in my ears and as Joel would advise, *if you cannot be positive, then at least be quiet.* Anyone who knows me can vouch that I'm a gabber—quiet is not in my blood—so I guess that only leaves one thing. Positivity fucking rules, right?

# chapter

## five

MOST PEOPLE LOVE THE WEEKEND because it means two days off from the daily grind, but not me. Saturday is always my busiest day of the week. I have five clients coming in today to get their makeup done. Three bridesmaids and the mother of the groom, and the other, a long time client, headed out for a night on the town with her boyfriend. Easy enough, no use in complaining, but it also means that I have to cut my workout short this morning to get into the salon on time.

That alone has me making all kinds of excuses as to why I can skip one measly day. I could've slept an extra hour, I worked really hard all week, I ate like a champ and didn't go over on my calories. If I bail on the cardio for one day, what's the crime? There is none! My rebellious decision is made . . . *until* I get my daily text reminder from G.I. Jane.

> *Jane: Morning Sunshine! Thinking about going to the gym burns between zero and zero calories. Get your ass in gear, babes! Xo*

As quickly as the guilt sinks in, I also remember that Tatum and I made a running buddy date today. "Dammit! I don't want to!" I cry into my pillow, wishing there was an easier way to melt this fat away. I mean, it's definitely vanishing somehow. I'm down twelve so the goal is getting closer, but don't I deserve a day of rest? God had one. It was Sunday. Can't mine be Saturday? I just want a break!

The phone rings on my nightstand and interrupts my pity party for one. I groan as I reach for it and scrunch my nose when I see it's Mom. It's not nice to dodge your mother's calls, but I know why she's calling and I'm not in the mood.

I answer anyway because she gave me life; I kinda owe her. "Hi, Mom. What's up?" As if I really have to ask.

"Have you spoken to Ashley yet?"

See? I knew it. "No, Mom."

"Madeline! I thought you said you would call her! I don't want to come off as the annoying, meddling mother-in-law and your brother—I can't say anything to him without him zoning out or brushing me off. I need you, Leni! You have to do this!"

What a Greek tragedy. Ashley and Rey have been talking about a destination wedding. My mother is up in arms. Nonna Rose and Papa Vito won't fly and Aunt Millie on Dad's side hasn't been off of Long Island since 1965. But this isn't my problem. "Ma, I can't tell them where to have their wedding. I know I said I'd talk to her, but just like you don't want to rock the boat, neither do I. I actually like my sister-in-law, she likes me, I want to keep it that way."

"What the hell are we going to do? Who gets married in Punta Cana, anyway? I've never heard of Dominicans making tiramisu! It's your brother's favorite. He needs to have tiramisu at his wedding!"

The eye roll of the century nearly gives me a migraine. I would totally deserve it, too. "I'll talk to them, Ma, okay? Can you leave me alone now?"

"No, I'm your mother, I haven't spoken to you all week. Are you avoiding me?"

"No, I'm busy."

"Doing what?"

"Living! Ma, really?"

"One day I'll be dead and you'll miss me, you'll see."

If I lost a pound for every time she used that one, I'd be a skeleton.

A loud huff escapes her when I don't respond. "You coming to dinner tomorrow?"

Regret pummels my resolve. If I say no, she'll get on my case all over again. "I don't know if I should."

"What? Why?" I can hear the heartbreak through the phone.

"Because I'm dieting, remember? Your menu isn't exactly full of the healthiest fare."

"Oh, stop! So, you have one bowl of pasta and only a few meatballs. No harm. I'll hide the bread."

Will she ever really get it? For a woman who wants her daughter to be thin, she's always trying to feed me. "No, I'll bring something with me. It's okay. I've got to go, though. I have a full schedule today and a few things to do before I get to the salon."

"And you'll call Ashley, too?"

"Yeah, Ma! I'll call her. Bye!"

"Bye," she sings. "Love you and you know you love me, too."

"Love you, Ma. Tell Dad I said hi and I'll see you tomorrow." I hang up, already feeling exhausted even though I just woke up half an hour ago. Talking to my mother will do that to you.

On the bright side, I'll have Tatum to bitch to. I guzzle down a shake with a shot of some green shit that seems to do the trick in holding me over until lunch as I slam the door shut behind me. Tatum's waiting for me outside, chugging down some Starbucks concoction that would shoot my calorie count to shit.

"Morning. You ready to do this?" I ask, love-tapping her on the ass.

"Am now." She winks as she tosses the empty cup into the trash can at the curb.

"Breakfast of champions?"

She nods, giving me pouty lips. "Rough night. Rougher morning. It was coffee or wine. And it's come to my attention that wine is not a socially acceptable beverage at eight a.m."

"Bummer." I giggle as we start to walk. "Want to talk about it?"

She shrugs, looking both ways before stepping into the street. "Nah, no use wasting time regurgitating my crap. To sum it up, work sucked, I had a crappy date with Paul, and my noisy neighbors kept me up all night so I didn't get much sleep."

I'm immediately sorry for my struggles, again. Seems I'm always inadvertently apologizing for my weight in some way or another. "Oh, Tay. You could have cancelled. I would have gone alone."

With a pat on my shoulder, Tatum smiles. "Don't be silly. I want to be here. I'm happy to cheer you on and to catch up with you, which reminds me. We're still on for tonight, right?"

*Shit! What's tonight? I totally forgot.* I feign recollection, seeing as I have no other plans anyway, and nod again and again. "Yup! We're on like Donkey Kong. What are we doing again?"

"Um . . . Netflix and Chill except I'm not booty calling you, and between binging on *Orange is the New Black*, we're redoing my resume. You totally forgot, didn't you?"

"Nope. It's on my calendar. Swear. Crazy Eyes and resume polishing. Nine p.m."

"Good. Now, let's get our groove on so I can go back to bed before the neighbors start in again."

When we arrive at the park, I take note of the usual suspects I've become accustomed to running into every day since I started my new routine.

There's the man with four dogs on two double leashes. He nods his 'hello' and I swear the dogs do the same. Next up is the thirty-something mother with her jogger stroller and her happy toddler. She lifts one hand from the stroller and waves at me. I return the gesture and smile. Coming round the bend are the boys from the track team. They have to be freshmen because they're scrawny and pimply, still not into their own. The first time we crossed paths they nearly slammed into me in an inseparable flock. Now when they notice me approaching, they part like the Red Sea, making room for me with brace-faced smiles and squeaky hellos.

"You're like the mayor, Leni! Look at you."

I smile, pride fueling my tired legs. "Yeah, I guess. It's only been three weeks, but these people make the track feel like home, ya know?" I look forward to their greetings and they encourage me to push further, bringing a warmth that can only be explained as *Cheers* syndrome, as I like to call it. You know, belonging to a place where everyone knows your name? I guess it's silly since none of them actually know my name, but the point is, I feel welcome. Part of the crowd. Akin to these folks sharing the track with me.

"Maybe you'll meet someone, huh?" Tatum nudges me and winks.

I roll my eyes and shake my head, dismissing her. It's not so far fetched, except that of the all the people who've been so welcoming and warm, there's only *one* whose attention I cannot seem to grab.

"Too bad, Fancy Pants won't even look my way." I pout.

"Who?"

"Oh, just this guy who's always wearing a snazzy pair of track pants. He's really cute—more like knee-buckling-hot—with a badass tattoo wrapped around his bicep and shaggy blond hair that bounces with his stride. Dude never looks up from the pavement to give me the same courteous nod that most of the other joggers do. Whatevs." I should rename him Rude Fucker, but I don't like to judge. Maybe he's having a bad day—consistently for the last three weeks. Maybe he's concentrating. Maybe he just doesn't want to give a chubby girl false hope in the form of acknowledgment. Who the hell knows. Either way, it's started to grate on me. More like, it's become a mission to get the guy to give me the time of day. I'm not asking for a wedding proposal, but a simple 'hey' would suffice.

"You need to up your game, girl! *Make* him look at you!"

"No. I have no desire to attempt flirting with a guy while I'm all sweaty and out of breath. Plus, I'd rather him *not* notice me until I've lost some of the weight. Better odds and all."

"Oh my God, this again? You make it sound like you're a leper. You're beautiful, you're smart, you're funny as hell. Any guy should be *honored* to flirt with you. You piss me off, so bad! You know that?"

I shrug, shaking off the lecture I've heard over and over. "What? I'm just being realistic. I'm used to it. It's okay."

"Well, stop being used to it. Go for what you want and if Fancy Pants is what you want, go forth and seize his fine ass. Otherwise, stop dwelling. It ain't a pretty look on you."

She's right. I know this. With each passing day I promise myself I won't let it get to me, but it always does. I'm one of those people who thrive on the acceptance of others. Pretty stupid goal for a fat chick with self-esteem issues, but I've done a good job of compensating where I'm lacking, the way Tatum pointed out. I want to scream at Fancy Pants, *People like me! Why can't you?* It's true, it's what's on the inside that counts. I've tried to follow that motto, but unfortunately, society has its ways of judging a book by its cover.

Thankfully today I have Tatum to overpower the voices in

my head. I quickly change the subject. "So, you're really thinking about quitting your job? You hate it that much?"

A long, aggravated groan erupts from her dainty mouth.
"Let's put it this way . . . every morning I wake up and pray I'll
take a stumble down the steps. I'd love to break a leg or, better
yet, both, so I can be laid up in bed on disability."

"That bad, huh?" I laugh.

"That bad." She bobs her head. "If I stay there any longer,
I'm certain I'll go to jail for mass homicide because killing my
boss won't be enough. The entire staff are assholes. I need out
before they dull my sparkle." She waves jazz hands in the air and
curtsies with grace.

This makes me stop dead in my tracks with laughter. "No
one can dull *your* sparkle, babe. You're glitterlicious! And after
we spruce up your already kickass resume, the chances of you
being put away for murder will decrease significantly."

"Sounds like a plan." We high five each other and then I see
something out of the corner of my eye that nearly makes me
stumble.

"Shit!"

Rounding the bend is none other than Fancy Pants. I don't
want Tatum to know it's him. Part of me doesn't want *him* to
see me with *her* because—okay, fine! Because she's perfect and
I'm not and if the first look I get from him is because he was really looking at her, I'll want to poke her eyes out. And she's my
best friend and thoughts like that about your best friend aren't
very friendly.

"My shoe lace is untied." I pull Tatum by the hand, dodg-
ing off course.

I focus on pretending to tie the shoelace that's actually already secured in a double knot, but I can't break my stare from
him no matter how hard I try.

Tatum follows my line of sight and slaps me on the ass.
"Leni! That's him, isn't it?"

"Ouch!" The slap stings and my screech turns heads. *His* head. And . . . *hers*. They look our way and then smile tightly. I smile back although I'm left thinking, *Who are you and why are you with my man?* He has a running mate today and she's everything I'm not. Tall, thin, tan, blonde, *perfect*. Before they noticed me they were laughing together. I can't help wanting to know what she said to bring that kind of enjoyment to his face. The enjoyment that vanished as soon as he made eye contact with me.

I quickly avert my attention. My gut burns with disappointment and, dare I say it, embarrassment. I'd be lying if I failed to admit that there were days I crawled out of my bed and dragged my ass down to the park just to get a glimpse of him. Stupid. I know.

I untie and retie the other lace just to keep busy waiting for him to be gone and then a hand hits the back of my head with a harsh thud.

"Hey! What was that for?" I rub the throbbing spot.

"How can he notice you if you're off cowering on a park bench?"

"Oh, give it up, Tatum. He has no reason to notice me when he has *her*." I plop onto the bench and Tatum joins me.

She wraps an arm around me and squeezes me close. "It could have been his sister for all you know. Why are you always so pessimistic? You're so much better than that."

"It comes with the territory. I don't know what else to tell you."

"Tell me you'll stop thinking you're anything *but* the amazing, loving, gorgeous best friend I know and love. Size isn't everything, you know?"

"That's definitely *not* what she said." I use sarcasm to mask the hurt.

"Definitely not," she giggles. "But it's what *I* said and I know what I'm talking about so when are you going to start listening?"

Time to shut her up before this gets sappy. I don't have time for sap. I need to finish my workout and get to work. Except, Tatum's always been there for me and I owe her something other than my gloom and doom. I recall the deal Ashley made with me at the bridal boutique and steal her idea. Fueled by my new-found battle against the bulge, I blurt out, "How about I make you a deal?"

Her eyes sparkle with wonderment. "Let's hear it." She rubs her hands together and bites her bottom lip.

"When I get to my goal weight—*if* I get to my goal weight—I'll put myself out there."

"You'll flirt with Fancy Pants?" She jumps to the edge of the bench.

"No! Geez, you're relentless. Forget him. He's taken. I'm talking about *other* hot, tattooed, shaggy-haired men. I'll even let you set me up."

She clutches her chest and gasps. *Shit!* I shouldn't have thrown in that last part. "Really? Really? Really?"

"Yeah, really. But not until that scale says the magic number and until then, I need you to let me complain about being on a diet, let me whine about being fat, and continue to let me wallow in my pessimism. You think you can do that?"

Her eyebrows scrunch in disgust. "You take the fun out of everything, Len. And when will you get it through your thick skull that the attention of a man won't fix everything. You need to feel worthy of *yourself*. A guy can't do that for you and it goes so much deeper than losing a few pounds."

Once again she's right, but this is all too heavy a convo for right now. I realize I have things to work on other than shedding some skin, but I'll deal with that later.

"Can we not? I made you a deal, you taking it or not?"

It takes her a second to give in, but then her pretty smile returns to her even prettier face. "Fine! You're on! Whine away, there's a silver lining with my name on it!"

While I'm enthused by Tatum's amusement, I'm not so sure I'll be able to hold up my end of the bargain. The whole idea of a full-on transformation scares the ever loving shit out of me.

"DON'T DO IT, LENI." TATUM'S calm warning reminds me of my mother's when I was a child.

"Shut up, wench!" I snap. I want no part of reprimands to-day. It was a bad one. The kind where your cravings get the best of you and your stomach speaks in tongues—growling and cry-ing for anything other than a freaking raw carrot or a tasteless cucumber slice.

"Come on, it's not worth it! You'll regret it later." My friend's hand is at my wrist in a death grip. *Geez, she seems more invested in this than I am.*

"Fuck off!" I pout and nudge her in the arm with a rather sharp elbowing.

"Ow, bitch!" That gets a rise out of her. "Put down the god-damn spoon and have a little self respect!"

I gape at her, the spoon dripping with a huge heaping of Rocky Road. "Did you . . . did you really, just—?"

"Yeah, I really just." She yanks the melted ice cream cov-ered spoon from my hold and stuffs it in her own mouth. After she licks her lips and fingers clean of *my* treat, she deadpans, "Deal or no deal, it's been three weeks and you've lost twelve pounds! That's two small newborns! That's amazing, Leni I'm so proud of you and you should be, too. So, why? *Why* would you ruin everything you worked for with this?" Tatum points to the quart of poison as if it's . . . well, poison.

"Shit, Tatum. I'm not snorting coke! I just wanted to treat myself. I had a shitty day and I needed something more than an ugly green vegetable to help me get through." I rise from the table with a loud scrape of my chair against the tile floor and head to the fridge. If I can't have my beloved ice cream, I'll have to settle for celery.

Tatum follows behind me, like a woman on a mission. "Do you hear yourself? That's the one thing you haven't admitted yet. You use food as a crutch, as some weird coping mechanism."

"So!" *Doesn't every woman?* I ignore her as I search through the fridge for something to accompany my crunchy veggie.

"So? So, you have me, your parents, and Reynold and Ashley! You don't need to turn to *food* when you have a shit day . . . turn to *us*! And what the hell was so awful about today that you decided to do *that*?"

"Again? Calm your tits. You're pointing to the ice cream container like it's a weapon of mass destruction."

"It is." She snorted with laughter but I didn't find anything amusing about this. "Your ass will spontaneously combust if you eat it. Because let's face it, Len, I know one scoop isn't gonna do the trick. Then, after you devour the entire quart you'll cry because you're disappointed in yourself and then your shitty day will turn into a shittier night and you'll find yet another food to comfort you in your time of need. 'Round and around . . . see the cycle, here?"

*Shit! She's right!* I still don't get why Tatum cares so much, though, so I brush past her, chomping on the green stalk of not-so-yumminess. I plop down on the couch, cursing her under my breath for being right and for being so effortlessly skinny and for having to deal with this damn day without a tub of Rocky Road like the good old days.

She joins me, sans ice cream spoon, and grabs my shoulders. Pivoting me so we're face to face, she demands, "Talk to me. What happened?"

I exhale, hoping to rid myself of the negative vibes, but when I sit straight up again my mood's still as sour as can be. It would be nice to get on with our plans for the evening, so I decide to unleash and get this out of the way. "Well, besides being snubbed by the hot guy at the park—*again*—I just had one of those oh-woe-is-me days."

"Elaborate."

I fight back tears, recounting my day from hell. "The three bridesmaids were awful. Like Kardashian awful. Everything they did and said reminded me of my insecurities and struggles. If they weren't paying me so well, I would have fucked up their makeup just to uglify them, but it wouldn't have mattered. They were flawless from head to toe and they knew it. Then, the mother of the groom gushed on and on about how her son had met the most amazing girl. It was love at first sight and they'd only known each other two months before he popped the question because 'you don't let a beauty like that slip away.'

"As if that wasn't enough sweetness to give me a toothache, Angie, my long time client, suspects she's getting engaged tonight. The guy is super hot and beyond amazing from what she's told me. I'm so happy for her because she's a sweetheart herself, but . . ." I release it all like venom, spewing it out with jealousy.

"Okay." Tatum interrupts before I can continue. "I get it, but this isn't the first time you've done up a bridal party, Len. You're around this all the time."

"I know that, believe me, but it just hit home today. I want that. I want to be the beauty that some man can't allow to slip away. I want the man, the ring, the happily ever after and the only thing stopping me is this!" I grab a large chunk of flesh from my middle and start to cry.

"No, honey," Tatum cries along with me, kissing my tear stained cheek. "Your ridiculous image of yourself is stopping you. Only *you* can change that, babe. No matter how much I try to make you see how beautiful you are from the inside out, my words are weakened by your self doubt. It starts with you, Len.

It's all you."

I cry for a few more minutes, wallowing in the struggle that's overcome me.

I've heard it before, but this time it sinks in. The reason why? I'm ashamed to admit it, but the vision of Fancy Pants and Perfect Tits frolicking in the park today caused something to click and inspiration to strike. "I'm sorry I turned this night into Misery with Madeline," I say as I sniffle and wipe away my tears.

Tatum uses her sleeve to help clean my face. "I'm your best friend. I'm here for you always, so no apologizing."

"What would I do without you?" I ask, smiling through trembling lips.

"You would have eaten all the ice cream and cried all the tears, so thank fuck I'm here to tame your pitiful ass."

Thank fuck is right. I never want to see another tub of Rocky Road again.

# chapter

# six

"GIRL! LOOK AT YOU GO!"

And go I did. "Shit, am I reading that right?" I stare at the numbers in astonishment. It's been three months since I entered hell and now standing on this scale is a little slice of heaven.

"Hells yeah, you are! 1-8-3. Leni, this is amazing!" Mandy shouts as she pokes my arm. "You should be so proud of yourself!"

I am. I so am, but I'm still in shock. I haven't been this weight since college. Since Alex. Not a happy memory. On the same token, I'm closer to my goal weight and in hindsight, it didn't take much at all. I said *hindsight*. What's the opposite of hindsight, because while I was going through it, it certainly didn't *feel* easy?

"Say something, you fool! Did you lose your ability to speak with all those pounds, too?"

"I'm . . . I'm . . ." Tears erupt and I start to cry like a blubbering fool. "I'm so . . . happy."

"Oh, baby. Then why are you crying?" Mandy helps me off the scale and pulls me into her arms where I unleash a river of tears into the crook of her neck.

It's an overwhelming feeling. To some, this may sound ridiculous because there are so many greater accomplishments in life, but this is mine and I'm gonna ride the happy train for a while. "I just didn't think I could do it. I haven't cheated once by looking at the scale, just like you said, and part of it was because I was afraid I wasn't making any progress."

"My ass! Look at you! Your old clothes have to be falling off. You had to know you were losing, Len."

"Yeah, but seeing the actual numbers make it real, you know?" I sniffle as I put my shoes back on and take another deep breath. *183.* What a beautiful number. Not perfect, but so much better than what I was before.

Mandy hands me my other shoe and lifts my chin with her finger so we're eye to eye. "This doesn't mean you go back to old habits. It piles back on a lot quicker than it melts away."

As if she has to remind me. "I know the drill, Mandy. I'm not dense. But, sorry not sorry, I'm treating myself tonight."

Her eyes go wide and her lips form a tight line.

Before she can scold me, I raise my hands in defense. "Calm your rock hard ass cheeks. I'm talking about a cocktail or two to accompany my grilled chicken and broccoli. Don't worry. I'm not about to ruin the way this feels." And oh, does it feel so damn good.

"That's my girl!"

If I weren't straight as a ruler I'd kiss her right on the mouth. As much as I wanted to kill her in the beginning, Mandy has become a hell of a friend. She's talked me off eating benders and cooled my jets when I was on the verge of giving up. I owe her. "Hey, why don't you and Jane join us for a night out? It'll be fun, and I owe you a drink for putting up with me and getting me to this point."

"Yeah? Who's us? And when are we talking about?" A genuine, appreciative smile dons her lips.

"Tonight? Me, Ash, and my friend Tatum. Girls' night. What do you say? Is it too last minute?"

Without much thought, Mandy nods her head and winks. "I think you've got yourself a date."

"Should Jane be worried?" I joke.

She leans in closer and whispers, "Nah, honey, we like to share sometimes."

My eyes pop to the size of double-stuffed Oreos. *Gulp.* I know I look good but this isn't the type of attention I was going for.

Mandy's laughter bellows throughout her office. She leans over, clutching her knees as she snorts. "I'm joking. Sorry. Didn't mean to scare you."

Always the butt of the joke. That's me. But not this time. Instead of letting her get the upper hand, I caress her arm in soft strides and arch a brow. "I've always wanted a little girl on girl action and with a little liquid courage and my new outlook on life, I might just be ready to cross an item off my bucket list and pull a Katy Perry—you do wear cherry Chapstick, right?"

It's Mandy's turn to gulp and my turn to snort at her open-mouthed disbelief. "Wh-what? Really? I'm flattered . . . but—"

"Gotcha!" I wink, pointing a not-so-pudgy-anymore finger in her face. "I'm all about that bass, babe, but it needs to have a drumstick, too. I'm just playing."

She shakes her head and sighs. "Save your flirting for the *men* at the bar tonight, 'kay?"

I grab my purse from the hook behind the door as I open it to leave. "Yeah, yeah. I'll text you and Jane the details later. Thanks for everything."

"Anytime. Now go rejoice in your slenderness. You deserve it."

I know I do. So instead of heading home to finish reading

the rest of the book I started last night, I march my ass right to Fifth Avenue for some retail celebration. Mama needs a new pair of skinny jeans. I never thought I'd live to see the day!

"WHAT ABOUT HIM OVER THERE?" Tatum nudges me and points to the model-like male sipping a martini. There's no denying he's hot, but I'm not quite ready to test that body of water just yet. I'm looking more for the down-to-earth dude with a beer and a concert tee. Not the enigmatic suit and tie stud. Besides, I don't have to hold up my end of the bargain just yet.

"I haven't reached my goal weight yet. You can't force me to do anything."

"Since when are you such a stickler for rules? Live a little, Skinny Minnie."

"Yeah, I wish." I roll my eyes and take another taste of my vodka tonic.

"If you roll your eyes one more time, I'm calling Mr. Martini over to slap your ass Christian Grey style," Ashley warns me with a devious grin. She's not joking. Remember what I told you about Vegas. Girl has balls for a dainty little goddess.

"I second that! I'm heading to the bar to grab Janie another drink. I don't mind playing wing woman. Might as well make myself useful." Mandy's quick to chime in, fitting right in with my favorite gal pals.

"What is this, a jump on Leni party? I thought you were my friends."

"We are your friends and we want to make this a *hump* on Leni party. Don't you agree, girls?" Tatum rouses the table with cat calls and the rest of the bar ogles our way. Half the onlookers raise their glasses to toast our good time—Martini Man included—the rest just glower.

"I said girls' night and I meant girls' night. I'm not prepared for anything more."

"Granny panties?" Ashley snickers.

"No!" I tsk. "Does your horny mind have no bounds?"

"I'm not horny, but you have to be! Your va-jay has to have cobwebs. When was the last time—"

"Ashley! Are you kidding? Not cool."

"Not cool 'cause it's true or . . . ?" Jane seems rather curious. I wonder if there's any truth to her wife's comment about sharing other lovers.

"Oh my God, guys. I'm not talking about my nether regions."

"Well, we should, because it's been a while—I should know—and I'm calling my wax girl right now to get you an appointment." Tatum whips out her phone and starts to swipe away but I snatch if from her before she has a chance to make said call to said wax girl.

"Stop it! All of you! First of all, if you must know," I lower my voice so the whole world doesn't hear. "I already have a very nicely groomed garden, thank you very much."

Tatum and Ashley share a prideful glance. What is it with these two? Is nothing sacred anymore? I ignore their happiness over my who-ha and continue. "And second of all, can I just freaking relish in this accomplishment for one second without having to worry about the next thing I want to cross off my list? I mean, cut a girl some slack. I've been skinny—well, skinnier—all of three minutes and the four of you are like Chuck Woolery from the *Match Game*."

"I think you mean Gene Rayburn. Chuck Woolery was the host of the *Love Connection*. Get your game show hosts straight, doll." G.I. Jane a Game Show trivia guru? Who woulda thunk?

"Whatever. You know what I mean." I roll my eyes.

"Ash, you saw that! Go get Mr. Martini! She rolled her eyes again." Tatum—the bitch who's supposed to have my back over every other chick at this table—throws me under the bus and sets Ashley dashing toward the bar.

"Ashley!" I call out. "Don't you dare!"

But she dares. Before I can hide under the table in embar-rassment, my soon-to-be sister-in-law—make that my soon-to-be-*dead* sister-in-law—is cozying up to one of the hottest speci-mens I've ever seen this side of the Hudson.

It's funny because when he comes over to introduce him-self, that's exactly what his name is.

Hudson regales us all for the next half hour, his eyes never leaving my fidgeting hands. No one else seems to notice it, but it's hard for me not to since I seem to have his constant atten-tion. No matter what he says, I can't stop squirming. He men-tions his French Bulldog puppy and I squirm. He goes on and on about an art show he attended at his friend's gallery last week, and I squirm. The dude belches, and I squirm. There is nothing that comes out of this handsome man's mouth that doesn't have me wiggling around in my seat and clenching my thighs with nerves.

"Leni, can I buy you another?" Hudson points to my empty glass and his pearly whites sparkle like the ones in the tooth-paste commercials.

This time, I don't squirm, but I do almost fall off my chair. "Um—um—you—"

Ashley cuts in and saves the day. "Yes, Hudson. Leni would love another. In fact, why don't you grab it and she'll meet you back at the bar after she freshens up."

I'm momentarily dumbfounded and I fear oxygen has stopped pumping to my brain. Did this guy really just ask *me*— out of all the beautiful women at this table—if he can buy me a drink? And did I just stutter like a bumbling fool and have my friend do the talking for me? *God, right about now would be the perfect time for a meteor to hit New York City like it does in so many end-of-the-world movies. Please, please, pretty please?*

But the world keeps on spinning and Hudson merely nods

as he walks toward the bar, looking over his shoulder for another glance at me.

When he's out of earshot, my fantastic four huddles close and giggles. "Leni's getting laid, Leni's getting laid," Tatum chants and the rest join in.

I look around to make sure no one can hear and my cheeks and ears become so hot and tingly I must be ninety shades of crimson. "Guys! Please! Stop it! You're making me uncomfortable."

"Oh, I bet Hudson can remedy that. Don't you think so, Janie?" Mandy does her best giddy girl, kissing her wife at the nape of her neck.

"I wouldn't know since he's doesn't have the kind of equipment I like to play with, but—I don't have to be a man-loving woman to see that that man digs you, Leni. You better cut the shy schoolgirl act and give him what he wants!"

"And what exactly is it that you think he wants? I have no idea what Ashley said to him to make him come over here, but I'm sure he's not at that bar pining over me."

"And that's where you're wrong, Madeline Moore." Ashley downs the last of her Cosmo and slams the empty on the table. "He asked if you were single before I even invited him to join us. Dude's definitely interested, so run with it and shut the hell up."

I'm usually quick with a comeback, but not this time. I'm floored. If Ashley's telling the truth, this is a first. A thousand negative scenarios run through my head, but I notice that he's alone, without a group of buddies to heckle with. Images of Alex and his frat boy dare make me uneasy, but this man is no frat boy and he's not with anyone who can dare him to do anything.

Could it be? Does *he* actually find *me* attractive?

"Say something, I'm giving up on you," Tatum sings.

I take a second to collect myself, to let it all sink in. I've worked hard and it's finally paying off. I may not be exactly where I want to be, but hell, Hudson doesn't know that and he doesn't seem to care that I'm a little curvier than most of the women here tonight. As much as it scares me to step outside my comfort zone, I deserve this and I'm going for it.

Lowering off the stool, I grab my clutch and smooth out my new top. Boldness takes over as I gulp the last sip of Tatum's wine and announce. "Well, butter my biscuit! I'm glad my garden's in good shape. If anyone needs me, I'll be over there flirting with *my* Hudson."

# chapter

## seven

I'M NOT BUTTERING MY OWN biscuit for very long. In fact, after two more drinks and lots of flirting, Hudson leans in with dreamy bedroom eyes and soft, sweet breath against my ear, "Can I take you back to my place, baby?"

*Baby.* Me? Baby! That term of endearment has never been uttered from a man's lips while directed at me. Unless of course you count the time my brother pointed at me at the fifth grade dance and announced that "nobody puts Baby in the corner" because I was sulking over not being asked to dance.

But this has a totally different, sexier, suggestive connotation. And I fucking *love it*. Something comes over me. Be it the alcohol, my new confidence, or the vibe Hudson's rubbing off on me, and I pull him by the collar and whisper back, "Yes, please. I'm all yours."

Hudson takes my hand and kisses my knuckles, then nods to the bartender for our check. I excuse myself to say my good-byes to my girls with a smile brighter than the north freaking star. I can already see the crazed looks on their face when I tell them I'm going home with Mr. Martini.

"Ladies," I interrupt their chit chat.

They all look up at me with puppy dog stares. I think I see Tatum wiping drool from her face as she slips her waggling tongue back inside her mouth.

"Wow. Were you guys watching us the whole time?"

"Yes!" They all broadcast.

"God, get a life."

"Who needs one when yours is so entertaining at the moment? Damn, Leni, that guy has not taken his eyes or his hands off you since you sat down next to him." Ashley is a giddy fool, beaming with excitement. I have to hand it to her. It's sweet that she's rooting for me.

"Well, it's time to call it a night."

Looking a little disappointed, Ash and Tatum pull their bags off their chairs, and Mandy and Jane rise from their seats. The four of them dig into their wallets and throw some money onto the high-top table.

Oh! They must've got the wrong idea. They think I'm going home with *them*. I reach into my clutch, pull out my lip gloss, and reapply it with a cocky smack of my lips. "You guys don't have to leave yet. I just came to say goodnight because Hudson invited me back to his place."

The look on Tatum's face is priceless. I wish I had my phone in my hand because I'd snap that shit so quick she wouldn't know what hit her. "Are you serious? O.M.G. You're serious!"

"As a heart attack. I'll text you in the morning. Thanks for celebrating with me." I act as nonchalant as I can when on the inside I'm screaming for advice and for someone to hold my hand.

As I turn to reunite with Hudson, I hear them mumbling behind me. Giggles, snickers, and oh my god's fill the air as I sashay my way back to the man who's about to cure my dry spell.

Ashley rushes up behind me, followed closely by Tatum. They both take turns barking out orders in the form of pert whispers.

"Make sure he wears a condom."

"Have fun."

"Be yourself; that's what snagged him in the first place."

"Call me if you need a ride home."

"Call me if he does anything stupid."

"Ride him like the stallion he is."

"Okay, that's enough. Goodnight. I'll call you tomorrow with a full report. Happy?"

"Ecstatic." Ashley croons.

"Delighted." Tatum beams.

"Buh-bye." I wave and find my way into the arms of a man who, two hours ago, was just a good looking stranger from a daydream.

THE WALK BACK TO HUDSON'S is surprising. He's chatty, funny, and polite. I find him reaching for my hand as we turn the corner after the bar, and I gladly accept his offer by tangling my fingers with his.

"I don't usually do this," he admits.

I find that hard to believe but I go along with his rouse. "I don't *ever* do this, so I got you beat."

"Not possible. A girl with your curves and those eyes—I was shocked when your friend told me you're single."

*Oh, Hudson.* Keep feeding my ego because the two pieces of grilled chicken I had for dinner aren't doing shit to curb my hunger. Fortunately, a different kind of hunger is at the forefront of my mind. "You're extremely flattering. Thank you." I don't usually know how to accept a compliment. Then again, it's been a while since a man had something nice to say about me.

We walk the rest of the way making small talk about the weather and simply enjoying each other's company. He stops a few yards from a building with a doorman outside. *This must be his place.* Before I have time to ask, I'm pinned against a brick wall with a strong, roving hand tugging at my hair. "Oh my," I breathe when Hudson's lips are an inch from mine, his gaze dark and seductive.

"I've been wanting to do this all night." It's the last thing he says before his lips crash to mine and a thousand sparks I've long since forgotten could exist flicker within.

I'm dying for control of my hands so I can grab his hair, his arms, his ass, but they're pinned against the wall above my head in the sexiest position I've ever been in. I moan against his mouth as our tongues slide and tangle together, and before I can fight the urge to break free of his hold, his lips leave mine and his arm is curled around my waist.

"Come. Upstairs. Now."

I never knew how sexy a demanding man could be. I mean, my dad's demanding in the "get me another brewskie, Josie" sort of way, but *this*—Hudson can order me around any which way he pleases.

I giggle past the doorman, float on over to the elevator, and once inside, Hudson narrows his dark stare my way, asking, "Ever do this before?"

For a split second I think he's asking me if I'm a virgin, but when I see him eyeing the elevator buttons I wise up. "No," I answer, biting my lip.

"Good."

With that, Hudson's finger presses the stop button and the elevator jerks to a halt. "Is this safe?" I ask, my nerves getting the best of me.

"Who cares," he states rather than asks, lunging at me with a look that can only be described as animalistic.

Holy shit! Mandy was right! Hudson just made me a gym

lover. I mean, I know it's shallow to think that he's only interested in me because I lost a little weight, but what else gives? Three months ago, I wasn't getting the attention of gorgeous men sipping martinis and tonight I am. Lectures from the past from loved ones ring loud and hauntingly in my head as Hudson continues to adorn my neck with warm kisses. *I am worthy. I always have been. I'm the same person I've always been. He's attracted to me because I'm me.* If I say it enough it'll become a mantra. 220 or 183, I'm still the same old Madeline Moore, but with a drop more confidence now that *I* like what I see.

"Madeline?" Hudson interrupts my thoughts, moaning against my neck as his tongue licks a trail inside the curve of my ear.

"Hudson?"

"I'm going to fuck you right here."

*Well, hello! Glad to oblige.*

"You can have me wherever you want me."

And have me he does.

Here, there, and everywhere.

Four times that night I scream out his name. Four times that night I nearly cry at how good it feels to be adored this way by a man again. Four times that night I swear I will never, ever, succumb to any of my old habits again. Because, damn it, the pain of pushing myself and learning to overcome the self doubt was worth every ounce of sweet ecstasy Hudson bestowed on me that night. The night I allowed a handsome stranger to fuck the insecurities right out of me.

# chapter

# eight

YOU KNOW THAT SCENE IN the *Sound of Music* where Julie Andrews spins around and sings *"The hills are alive with the sound of music?"*

Well, that's me this morning. Except, instead of bellowing from the grassy knolls and mountains of Austria, it's just me, in my shower, singing the praises of last night's tryst with Hudson.

What a few orgasms and some manly hands all over your body can do to lighten your mood. Not to mention, your ego. There's something to be said about being worshiped by a man's lips and adored by his tongue. *Mmmm.* The thought has me weak in the knees all over again.

It's been years—I mean, *years*—since I've felt this good about myself. Hell! This good in general. Call me crazy, but I really don't care that it took a man to breathe that kind of confidence back into me. There's a first step to every process and I'm ready to follow through with the rest.

As I rinse the shampoo from my hair, I lace my fingers

through the long locks the way Hudson did when he kissed me. While I lather my body with soap, I trace the curves of my new and improved shapely body, mirroring the stroke of his hands. "Oh, Hudson," falls from my lips as my fingers dip between my legs and emulate the deft motions of the man whose name I recited over and over again last night. I bring myself to rapid breaths and erotic groans, an inch away from release. My impending eruption is cut short by a pounding on the bathroom door.

"Leni, you bitch! You never called. Hey, you okay in there? I thought I heard you—oh, shit!"

*Oh shit, is right.* I thought I was alone and here I am moaning and groaning with my fingers buried in my garden and my best friend as a witness. "Be right out!" I yell, wrapping up my long, luxurious shower with a turn of the knob to run colder water. *Snap out of your sex-fog, Leni. She's gonna want a full report, STAT.*

Faster than you can say orgasm stealer, I'm out of the shower and semi-ready to face my friend and her inquisition. I wrap a towel around my hair and another around my body as I smudge the steam from the vanity mirror. Refreshed—regardless of my lack of um . . . garden exploration—I inhale the thick, foggy air and smile at my reflection. "You did good, Leni. Be proud."

When I open the door, Tatum's impatiently swinging her legs over the arm of my couch while flipping through Vogue. "About damn time, sexy lady. I was about to call the search and rescue party when you didn't answer any of my calls!"

Relentless. It should be her middle name. "Sorry for making you worry, even though I know you weren't *really* worried, just nosey and mad that I didn't call you as soon as I stepped out of Hudson's reach."

"Yeah, yeah, yeah . . . now tell me all about that reach! How was it? How was he? Is he your new beau?"

*Whoa, Nellie.* Seriously? "First of all," I twist the Q-tip inside my ear with one hand and remove her legs from the arm of my off-white tweed upholstery with the other. "This isn't a barn. Second of all, what ever happened to respecting the privacy of others?"

"Privacy?" she laughs, amusing no one but herself. "You screwed that theory in eighth grade when you made me *show* you how to insert a tampon. Plus—I heard you in there." She points to the bathroom with a smirk. "I'm used to getting a nice welcome, but *that*—oooh, aaah, ohhhh—was pretty fancy, Len. Thanks. I'm flattered!"

I snatch a throw pillow from behind me and toss it at her head. "Way to embarrass me, bitch! With friends like you, who needs enemies?"

Tatum's laughter turns into guttural cackles followed by excessive snorts. She raises her hands in surrender and shields her face from any further pillow flinging. "Continuation from last night, or remedying what *didn't* happen?" She peeks through her fingers, testing the waters.

"Continuation," I mutter, my cheeks flushing.

"You, dirty, dirty, ho! I'm so jealous!"

"Why? You have a guy, and plenty waiting in the wings. What's it to you if Hudson rocked my world—four times last night?"

"Four! FOUR! Oh my God, Leni's back!" She catapults from the couch and rushes over to the widow, drawing my curtains with a loud grind of the grommets against the rod. "You hear that, world? She's back and better than ever!"

This time, I laugh, allowing the humor in the moment to engulf me. It's a good thing. I'm not the butt of the joke this time. Now, I'm the belle of the sexscapade ball. "Would you sit down and stop your nonsense?" I beg. She's entertaining, but I have to get to the market and then to my parents' so I don't exactly have all the time in the world to gush on and on about my special night.

Sensing my haste, Tatum sits next to me and looks me up and down.

"What?" I ask when she doesn't say anything.

"You look different."

"Well, I lost 37 pounds. That could be it."

"No, that's not it. I've never seen that part of you, you know that. You could be 600 pounds and you'd still be my gorgeous, funny biffle. But today—you look different! It must be the after-sex glow?"

I touch my face and smile. "Maybe."

"So, I guess you're not in the mood to share *everything*, but I have to know—how did you leave off? Do you think you'll see him again?"

The million-dollar question. I thought about it on the cab ride home last night, before I drifted off to sleep at home, and as soon as I woke up this morning. The answer's been the same every single time. Without a doubt. "No."

"No? Why? You did say four times, didn't you? That means he was good in bed and he was totally hot, so what gives, huh? Is his dick crooked or something?"

"Oh my God, Tatum! No! His dick is perfectly straight and just the right size."

"Oh, so he was tiny?" She whispers the last word as if Hudson might hear her from across town.

"How do you get *that* from what I said?" See? Relentless. "If you must know, he was very well endowed both in length and girth, okay?"

"So? Then why don't you want to see him again?"

And that's the *gazillion* dollar question. The other one I've been thinking long and hard about. After debating, I've come up with an answer that I'm happy with whether or not Tatum agrees. "Because I'm better than that. And before you question me, let me explain."

Tatum slouches against the couch cushions with a look of

confusion tainting her features. With an outstretched palm and
a nod of her head she gestures for me to continue.

"I feel like a new person, Tay. It took hard work to get here,
and while I absolutely *flooooooved* the attention Hudson shelled
out, I can't feel good for a guy. I have to feel good for *me*." What
my friends don't know is that in addition to working out my
body I've been working out my soul. I decide to confess what
I haven't told anyone. "There was this day, about two months
back, when I had to literally force my boss to keep me late so
that I couldn't get to the fast food joint before they closed."

"Oh, Len. Why didn't you call me? You know I would've—"

"Of course, I know, but that's not the point. I didn't want to
rely on you or Ash or *anyone*. I wanted to win the battle over my
sucky willpower."

Tatum places a hand on my arm and smiles, allowing me
to continue. "That night, once it was safe to walk the streets
without the temptation of Mickey Dee's or the sort, I went
home and did some research. You're going to shit yourself, *but*
I ordered some of those Joel Osteen books Ashley always talks
about."

"You didn't?" You'd think I admitted to hooking myself the
way Tatum's mouth falls open.

"I did! And you know what, Preacher Man is pretty amazing! I learned so much about motivation and self worth from
those books and now I know that guys like Hudson can't make
me happy. It's up to *me* to make me happy. I looked past the
holy sermons about Jesus, The Lord our Savior, and grasped the
deeper meaning."

"Being?" She furrows her brows but her eyes twinkle with
understanding.

"I don't need a guy to make me feel thin and pretty anymore. I may not be perfect now and I probably never will be,
*but* I'm the best me I can be. Hudson certainly put a little boo-
gie in my booty and I'll always remember him for that, but just

because one hot guy gave me attention doesn't mean I have to marry the dude, either. Maybe this is the beginning of a new era, you know what I mean?"

"The slutty, one-night-stand era?" she muses with a wink.

"Something like that." I laugh.

She tackle hugs me and almost knocks the towel off my head. "I'm so proud of you!"

"Can't. Breathe. Over. Here." I manage to get out.

Tatum backs up and stares. "You've managed to lose *and* gain all at the same time."

"Yup! Imagine that?"

"No, imagine the look on Mr. Martini's face when you don't accept a second date."

Oh, yeah. That. "Well, we did exchange numbers, so you never know if we'll cross paths again, but for now—I want to learn to love *me* before I share that love with someone else."

"Wow!" Are those tears in my best friend's eyes? Why, yes. I think they are.

"Don't you dare cry!" I get up from the couch and undo the towel, my wet hair falling around my shoulders.

"I can't help it," she whines. "I've been telling you this for so long and to finally hear you say it yourself—I don't know. I just feel . . . I'm so happy for you!"

"I'm happy for me, too," I admit, honestly believing that statement to the core.

The rest of the day leaves me feeling just as hopeful and energetic. After Tatum leaves, I head over to the farmer's market for fresh fruits and veggies so I can stick with the program. I don't cringe at the sight of a carrot the way I used to, and broccoli is no longer a dirty word. When I'm done unpacking the groceries and tidying up my apartment, I head over to my parents' for dinner and ready myself for more Ashley and Reynold wedding talk. Again, this was something that used to make my stomach coil until the point of agony. But now, this new outlook

has me seeing things in a different light. While I'm no longer fixated on a weight loss goal, I'm one hundred percent focused on
my happiness goal. As my new friend Joel would say, *if you want
to be happy, you have to be happy on purpose.*

IF ASHLEY EYES ME WITH that look one more time, I might
just smack the wily smirk off her face. I texted her on the way
to Mom and Dad's and begged her not to mention the Hudson
situation. I have nothing to be ashamed of, but I also don't need
my parents or my brother knowing about my love life, or lack
thereof.

She prodded with a few questions and I summed up my answer the way I did with Tatum at my apartment. With my two
closest friends content and my unfuckwithable level through the
roof, I decide that this is the time to back Mom up and express
our concerns about the destination wedding thing.

"Guys," I interrupt Reynold and Dad's baseball banter.
Everyone's attention darts my way and I gulp down the fear of
pissing Ashley off. After all, if anyone has a right to be pissed it
should be me. Granted, the result was spectacular, but she was
the one who took it upon herself to approach Hudson and get
the ball rolling—without my permission.

"What's up?" Reynold asks, clueless.

Ashley still has the smirk on her face, and Mom is waiting
on bated breath because I have a feeling she knows what I'm
about to do. *Please don't let this be a shit show.* I've never argued
with Ashley and I don't want a reason for her to dislike me.

I shoo away the fluttering of nerves and just spit it out. "So,
I've been doing some digging around—well, mainly some eaves-
dropping during my sessions with the brides—and I have a list
of some really unique and trendy wedding hot spots."

Ashley scrunches her nose and tilts her head. *Shit. I*

*overstepped, didn't I?* Insecurities knock my ballsy confidence back down to Smurf size. "But you know Rey and I have been thinking of Punta Cana."

"I know, but—" I tread lightly and evaluate everyone else's reactions. Reynold seems interested, Mom is cheering me on with a megawatt smile and big, round eyes, and Dad's still stuffing his face. Ashley, on the other hand, is unreadable. "Ash, before you shoot it down, can I show you some of these?"

I excuse myself from the table to grab the binder I prepared just for today. I used to envision an elaborate wedding for myself one day, and seeing as that's not on the horizon for me just yet, I'm happy to share the wedding planning wealth with Ashley.

To my surprise, when I scoot between my brother and his bride-to-be, their attention can't be stolen away from the pages upon pages of swatches, menus, venue details, and honeymoon spots. Ashley becomes overly excited when she notices the page I've dedicated to the winery she and Reynold visited last year for their anniversary. "They do weddings? How did we not know this, babe?"

With the two of them enthralled in the binder, Mom creeps up behind us and whispers a sneaky little *thank you* in my ear. That afternoon—besides eating the proper, non-gargantuan portion of Mom's baked ziti and eggplant parm—I feel a surge of accomplishment I haven't experienced in a while. Ashley and Reynold decide to check out a few local spots and to not put all their eggs in the Punta Cana basket. Mom is over the moon excited that Nonna, Papa, and Aunt Millie might actually get to attend the festivities, and me—I have a new pep in my step that makes me feel unstoppable.

# chapter

## nine

EVER GET THIS FEELING WHEN you first pop your eyes open in the morning that your day is destined to be brilliant?

Well, I've had that uplifting positivity infused through my veins all week. And the destiny gods have most certainly delivered with good juju. Call it a fluke, or just a streak of good fortune, but I'm calling it *it's about damn time Leni sees the light.*

On Monday, I got the call that our team at the studio was requested on a photo shoot for an up and coming swimsuit line. To say I was thrilled is an understatement. Something like this is a huge deal in the makeup world. It means my name is getting out there—somehow. And *my* name on anyone's lips means great things in this industry. Doors could open, opportunities might arise, shit could get real. All pluses in my book.

Then came Tuesday, when two of my regular clients gave me rather large, unexpected tips. One loved the risk I took with her eyebrow shaping (she'd been sporting the Brooke Shields 80's look a little too long). The other was simply in a good mood and felt like paying it forward. Thank you very much, have a nice day.

When Wednesday rolled around, I hopped on the scale for weigh-in day and found I'd lost another two pounds. There were weeks I'd lost more, less, and even zilch. But I hadn't gained since I started and to me that's winning. And I'm not talking about the Charlie Sheen type of winning. The continuous dropping of pounds means I've not only stuck to a plan but finally figured out how to change my lifestyle. Any health nut will tell you *it's not a diet, it's a lifestyle* and I've become a firm believer in that philosophy. Like I said, I've seen the light.

Yesterday my luck continued when Hudson texted me. It's becoming a normal thing and quite honestly, I enjoy the attention, but I've yet to accept his offer for another "date." One, because he's made it clear that his definition of date is more like a booty call, and two, because, well, like I told Tatum, I'm learning to love *me* and it ain't happening overnight.

I've definitely become more comfortable in my own skin, and part of that is because of what I see in the mirror, but the rest of it can only be explained as a come to Jesus moment. For once in my life, I get it. Looks aren't everything. Happiness comes in other shapes and forms, and I'm not talking about that apple or pear shape analysis of the body that society makes you obsess over. I'm a cool chick and people dig me. *That's* happiness; the only kind I should've ever cared about. So, I'm rolling with it and stringing Hudson along until he either moves on to the next curvy chica or accepts that the only thing I can offer him right now is a discounted eyebrow threading or my friendship.

Today feels no different as I step out onto my favorite path and turn up the volume to a Milky Chance tune that I adore. *Stolen Dance* echoes through my ears and gets my heart pumping and my arms swinging in time to the catchy beat. I always find myself mouthing the words to my favorites, and wonder if people see me and think I'm cuckoo. I honestly don't care because I'm in my zone and as Starship would say, nothing's gonna stop me now.

The air is crisp and the leaves have started to fall, Mother Nature's way of readying herself to welcome the season I love best. I close my eyes and breathe in the scent of dewy, fresh-cut grass and damp, musty tree bark. And then it hits me—*BAM!* Literally.

*Holy shit that hurt!* The unexpected impact causes me to fall flat on my ass. The initial pain overwhelms my skull. *The world is spinning.* I cover my eyes to rub the throbbing sensation away. *Where did that tree come from?* My vision is blurry so I blink to clear it, but it remains unfocused, further confusing me. "Mother fu—" I start to whine, but I'm stopped by a helping hand at my shoulder.

"Oh my God! Are you okay?"

I can't make out the person or the voice because my eyes are busy scrambling around in my head. I try to look up, but something wet is dripping down my face and over one of my already clouded eyes. "Shit! Is that blood?"

"Yes, you're bleeding. We need to get you to the hospital. Can you tell me how many fingers I'm holding up?"

*No! I can't even tell who the hell I'm talking to!* "Um," I squint and try to make his fingers out, but no dice. "No," I wince, suddenly feeling queasy. Before I can control it, I'm yacking all over this helpful strangers running shoes. "Oh my God! I'm so sorry." I don't even know if he can make it out through all the puking, but guess what I do make out. His shoes. As in *his*. Yup! My valiant knight in shining Under Armor is none other than *the* Mr. Fancy Pants.

"Holy shit!" I slap my hand against my forehead and with that little bit of pressure against my already bruised head, I feel myself falling, falling, *falling* . . .

"WHERE AM I?" I ASK, looking around the room. It's a hospital room, and I'm wearing a green cotton gown—with my bare ass exposed—laid up in a hospital bed. The harsh reality startles me and I jerk upright to take in my surroundings.

"Whoa! Relax. You might pass out again." I didn't know I had company until he spoke and now that he has, I wish I would collapse unconscious again.

"Oh, hi," I whisper, wishing I could disappear into thin air. "What are you—why did you—" I don't even know where to begin. My words are a muttered mess and my brain literally hurts.

Mr. Fancy Pants approaches me with a gleaming smile. And dimples. The dude has not one, but *two* insanely adorable indents in his scruff peppered cheeks. "I'm Lane. It's nice to actually *meet* you." His voice is soft and gravely. Exactly as I imagined it would be. You know, like when I daydreamed about him whispering sweet nothings in my ear. And *Lane*. Isn't that something. Leni and Lane sounds so cute in comparison to Leni and Mr. Fancy Pants.

"Hi, Lane." I finally drag my thoughts out of La La Land and back to the gorgeous specimen who saved me from the evil tree and who allowed me to—*oh my God, I puked on his shoes.* "Crap! I am so, so sorry I hurled on you." I bring my hand up to my eyes to hide my embarrassment.

Lane laughs—a deep, throaty chuckle that sends tingles to my garden—and shakes his head. "No worries. I had to get a new pair soon anyway."

"Yeah, you probably wore them out with all that running you do, eh?" *Eh? What, am I Canadian? And way to point out the obvious. Stalker much?*

"No more than you." He smiles again, staring a bit too long at the spot above my left brow that won't stop throbbing.

I should ask him what he's looking at, but my mind can't

detach itself from what he just said. "You've seen *me* running?" I ask, squeaking like a shy little mouse.

His face lights up with recognition and a glint of humor in his green eyes. "Of course I see you. In fact, you've got quite a reputation, you know?"

"Huh? I do?" Now I *really* know I did a number on my head because I must be confusing his words.

He pulls the chair beside my bed closer to me, sitting and making himself comfortable. "Yeah, the other runners call you Karaoke Girl."

*Other* runners? Is there some secret club? And Karaoke Girl? What in the ever loving—?

Sensing my confusion, he answers, "You sing out loud to your music. It's cute."

"*What?*" Okay, I'm dreaming, right? Or I'm dead. *That's it!* When I hit that tree I died and went to heaven and now God is allowing me to live out every single one of my fantasies because he cursed me with the chubby gene and I deserve everlasting happiness in the afterlife.

He leans back in the chair, flashing another bright, warm smile. "Why do you look so shocked? We find it rather entertaining."

"*We?*" I was once starved for attention. Now that it seems all eyes are on me, I take it back.

"The regulars." He sniffs as if I should know what he's talking about. When I shake my head in misunderstanding, he continues, "*We've* been rounding that track for the last few years and what started out as a *hello* every now and then turned into a sort of, I don't know, common ground, I guess."

Understandable. I get that comradery vibe in the park, too. Funny, though, since I never actually thought to talk to one of the *regulars* and I never witnessed Lane speaking to one, either.

"But I always see you alone." *Except of course that one time, with that one chick that I'd rather not bring to your attention since you* haven't brought her around again and I'm secretly hoping you broke up, if she was indeed your girlfriend. And now she's moved on and you're all sad and you're here and you saved me and . . . will you marry me?

My thoughts trail off but Lane goes on. "Nah, not true." He shrugs his muscular shoulders. "You and I just never seem to be on the same timetable, but after we pass each other I usually catch up with Ronnie or Saul. Other times it's Jenny and Karen."

"Huh," I muse. "There's a whole world of you people out there that I never knew about."

"Don't be crazy. You know who they are, too. Ronnie's that guy with the four dogs. Saul is the red-headed dude with the dark shades. And Jenny and Karen are the twins. Karen usually has her jogger stroller. The little guy in there is her son, Liam. And Jenny—" He huffs before he can finish his thought, his voice lingering on her name. I bet she's the girl I saw him with that time.

Instead of allowing him to reflect on this *Jenny*, I cut him off. "Well, I still feel like an outsider to your secret runner's society. I don't know jack about all of these *regulars*, but they all seem to know me, is that right?"

"They sure do!" His thick chest rises and falls with silent laughter.

"Hey! So, I'm some comedy act to all of you?" Madeline Moore, the perpetual butt of the joke.

Lane notices my embarrassment and reaches over to rest his hand on my arm. I almost pass out again from the gentle gesture. "Not at all. Like I said, it's cute. And you have a really sweet voice."

*Humina, humina, humina.* My mouth falls open at his sweet words. I'm momentarily speechless. Thank God for head injuries—blame it on the brain.

Lane and I spend an awkward moment in silence, evaluating each other's faces as if really seeing each other for the first time. I take note of the barely noticeable curve to his nose and the small scar underneath his right eye. *Beautiful imperfections.* His five o'clock shadow is scruffier than usual, but it's sexy and colorful, bits of auburn and deep orange intertwined with the same ashy blonde on top of his head. His eyes are the greenest I've ever seen and I've seen and taken notice of lots of eyes in my line of work. The deep jade hue doesn't even compare to that of any I've seen on a woman. This man is perfection. And I'm only looking at what's above the neck. I can only imagine what the rest of the package is like underneath that heather grey, sweat-damp, body-hugging—

"Madeline Moore?" A man wearing a white lab coat waltzes into my room and steals every ounce of goo-goo goodness out of my moment with Lane.

Lane snaps out of the haze we were both under and zips out of the chair. He starts to excuse himself, using my full name. "Madeline," it sounds like honey dripping off his tongue. "I should go. The doctor probably has some—"

"No!" I blurt out, every molecule in my body urging me to make him stay put. "Please, stay?" It's a desperate plea. I, myself, recognize the pitiful despair lacing my tone. The doctor arches a brow, indicating he recognizes it, too. And Lane—handsome, caring, fancy-pants-wearing Lane—he narrows his gaze and looks deep into my eyes, letting me know he senses it too.

In this moment he can either run for the hills to avoid whatever strange twist of fate allowed this to happen *or*—God willing—he can throw Karaoke Girl a bone.

Lane tilts his head and I'm certain he's about to crush my dreams, but when he opens that sexy mouth of his, he says, "Sure. I'd be happy to. I'll just wait out in the hallway while the doctor updates you. Sound good?"

"Sounds perfect. I'll be—uh—*obviously* I'll be right here." *Duh, Leni.*

"Yeah. I think you're stuck here for a bit." He laughs again, this time focusing on the ground. Would ya look at that? Mr. Fancy Pa—I mean, Lane is nervous!

I grin brightly and nod in the direction of the door, so as to not put my foot in my mouth the way I usually do when I'm around the opposite, very gorgeous, sex. Lane bows his head in agreement and strides out the door, leaving me to gush like a giddy school girl to the only one left to listen. This poor doctor has no idea what he's in for.

# chapter

# Ten

AFTER THE DOCTOR DOES A thorough examination and gives me a full report, I give myself a reality check. *Yeah right.* If I weren't so nervous I'd scramble my brain further, I'd be jumping up and down and fist-pumping to my heart's content.

Unfortunately, according to doctor's orders, I have to take it easy for at least a week. My injuries earned me an overnight stay at Mount Sinai so they can run a brain scan and make sure there's no internal bleeding. *Good times.* It could be worse, though. I could be here alone. Instead, I have a handsome man who came to my rescue waiting out in the hallway for the all clear.

"All clear," I yell, praying he's still out there and wasn't just pitying me before.

When Lane appears in the doorway in a pair of green scrubs that compliment his eyes, my heart thumps uncontrollably in my chest. Thank God I'm not hooked up to some heart rate monitor. It'd be a dead giveaway.

"You changed?" My bottom lip involuntarily winds up trapped between my teeth.

"I did," he answers, sauntering back into the room. Sitting at the foot of my bed, he runs his fingers through his unkempt hair. "I was a sweaty mess and, you know, the vomit wasn't a really good look for me."

*Oy vey. Why me?* Flirting and vomit don't usually go hand in hand. "I really am sorry about that. I'll give you the money for a new pair of sneakers and to launder your puke splattered clothes."

"Don't be silly, Madeline. I'm just glad I was there to help. They'll take good care of you here."

"Please, call me Leni, and how would you know? You have an in?"

"As a matter of fact, I do. I'm a geriatrics nurse here."

"Really?"

"Yup. How do you think I scored this awesome get up?" His hand scans the length of his body.

I'm totally impressed. This man is full of surprises. "I thought you just flashed your prize winning dimples and the scrubs fairy magically appeared."

Lane's head tips back when he laughs, his Adam's apple vibrating in his thick neck. "What is it about women and men with dimples? I don't get it."

"Well, being you have quite the killer pair, you should be used to it by now."

He shakes his head, dismissing my compliment, and then focuses on the bandage over my eye again. "So, you gonna live?"

I reach to touch the sore spot and flinch. "Looks that way, but I probably won't be at the track for a while. I was told to *take it easy* for a bit."

It could be the state of my muddled membranes but I swear I see a hint of disappointment dance across Lane's face.

"Gonna miss me?" I joke, a boldness overtaking me that I

never knew I possessed.

"Maybe." With a tilt of his head and a tight smirk, my knees go weak. *Thank you bed for keeping me horizontally safe.*

I've never been good at the flirting thing, but I'll be damned if I'm about to end this here and wait for another run in with a tree to get us together. I opt for honesty, rather than blundering with a try at seduction. "Can I ask you something, Lane?"

"Sure. What's up?"

"How come you never spoke to me before?" I'm not sure I want his answer—or some lame excuse—but it's too late. Cat's outta the bag.

Lane shifts on the bed, looks down, and fingers a loose thread at the hem of his shirt. I've learned the art of body language over the years and this is the second time this should-be-cocky-and-confident man has given way to his nerves. "I guess—I don't know, you were in your zone and I didn't want to bother you. Besides, you're kind of intimidating."

*Yeah, okay.* Now it's my turn to laugh my ass off. The snort that escapes me puts Miss Piggy to shame and gives Lane something to gawk at. "*Me?* Intimidating? And what, pray tell, is so intimidating about someone like *me?*"

His expression turns serious; it's the first time I've seen him frown. "Someone *like you?*"

"Yes," I admit. "I'm not exactly in the same stellar shape as Karen or Jenny and I've been described as many things, but intimidating is definitely not one of them."

"Well, then call it a first." I expect him to stop there, but he zones out for a split second and then turns back to face me. "Before today, you didn't really know anything about me other than that we run on the same track. I'm not sure what impression I gave, but contrary to popular judgment, I'm a quiet guy who keeps to himself a lot. I also don't know much about you, but from what I've seen—you're a beautiful woman with genuine determination, albeit it *clumsy* determination, and a really pretty singing voice. My brothers get on my case all the time for being so shy around the ladies, but yeah, everything I've just described about you is *very* intimidating to me."

*Gulp!* Stop the presses. I need to play the lottery because today, my friends, is Madeline Moore's lucky fucking day. "Wow, Lane. Please forgive me while I pick my chin up off the floor, but, dude, you just made my year."

He does that throaty chuckle again and his eyes sparkle with amusement. "Glad to be of service. And speaking of . . ." He reaches in his pocket and takes out his phone, checking the screen. "My shift starts soon. I should get washed up and start my rounds."

I can't help the surge of disappointment that washes over me. I attempt my best sexy-pout and it earns me a playful poke on my leg.

He rises from the bed and straightens out a few wrinkles in his scrubs. "Tell ya what. I'll come check on you during my break. That is, of course, if you want company?"

Eager Beaver wants to come out and play, but I know better. Rather than acting like some overzealous geek, I smile, a genuine one that reaches all the way up to my eyes. "I'd like that a lot."

"Great. Get some rest and I'll see you later, then." He turns to walk out of the room but looks over his shoulder when I call out his name.

"Lane?"

"Yeah?"

"Thank you for everything. The next time I bump into a tree—because, knowing my track record, it *will* happen again—I hope you're there to save the day."

Lane grins widely, his dimples showing again. "You got it, babe."

He exits and sets off to the land of blue-haired biddies and wrinkly old men. I'm left swooning and squirming, oozing with excitement over the last amazing hour of my life.

"YOU SMACK INTO A TREE and the universe applauds you! Way to go, Leni cakes!"

As soon as Lane was out of earshot, I grabbed my phone to call Tatum. Within fifteen minutes of telling her about my tree mishap, the hospital, and Lane, she's at my side, feigning good bedside manner.

"Tay, can you refill my water glass? The pain meds are making me parched."

She scowls as she slops water from the tiny plastic hospital carafe, dripping some over my barely covered legs. "Less drinking, more talking. I want to hear everything. Every. Last. Detail."

I scarf down the water, practically choking it down because of the way my best friend is eyeing me. When I'm done, she grabs the cup from my hand, slams it down on the swivel table and then rolls it out of the way. "*Un*parched?"

"Yeah." I nod.

"Speak."

For fear of losing a limb, I blabber on about everything that unfolded over the last few hours. I can't help but smile each time my lips speak his name. Like anything else in my life, however, I vow not to get my hopes up about any of it. Besides, I've been avoiding anything with Hudson all this time for the greater good. *Me.* I need to do me before I can do anyone else.

"And that's it in a nutshell," I finish with a drawn-out sigh.

Tatum's eyes flicker with enjoyment; her lips curl with glee. "Well, that's quite a large nutshell. He totally digs you, you know that right?"

"I know nothing of the sort."

She *tsks* away my negativity and gets serious. "You said he's coming back to visit with you when he's on his break?"

"Yup."

"He stayed with you until you were conscious?"

"Mmm hmm."

"He didn't lose his lunch when you lost yours all over his shoes?"

"Nope."

"And he called you beautiful and intimidating?"

"Uh huh."

Tatum leans over the length of my body and grabs my shoulders, shaking me. "Leni! Wake the fuck up! All this time you've been avoiding Mr. Fancy Pants and he's been pining over you! You, my friend, are on a roll, and I think it's time you accept it!"

Pushing her off me, I wince at the wave of dizziness her shaking caused. "Wanna watch it? Head injury here," I bark.

"Oops! Sorry. But really, Len. Think about it."

She has a point. I have to hand it to her. Ever since Hudson, I've been riding this wave of male attention that's nothing short of fantastic. That being said, I could *never* allow something so trivial to get to my head. I'm not that person. Never was. And no amount of weight loss will *ever* make me be.

"I don't know," I muse.

"What's not to know? You've wanted this for as long as I've known you—the attention of a hot guy who actually seems to like you for yourself. Why can't you embrace it and see where it goes?"

It seems easy enough. In fact, I'm half convinced it's time to pull up my Hanes Her Way and be a big girl, but reluctance rules my roost. Uncertainty undulates my utopia. I'm a chicken unwilling to crash land from the coop.

"We'll see," I finally concede, sinking my head into the not-so-plush hospital pillow. "Who do you have to blow for a decent pillow around here? Can you text my mom to bring me a better one? I'll never get through the night with this."

With a disappointed frown, Tatum rises from her seat on the bed and comes over to fluff the lifeless pillow. "I have a feeling that's not the only reason you won't be able to sleep comfortably tonight," she murmurs.

"What was that?" I should ignore her stubborn persistence, but I'm not one to allow someone else the last word.

Dancing around the room like a fool, Tatum clutches her heart dramatically. "Oh, Lane! I love your fancy pants. Can I take them off for you?" She smacks her lips and makes kissy noises as she moans and groans his name.

I snatch the useless pillow from behind my head and fling it at her. "Would you stop? You're so freaking immature! Enough already!"

Tatum deflects the pillow and continues tormenting me. "Lane, my hero. You saved me from that big bad tree Now, show me your big bad co—"

"Knock, knock." Tatum freezes and me? I'm on fire. I imagine I turn a shade of red that's not even on the color wheel. "I can come back if I'm interrupting something . . ."

*Okay. I just died. I need to be dead, buried, gone.* "Um . . . come on in, *Lane*." I accentuate his name and give Tatum a death stare that makes the beautiful palette of colors drain from her perfectly made up face. "My friend here was just leaving." I have no idea what Lane's heard, if anything, but the best way to avert the crisis is to avoid it.

"I was not," Tatum has the balls to say, her mouth agape.

"You were, too. Remember? You have to get to the pharmacy before it closes so you can get your wart cream."

Tatum turns to face me so only I can see and mouths the word "bitch" while narrowing her eyes. She quickly recovers after taking a deep, take-one-for-the-team breath. "Oh yeah." She glances at her wrist—she's not wearing a watch—and straightens out her shirt. "Would ya look at the time. I should head out." I'm awarded a tiny kiss on my forehead, accompanied by a subtle growl, and then she starts for the door where she meets up with Lane. "I'm Tatum, by the way," she says, with an up-to-no-good swagger.

"Lane," he reciprocates, taking her hand and shaking it. I don't miss his eyes darting down to where their hands meet. He quickly pulls away from her grip with a nonchalant brush of his palm on the leg of his pants.

I laugh to myself, content with my revenge. Serves her right, after all.

With one more glance my way, she sets out to leave. "Well, it was nice to meet you, Lane, and thank you for taking care of my klutzy friend. She owes you a date. Ta ta, for now." Wench had to get that last jab in, didn't she?

She waltzes out the door and on her merry way and the evil witch leaves me alone to explain myself to a very perplexed Lane.

# chapter

# eleven

TURNS OUT I HAVE A pretty thick skull—as I've always been told. Even so, I hit it pretty hard and in just the right spot, causing a mild concussion. The doctor discharged me with orders to stay off my feet—no work, no exercising—for a week. I'm not gonna lie; I definitely don't mind the idea of a break from everything, but this'll be the first time since I started with Jane and Mandy that I'll be inactive and I'll have to rely on eating really strictly to make up for the calories I won't be burning. And after Mom's trip to the grocery store for comfort food, that's gonna be a problem.

"Ma, really? Are you trying to sabotage me?" I hear the bag of chips crinkling as she removes it from the shopping bag. There's no mistaking the glorious sound of salt and vinegar Lays.

"What? They're reduced fat." Mom shrugs and stores them in my cupboard, inside the empty hole that was once a well stocked mother lode of goodies.

"They need to be gone. Out. Take them home with you. I can't deal with the temptation. I *won't* deal with the temptation. Hence the banishment of the chips."

"Geez, Leni. I just wanted to make sure you had all your favorite snacks. Crucify me, why don't ya!" Her pout could put a five-year-old's to shame.

All snacking aside, insulting her wasn't my plan. She's only trying to help. "I'm sorry. I know you mean well. I'm just—I'm a little on edge." *More like all kinds of weirded out due to my Lane situation.*

Mom unpacks the last of the food—that'll wind up going home with her anyway—and comes over to me on the couch. Just like when I was a kid, she brushes the loose strands of hair from my forehead and places a tender kiss there. "Well, then this little rest came at a good time, sweetheart. You've been running yourself ragged. You're allowed to take a break."

If only it were that simple. I hate disappointing clients, and I've gotten used to my workout routine. If the doctor hadn't made me so nervous about the after effects of a concussion, I'd tell him to go scratch and continue on with my business as usual. Besides, Lane gave me an earful too. *Him* I'm okay listening to. *His* word is gospel.

Just thinking about Lane and how he sent me off with such care and concern sends a smile creeping to my lips and warm fuzzies up my spine.

"You're doing it again." Mom interrupts my dreamy thoughts with a discerning nudge.

*Damn it.* Does this woman miss nothing? "Doing what?" I'm not going there with her. If I thought Tatum was bad, Mom's inquisition will go down in history, far superseding the one that took place in the medieval times of Spain.

"You're in La La Land. Just like you were last night when Daddy and I came to visit, then again this morning when I came to pick you up. And it was the same for most of the car ride home. What gives, Madeline? I'm not stupid. I know when something's going on." That she does, but I'll be damned if I'm about to tell her that *something* is a guy who has my heart beating at the pace of a marathon sprinter.

A good actress I am not, but I try my best at sick-patient improv by bringing my hand up to my bandage-covered bump. "You heard the doctor, Ma. He said I could have dizzy spells and migraines for a while. That's all. My head still hurts." I throw in a wince and bite my lip for good measure.

"Oh, baby. You poor thing." She lifts off the couch like a jack-in-the-box and reaches for a throw blanket from the love seat. Draping it over me, she guides me into a more relaxed position. "Here. You lay down and take a snooze. I'll start some chicken soup."

Crisis averted. I do as I'm told and settle against the pillow, resting my eyes. Before my mother can chop an entire carrot, I'm out for the count.

I'M NINETY-NINE-POINT-NINE PERCENT POSITIVE THAT when the doctor said to take it easy he didn't mean having my entire family and my best friend over to play a heated game of Bullshit.

"Bullshit!" Reynold shouts, throwing his cards down on the table. "There's no way in hell you have that card."

"Do you?" Tatum taunts, clutching her hand to her chest.

"No, but—"

"But nothing," she cuts him off with a wicked grin. "Do you call Bullshit or not, Rey? Going once, going twice . . ."

Reynold observes the rest of the players with an intense stare that would better serve him as an FBI interrogator. Everyone else remains stoic, focused on their cards or the intricate wood grain in the table top. I will never understand how such a silly, childish game like Bullshit can turn into DEFCON 5.

It's time for them to go. My head hurts, I'm tired, and if Reynold doesn't win this game—he's the sorest of sore losers ever—all hell will break loose. "Abort mission!" I shout from my reclined position in the living room. I haven't moved all day because whenever I tried it felt like the world was teetering back and forth unnaturally on its axis.

"What's the matter, Leni? Nauseous again?" Mom abandons her cards to rush over to me.

Tatum and Ashley follow suit, leaving Reynold to scour through the scattered cards and Dad to clean up the table.

They huddle around me as if I'm some endangered species on the verge of extinction. "Back off, mother hens. I'm fine. I just need some peace and quiet and your Bullshit screaming hasn't exactly allowed me that small luxury."

Mom pats my head lovingly while my two closest friends gang up on me.

"Someone got the fun knocked out of her when she smacked into that tree." Tatum elbows Ashley, who responds with another snarky quip. "Yeah, I think I know just the right person to force it back into her."

The two share a scheming chuckle that perks Mom's ears up at Border Collie attention. "Huh? Who are you talking about? What did I miss?"

"I'll murder you," I mouth, glaring at my supposed friends.

Apparently the look of death I give Ashley does the trick because she quickly changes the subject. "Josie, did your son tell you we picked a wedding date?"

Mom's concentration is diverted from me and fixated on my card-hunting brother. "No! What do you mean? Reynold, you little shit!"

Rey shrugs it off and goes to the fridge to help himself to another beer. "Girl stuff. I figured Ashley already told you."

The happy couple goes back and forth, placing blame on

the other for not sharing the details. It's late breaking news to me too so I'm all ears. Even if they're ringing from the unnecessary racket.

Tatum, sensing my mental combustion, breaks up the family feud with a loud, well-practiced whistle from between her fingers. "Whoa! Stop the bickering! Just tell us already."

The room falls silent—momentary bliss—and Ashley beams. "It turns out the winery Leni suggested had a last minute cancelation. We'll have to pull a lot of strings and ask for tons of favors to get all the vendors lined up, but this seemed meant to be so . . . we're getting married on November eighteenth."

My brother joins his bride in the living room and nuzzles into her neck. It's plain to see they're happy with their decision, but Mom and I set off into sudden panic mode.

"November eighteenth? As in *this* November eighteenth? That's less than two months away! Definitely not sufficient notice for the out-of-state family. I have to get a dress. The caterer. Your shower, Ashley! There's not enough time. It can't be done!"

I allow my mother to spew her tirade of worries while my own mini-monsoon of concerns bombards my already throbbing brain. *I still have so much to loose. I imagined I'd have more time to get in shape. And find a date. What the hell are these two thinking?* And then it dawns on me. "Are you knocked up?"

"Leni!" Ashley scolds in shock, but all eyes are on her. Even Reynold's.

"Well? Are you, dear?" My mother's face is a mix between scared shitless and overjoyed. If the tables were turned and I was the one who was potentially preggers out of wedlock, she'd have whipped out the wooden spoon and chased me around my own apartment.

"No! Of course I'm not pregnant. Wow! I had no idea you'd all be so skeptical and judgmental over this. I imagined everyone would be happy that we've decided to do this sooner rather than

later. I guess we can call the venue and see what they have a little further out. I don't want to cause any problems for anyone."
Ashley's on the verge of tears, rambling on and on while she
paces. I have to hand it to her—if this were me and my fiancé's
family had pulled the shit show we just pulled, I'd be waving
sayonara to the whole lot of them, including my non-supportive
husband-to-be. But not Ashley. She's a saint. I'm almost positive
she'll be canonized when she gets through those pearly gates
just for dealing with all of us.

The room is in a quiet commotion of hushed whispers
in separate corners. I can't take the pathetic look of defeat on
Ashley's face and my brother's hum-de-dum, blasé attitude
about something that has his girl so upset.

I'm usually the *not my circus, not my monkeys* type of gal, but
I've seen enough and God help me . . . I want this night over
with for once and for all so I can get the much needed rest I was
prescribed. "Ashley, don't you dare change a thing! This is *your*
big day. No one else's."

"Hey, it's mine too." Reynold finally speaks.

"Oh, shut it, nitwit. *Now* you want to say something?"

Thankfully, Reynold gets the point and zips his lips, leaving
Ashley and I to our moment.

"Ash," I amble over to her slowly, gripping her shoulders
with a tight squeeze. "If you want to get married to my ass
of a brother on November eighteenth, then get married on
November eighteenth. We'll figure out the details—*together*, if
need be—and make it work. This is about you and Reynold and
anyone who has boo to say about your date being inconvenient
for them needs to reevaluate their place in your lives. Got it?"
I realize I've dug my own grave and put a nail in the coffin by
backing up her cockamamie plan, but the girl is in tears. I can't
have that. Not on my turf. So what if I don't have a date? Who
cares if I'm not down another twenty pounds. All eyes will be
on Ashley anyway. It's not my day. It's hers.

"You really mean that? You don't object?" Ashley swipes at an errant tear and it's as though it's only me and her in this room full of watchful eyes.

"I could never object to finally having you as a sister. You know I love you. You're my best friend."

"Hey! That's my job!" Tatum butts in from behind me.

I roll my eyes and turn to her with reassurance. "Yes, Tatum, you are and always will be my bestie for life, but Ashley is too, so deal with it."

"I'm just messing with you. You know I love her, too." She comes over to put one arm around me and the other around Ashley, pulling us in for a group hug. "I know I have no say in this, but I'm with Leni. Go with your gut. Don't listen to these crazies. Love ya, Mr. and Mrs. Moore!"

Mom and Dad grunt from the kitchen and Tatum retreats to kiss their asses and help Dad tidy up the rest of the mess from this evening.

Left with Ashley and my brother, I reiterate my honest feelings about the situation. "I'm serious, guys. If that's your date, stick with it. Do what makes you happy."

The two lovebirds gaze at each other and smile before falling into a warm embrace. "November eighteenth it is!" Reynold sings, lifting Ashley in the air and swinging her around.

I quickly dart my attention to my mother who's no longer a deer in headlights. There's no doubt this will make for millions of side conversations and late night complaints, but for now she's content because her little prince is content in the arms of his saintly princess.

My work here's done, or so it seems, because Reynold and Ashley are engrossed—emphasis on the gross—in a lip lock fit for a late night Cinemax flick. The public display of affection churns my stomach and reminds me of my concussion and its possible aftermath. "Okay, now, everyone get out! I need my beauty sleep." I don't care that it's blunt, I don't give a crap that it's rude. I'm done with this day and I'd like to end it on a happy note.

My family starts to disassemble and I find my spot back on the couch that has housed my ass for the last six hours or so. Just when I think the crew is set to sail away off into the night, there's an unexpected buzz at the door. *Damn it all to hell! I was this close to silence. What now?*

Total blackout moment. Did someone call for takeout and forget about it? I could swear I paid the paperboy last week. "Who the hell could that be?" I'm clueless. And did I mention how dog-tired I am?

Everyone takes turns kissing me goodbye on their way to the door and Mom scurries past to answer it with her purse already in place on her shoulder. "Let me get it."

I gladly accept her offer and stay put. However, when the door swings open and I see my surprise visitor, I'm on my feet in 2.2 seconds. "Lane? What are you doing here?" I don't know if the words are audible because my tongue has become a dried up slab in my mouth and my pulse is thundering in my ears.

"Well, lookie what we have here," Tatum goads.

"Is that *him*?" Ashley rushes to her side, whispering.

"Leni, who's this?" Mom's oblivious. *Thank God.* I'd like to keep her that way, too.

It's my turn to be the deer in headlights. I'm momentarily speechless until I notice the bouquet of daisies in Lane's hands. "Um, everyone. This is my friend, Lane. Lane why don't you come in. They were just heading out. Let me say my goodbyes and I'll be right with you."

The poor man simply nods and makes his way past every curious bystander to this very awkward greeting.

One by one, I usher my now unwanted company out into the hallway. Questions fly and giggles ensue, but this has been one long ass day and I have a—I have a *Lane* waiting for me. Inside *my* apartment. "You all need to leave. Now. Thank you for taking care of me today, but if you don't scram—like right now—I'm disowning every last one of you."

I don't give them time to object or intercede. Instead, I squeeze past a baffled Dad, Mom, Reynold, Ashley, and Tatum and slam the door behind me. Once back inside, I lean against the door and let out the longest sigh known to womankind. Lane's spellbinding smile–dimples and all—is what infuses the air back into my lungs.

# chapter

## twelve

*COLLECT YOUR THOUGHTS AND CALM your tits. Be cool, Leni.*

"How did you know where I live?" It's the first thing I blurt out. Totally *not* cool, but really. How'd he find me?

Lane approaches me and clears his throat. "Hi, to you, too," he jokes, extending the beautiful arrangement of daisies. "These are for you, by the way."

I accept his kind gesture and bring the flowers to my nose, inhaling their mild but pretty scent. "Lovely. That's very sweet of you and thank you so much, but—"

Before I can ask him the same mundane question again, he interrupts by taking something out of his pocket. "You left this at the hospital."

*My phone.* Stupid me. I hadn't even realized it was missing. With all the fuss while I was being discharged and then the train wreck that is my family, I never even noticed. I take it from his hand with a smile. "Wow, what a dumbass I am. Thank you; you saved me a lot of trouble. I really appreciate it." Suddenly, I don't care that he came here to return my phone, or how he got my address. I'm just overjoyed that he's here. *Here.* In *my* apartment. With flowers for *me.*

"Why don't you sit down and I'll put these in a vase. Want a beer, coffee, some left over chicken soup?" I'm rambling in true Leni fashion because even though I'm supposed to be sitting still, I can't. My brain is on overdrive and my pits are sweating something fierce. *Lady Mitchum, don't fail me now.*

"No, I'm okay. I can't stay long, and you should be resting." Lane squirms uncomfortably on the couch as I fill my favorite antique crystal vase with the daisies. It dawns on me that I've always been the one to purchase the flowers to fill this vase. This is a first. A very lovely, unexpected first that I want to savor forever and ever and ever.

Giddiness overwhelms me as I return to the living room and place the flowers on the coffee table. I take a seat next to Lane and *exhale.* "I've been resting since I got home and then my family made it absolutely impossible to think straight, so while I'm sure my concussed head needs a break, I'm happy you came by. It's a nice surprise." Everyone's always told me honesty is the best policy. I just hope my honesty—the kind a fool wears on their sleeve—doesn't bite me on the ass. I've got plenty to chomp down on, so this could be a problem.

"I hope I didn't kick anyone out?" Lane offers.

"Oh, no, that was all me. They have a tendency to overstay their welcome." I lean back and tuck my feet underneath my bottom, directing my focus on the fine man beside me. Mr. Fancy Pants is in my house and I might get a case of the nervous Nellies because I simply don't know what to do with myself. Instead of fidgeting or ogling him like a buffoon, I return to my original question. "So, how'd you get my address, super sleuth? Am I that easily accessible or are you seriously a spy?"

He flashes me those adorable dimples and runs a hand through his hair. "When I came to your room to say goodbye, you had already left. The nurse who was on shift while I was visiting you yesterday spotted your phone and assumed we were friends."

"She assumed wisely," I affirm. "Any guy who barely knows me and then stays by my side to make sure I'm okay after my clumsiness leaves me with a concussion is a friend in my book."

Lane's nervousness seeps through his masculine façade whenever I'm assertive. It's cute. I take note of how his cheeks brighten underneath the coating of scruff as he stares at the gigantic smile he's brought to my lips. "I was happy to help. I couldn't leave Karaoke Girl lying there in a pile of leaves on the ground."

The silly term makes me scrunch my nose. "Yeah, about that. I think we need to nix the nicknames."

"Nicknames? *Plural?*"

I hide my eyes with my hands at what I'm about to confess. "I may be Karaoke Girl but *you're* Mr. Fancy Pants."

Lane chuckles and then looks down at his scrubs, then back up at me with raised brows. "Fancy Pants? Me?"

Regret for opening my big fat flapper scorches me from the inside out, but since I've already spilled the beans, I might as well follow through. "Remember how you said you, um . . . noticed me . . . on the track?"

"Yes." He tilts his head.

How do I say this without coming off as a crush-crazed stalker? I can't exactly tell him I've been wishing, hoping, and praying that he'd give me the time of day. Flippancy is a wonderful thing, but it's not my forte. "Let's just say, the first time I saw you, you had on these fancy trainers that the real deal runners usually sport. I was impressed and—" I will not dare admit that they were so gorgeously tight he left nothing to the imagination and I loved every second of it.

"And?" he prods when I take a second too long reminiscing the glorious sight.

"You just always look so . . . athletic and . . . *fancy*."

Lane's lips curl up at the ends as he leans back against the cushions. "Fancy?"

Realization sets in. I hope he doesn't think I'm insinuating—"I meant it in a good, *manly* way. Promise. The pants are a good thing. All of them. I like all of your pants."

My rambling scores me another throaty snicker. "Mr. Fancy Pants and Karaoke Girl. Would you look at that?"

Look at that, I do. In fact, in my mind's eye I stare at that blend of perfection a little too intensely. I want nothing more than to explore this adorable, almost-comfortable flirtation we have going on here, but I hold back at the risk of coming on too strong, too soon. Before yesterday, Lane was just a stranger. Today, we're friends. I'll take whatever small victory I can and run with it for a while before I give away the whole cow to someone who might not even want the milk.

I fidget under Lane's watchful gaze, and then put myself in check. "Well, you're here and that's great, but I still don't know how you were able to find me."

"Oh, yeah, that. Um . . . well, I had your phone and no way to contact you since it has a security passcode. So I pulled a few hospital staff strings and got hold of your chart. Does that make me a creep?" The innocence in his eyes is heartwarming. The more time I spend with Lane, the more I believe he has no freakin' clue how good looking he is.

"Creep? Absolutely not. I say it shows dedication. Dedication well appreciated, too. I'd be lost without my phone for too long and you saved me a trip back to the ER which, no offense, I know *you're* there, but I really don't want to visit again any time soon."

"None taken. That place is a zoo most of the time. I don't blame you."

We share a mutual laugh and a few sidesplitting jokes about the wackos occupying the emergency room triage.

For the next thirty minutes or so Lane and I chat about my recovery. Not only is he the total package looks-wise, but the guy's a total brainiac. He could've been a surgeon, but he decided to go his own route when his grandfather had a stroke and they bonded while he literally nursed him back to health. I cry tears for a man I never knew when Lane describes how he held on for dear life to the old man's hand as he took his final breath.

Every time Lane opens his mouth something refreshing and inspiring comes out of it. I must admit, I initially judged the "Lane Book" by its cover—as in, I never imagined a man as hot as he is could also be so kind and friendly. Maybe the moon's out of whack or something because lately, every stud I run into is as nice on the inside as they are on the outside. *The tide's changing, Leni. Get yourself caught in its delicious undertow.*

Sounds good to me, but suddenly the only wave rolling my way is a nasty case of nausea. I jump up from my seat right in the middle of my discussion with Lane and beeline it to the bathroom without so much as a warning.

"Shit! Leni?" I hear him call from behind me.

Out of fear that he'll follow me inside and witness another episode of the Upchucking Wonder, I slam the door and lock it before becoming one with the toilet. My stomach empties violently, the front of my head pounding with every lurch. When the queasiness finally subsides after what feels like hours of retching, I rest my face against the cold tile floor and then there's a soft knock at the door.

"Leni, I know you swore off the ER for all of eternity, but I'd be happy to take you to make sure everything checks out okay."

Sweet, wonderful, caring Lane. The sound of his voice soothes my otherwise unsettled insides. The doctor warned me that I could experience more vomiting if I didn't rest, but I had no idea entertaining a few visitors and lounging around in LuLaRoes wasn't considered resting.

With a mere second to take stock of the now-emptied state of my stomach, I feel as if the worst is over. "No. Thank you, though. I feel much better. Let me wash up and I'll be right out."

"Okay. Do you have any ginger ale in your fridge?"

"Yes." *Thank you, Mom.* She always makes sure I have a bottle lying around like she did when I was a kid.

"Do you mind if I go into your cabinets and pour you a glass?"

"Not at all."

"Okay. Take your time. I promise not to snoop around."

I bite my lip and giggle, brushing a few matted clumps of hair from my clammy face. I should be worried this man will be the death of me, but he's already breathed new life into me just by being in the right place at the right time.

AFTER I FRESHEN UP AND join Lane on the other side of Pukesville, he orders me to bed and starts tidying up the apartment.

"You don't have to do that." I reach for the glass he's unnecessarily washing in my sink and my fingers brush the back of his hand. Our eyes lock and we share a silent moment of unspoken desire. At least that's what I'm calling it, because one single millisecond of my skin stroking his has me in a tizzy.

"I've got it. Really." He finishes soaping up and rinsing the glass, our moment gone as quickly as it came.

Once the glass is cleaned and dried, he wipes his hands on the dish towel that's hung over the faucet and then turns to face me. If there was one way to describe the aura in my kitchen right now it would be that awkward first date / first kiss scenario that everyone in the dating world from sea to shining sea has experienced at least once.

I gulp away my insecurities, begging my nerves to take a

hike. I'm dying to ask Lane to hang out again—not necessarily a *date,* but just more time together—before I lose my chance and my grip on my non-existent balls. I take a deep breath and close my eyes—dramatic much?—and open my mouth to get on with it.

"Leni." He beats me to it, shutting me up with those delectable dimples. "I know this will sound weird, but . . . other than your trip to the bathroom, I had a lot of fun tonight."

*Hallelujah.* We're on the same page of this crazy book. "I know exactly what you mean and I was actually going to ask if you'd like to hang out again some time."

Lane's features relax and his tight posture slackens. "I'd like that a lot."

"Me, too." If a heart could take flight, mine would sprout wings and fly right the fuck out of my chest.

"Can I have your number?" It escapes from his mouth in a breathy murmur. *Why on God's green Earth is this man shy around me?*

This whole thing feels like high school. Or how high school *should have* felt had I not been shunned from coolness. Either way, I'm loving every second of our adolescent-like exchange. "Of course!"

I waltz over to the junk drawer with a Fred Astaire bounce to my step and pull out my whimsical "portable therapist" notepad. I scribble my cell number above a comic bubble that reads *It'll be okay. I hope.* Ignoring the quote on the ridiculous gag gift from Tatum, I slap the paper into Lane's open, waiting palm. "Sorry. This is the only thing I had handy."

He reads it and then his eyes meet mine. "You're already more than okay, Leni." This time his voice is so low it's almost inaudible. Before I can comment, he retreats and tucks the paper inside his shirt pocket. "I better be going. I'll shoot you a text tomorrow to see how you're feeling?"

"Sure thing." I follow behind as he heads for the door,

unsure whether it's the concussion or pheromones causing my
loopiness.

Once at the threshold, I lean across him to let him out. If
I could avoid letting him go, I totally would, but it's late, I need
to rest, and I'm pretty sure I have some leftover puke nuggets
in my hair somewhere. "Thank you so much for returning my
phone *and* for the flowers. You're very sweet."

Lane smiles and bows his head, placing a hand on my shoulder. "It was a pleasure. Take care of yourself so we can maybe
share a morning walk on the track next week."

"That would be wonderful."

Before I can react to what he's doing, Lane's leaning in,
our faces mere inches from each other, and then his soft lips are
on my cheek. He lingers, his beard tickling my skin, before he
withdraws and says, "Good night."

I think I return the phrase, but I'm not sure because I'm
left in awe, staring at the image of Lane leaving my apartment.
What just happened? And how? I'm not complaining, because
that would be plain old dumb, but I'm not sure I know how to
handle all these emotions without a box of chocolate and a gallon of wine.

# chapter

## thirteen

IF I'M LAID UP IN the horizontal position for one more second, I'm going to commit Hari Kari. It's been seven full days, zero vomiting or headaches, one overbearing mother, two fading bruises, many sweet texts from Lane, and now that I'm standing on the goddamn scale—aka the devil incarnate—five more unwanted pounds. I had a feeling this would happen because of my couch potato status, but it still sucks. If only they could come off as quickly as they creep back on.

"Damn you!" I stare down at the number, blinking as if doing so will make it magically transform to something lesser. Disappointment floods my flaccid muscles and I make the decision to take matters into my own hands. Screw the doctor! I mean, I can't be the first jogger to become one with the trunk of a good ol' maple. Surely there are tons of cases where people bounced back right away and went on to continue their training.

So help me, God, I want to be one of those people, because in the past I was the total opposite. An obstacle would deter me and cause me to abandon my mission. It happened after I was ridiculed at fat camp and the diet pill debacle. And it really spiraled out of control after I was rejected by Alex. But not today. Today's the day I don't allow the tree mishap to define me. Today's the day I seize the moment and prove to my inner chunkster that I've changed, for the better.

After I inhale a quick shake for breakfast and stuff my thighs into my favorite running pants that were definitely not this snug a week ago, I lace up my sneakers and head to the park. The weather's beautiful and I'm taking advantage before the warm fall breeze turns cold and blustery.

It's only been a week since I've been here, but I've missed this place and I'm happy to be back. I stretch my limbs and shake them out, then plug my earbuds in. Not even two minutes after finding my familiar groove the music is interrupted by an incoming call. I brace myself to see my mother's name appear on the screen, but to my surprise it's my boss.

"Hello?" I answer, slowing my jog to a brisk walk.

"Leni! How are you feeling, love?" Raven's bubbly voice warms my spirit. I seriously hit the jackpot when she hired me. She's a doll, and her knowledge of cosmetology is off the charts.

"Much better. In fact, I'm out for my first run since the accident and I was going to call you when I got home to figure out my schedule for the week."

"Perfect, because I have great news!"

Raven's great news is always epic. I veer off to the edge of the path—no trees in my way this time—to ready myself for whatever she's got up her designer sleeves. "Tell me, tell me, tell me!"

Raven giggles and then divulges the monumental information. "The swim suit shoot turned into a full on runway show. They want our team on set in Miami in three days. Do you think you're clear to go?"

"Yes!" I don't even think about it before I answer. Come hell or high water, I'm on the next plane to Miami. This is a dream come true, and I'd rather risk another membrane rupture than miss out on it.

"Don't you need to check with your doctor first?" Raven's voice is laden with concern. Of course it is. She's a mother of three and one of the kindest people I know.

She won't just take my hasty word for it, so I try my best to reassure her. "The doc said one week. I followed his orders to the T and stayed off my feet—nothing but soap operas and smutty romance novels for seven days. The bruising's almost gone and I've actually been feeling like my normal self for the last three days. Come to think of it, I probably could've returned to work sooner."

"No, no, no. Don't be crazy, Leni. I didn't need you fainting in the studio while you were with a client. We took the proper precautions and I'm glad we did because . . . now you're nice and rested for Miami."

*Squeeeee!* "Really, really, really? I can go?"

"Of course you can go. You're my top girl. We need you. Now, go reenergize your cute buns on your run and I'll email you all the details as soon as we get off the phone."

I shake my booty and break out into a happy dance right there on the edge of the trail. "Thank you! I'm so excited you have no idea!"

"Good. Bring some of that excitement down to Miami with you. I'm calling a meeting tomorrow afternoon with the team to get everyone up to speed on what to expect. See you then?"

"Yes you will! I'll pick up the coffee?"

"Please. Thanks, Len. Have a good one."

I hang up with Raven, so thrilled with the news that my usual four mile run turns into six. I should be rusty from not working out all week, but my excitement about Miami fuels every last molecule in my body to push as hard as I can.

THAT AFTERNOON, I ATTEMPT TO start packing for the trip, but it becomes more a game of fling-the-clothes-around-the-room than anything else. There is not one item of clothing that fits properly, and while that should be a major triumph in my eyes, it's a frustration I hadn't planned on. What used to be too small is now out of date from sitting in my closet too long in anticipation of pound droppage. My old, stylish favorites are now saggy and frumpy thanks to my progress. This means I'll have to go shopping, and anyone close to me knows I'm not exactly a bubbly, cheerful shopper. Give me a department store full of wall-to-wall makeup and hair products and I'm in heaven, but clothes and dressing room mirrors . . . just call me Linda Blair, minus the pea soup.

I'm not up for the challenge alone, so I shoot a group text to Tatum and Ashley, begging one or both of them to join me.

Tatum is first to respond with the eye-roll emoji and a snarky response that reads: *Shopping with you requires Xanax and earplugs. Ashley . . . wanna take one for the team?*

Holding back, I tap my foot awaiting the three tiny dots indicating that Ashley is typing out a message. When it pops up on the screen, I nearly toss the phone alongside the mountainous pile of clothes gathered at the foot of my bed.

> *Ashley: Wish I could, but Rey and I have to meet with the florist tonight. Sorry. Tatum, be a pal. Isn't that what friends are for?*

> *Tatum: Have you ever endured a shopping trip with our dear old BFF?*

> *Ashley: Maybe once*

> *Tatum: And you survived unscathed?*

> *Me: GUYS!!! I'm right here!!!!*

*Ashley: Sorry, babes. Next time?*

*Tatum: Honestly, I would if I could, but Paul is coming over and I haven't seen him all week. Rain check?*

Defeat is a terrible thing, but I can't say I blame them. The wedding has everyone in a time constrained dither and I have been known to get up close and personal on a not so appropriate level with the fitting room attendants at Saks.

*Me: It's okay. All's forgiven, wenches. I guess I'll have to find a Miami-suitable wardrobe all by my lonesome.*

*Ashley: Yay, Len! So excited for you. I'll call you after my class to get the whole scoop on the trip.*

*Me: Sounds good.*

*Tatum: Hey! I have an idea! Why don't you ask your new beau, Mr. Fancy Pants, to tag along?*

Every phone conversation with Tatum has to have an expiration date. This one came rather quickly.

*Me: Okay, and that's the beauty of modern technology. I'm leaving this chat. Bye, girls, thanks for nothing. Speak to you later, Ash.*

With that I turn off the text notifications on the group chat and throw myself onto the mattress with a dramatic huff. My head sinks into the plush pillow and just as my lids descend over my tired eyes, the phone buzzes against my stomach with another alert.

I don't want to look because it's probably just Tatum torturing my life again, but I lift it up and instantly reawaken at the sight of his name.

*Lane: How's my favorite patient today?*

Aw. I'm his favorite patient? My thumbs tingle as they race

to respond.

> *Me: Hey, I'm good. Thanks for asking. Missed you on the track today.*

Too much? That was too much, wasn't it?

> *Lane: You should have texted me! I would have met you. In fact, that's another reason I was texting. I'm heading for my run now.*

Of course I missed him by a smidge. Story of my life . . . too much or too little, no moderation.

> *Me: Damn, would've been nice to have some company. Next time?*

> *Lane: Definitely. I can't tomorrow but maybe Wednesday?*

If it weren't for bad luck, I'd have none.

> *Me: Leaving for Miami Wednesday morning.*

> *Lane: Oh, nice! Business or pleasure?*

> *Me: Business. Swimsuit runway show.*

> *Lane: I knew you had to be a model! My gut is never wrong.*

Snot flies out of my nose as I snort at his ludicrous mistake.

> *Me: You better check that gut, buddy. I'm not strutting anything on the catwalk. I'm a makeup artist. My team was hired for the shoot and the show.*

> *Lane: Well, it's their loss then. It should be you up there. I'd pay anything for a front row seat.*

*Oh my, my.* This is either one of those cases of texting balls or Lane is just a genuine sweetheart. My cynical nature finds it hard to believe it's anything other than a daring compliment masked behind the security of the phone. I can't even muster a witty reply because I'm not used to being on the receiving end of flattery. Rather than come off as insecure, I change the subject.

*Me: No work for you today?*

*Lane: Nope. Twelve hour shift tomorrow.*

I can leave it alone or make good on what I told him last night before he left. Is it too soon to cash in? My fingers decide to take the reigns without consulting my brain.

*Me: Doing anything later? I could use a shopping buddy. If you're game.*

Did I really just ask him that like he's some girlfriend you drag to the mall to try bras on with? And what if Tatum's right about my shopping rage? I have to come up with another plan. Quick.

I start to type out an alternate idea—movies, bowling, anything—but Lane's text beats me to it.

*Lane: Sure, only if you let me take you to dinner afterwards.*

For the second time in one day, I praise the gods of modern technology. If texting had never been invented, this would be an awkward phone conversation, and the ear-splitting squeal that just rocked my body would have sent him running.

I compose myself and answer with trembling fingers.

*Me: You sure? I don't want to put you out, it's just that I have to get to the shops so I can pack before the trip.*

*Lane: You're not putting me out. I'd love to join you. Text me what stores you want to hit up and I'll think of a restaurant in the area so I can make reservations. Meet at your apartment at 3?*

Good-looking, sweet, and thorough. Me likes.

We end our very productive text with a confirmation, and I bust a few very unattractive moves around my bedroom. Out of breath and adrenaline pumping, I psych myself up to call Tatum for outfit advice. She's going to flip. I can hear her now. Surely, she'll take credit for this being her idea in the first place.

Okay. Maybe I'll wait to call her until I can bask in the joy of first date butterflies a few minutes longer.

# chapter

# fourteen

HA! SUCK ON THAT, TATUM. There were no outbursts at Bloomingdales or casualties at Urban Outfitters. And because I wore my favorite comfy Chucks, rather than the wedge boots she suggested, my dogs aren't barking and Lane and I can enjoy a nice stroll through the narrow cobblestone streets of the West Village. Rather than cram into the grimy subway, we carelessly promenade Wooster and Prince Streets, soaking up the natural art all around us; quirky boutiques, antiquated buildings, the hum of the melting pot of tourists, transplanted residents and real-deal natives of the city. In my former days, I would celebrate my enjoyment with a dirty water dog from a street vendor as an appetizer, but since I'm being good, and want to keep the streak of non-embarrassment going, I'll restrain.

"Ready to eat? All that shopping made me hangry!" Lane snarls as he politely grabs the bags out of my hands and meshes them with his own.

"Hey, you weren't complaining when you scored the

buy-one-get-one designer wife beaters."

He arches a brow and nods. "This is true. And why you New Yorkers call it that I will never understand."

"What? A wife beater?"

"Yes, it's kind of stereotypical, don't you think? I don't plan on beating on a woman every time I wear a white cotton tank."

"I get your point." I laugh as a hasty cab driver nearly clips my ass while waiting at a corner to cross one of the not-too-crowded streets of SoHo. "But I guess it's just one of those things you mid-westerners can't relate to."

During one of our conversations at the hospital this weekend, Lane told me all about his upbringing in Illinois. He lived there most of his life, until he moved to New York to attend college. While he hadn't grown up on a farm, wrangling cattle and such, I like that he's more mellow and laid-back than the guys from around here. New Yorkers like myself are known for being quick and abrupt, sometimes brash and forward. *If you don't like it, fugetaboutit!* It's easy to see that living in the city all this time certainly hasn't tainted Lane's easy going nature. It's refreshing.

The insecurities that are usually at the forefront of my mind seem to melt away in the easy silence between the two of us. We walk inches apart, wordlessly enjoying each other's company and that, too, is rather invigorating.

I follow Lane's lead as he crosses the busy, buzzing intersection and hangs a left on the next block.

"So, where are you taking me again?"

"La Esquina," he says, with an adorable attempt at a Spanish accent. "You did say you like Mexican, right?"

"*Si, señor.* It's my favorite." And it is, but suddenly I'm starved from all the shopping and walking and drool has accumulated at the corners of my mouth like a rabid animal. *No bueno* when you're worried about what kind of diet friendly meal you can get at a place that's known for its smothered corn on the cob and the most kick-ass *queso* north of the border. Even though the jeans I purchased earlier are three sizes smaller than my norm, the five pounds I put on during my recovery and the Mexican feast looming ahead bring my spirits down.

"Then why the long face?" Lane must notice the apprehension in my slowed pace and he bumps his hip with mine.

"Ugh. Calories." Not something I'm proud to admit to a prospective date, but it's the truth and I feel comfortable enough around Lane to let it out.

"Oh, don't be crazy. You worked out this morning and we've been walking all afternoon. You're allowed to live a little, Leni. Trust me."

"Easy for you to say," I mutter under my breath just as we approach the hostess stand outside the building made to look like a very unassuming diner.

Lane places a hand at the small of my back, grazing the dip where my butt becomes bubbly, and escorts me closer to the hostess. The raven-haired beauty eyeballs the two of us as if we're a pair of mismatched socks. No doubt she sees me as the one with the ugly holes at the toes.

"Reservations for Sheffield." Lane breaks Miss Judgmental out of her stupor and she reaches under the wooden podium for the menus. I don't miss the confused slant of her brow as she appraises how close Lane's body is to mine. *Yeah, chola. He's with me. Fuck off.*

"Right this way." Bitch sways her mini-skirt clad hips dramatically as she leads us through the dim, cozy atmosphere.

I take in the quaint yet lively room, appreciating that Lane thought to take me somewhere so romantic. I would've never guessed it had such a classy Latin flair from the outside. Looks are deceiving—maybe that's the theme of the night. The root of that belief takes hold and burgeons within me. Regardless of the disapproving glare from our hostess, I boldly take Lane's hand in mine and squeeze with delicate fervor.

Placing the menus on the table, she politely hums, "Enjoy

your evening."

"Oh, we will." I smile the fakest smile known to man and curtly wave her off.

The warmth of Lane's hand leaves mine as he pulls my chair out for me. "This table okay?"

It's secluded and toward the back corner of the dining room, but in full view of the band at the far end of the room. "It's perfect. Thank you."

Lane removes his jacket and hangs it over the back of his chair before sitting. His olive-colored Henley makes his eyes look greener than normal even in the faint candlelight. And those arms. Guns, I tell ya. Lethal, sexy, weapons of mass ovary destruction. To think a man with such a perfect physique just had his hand entwined with me—a woman on the total opposite body-shape spectrum.

The waiter interrupts my self-doubting to ask if we'd like to order cocktails.

I start to ask for a water with lime, but Lane lays his hand atop mine. "Allow me?"

I nod with a curious smile and listen as he recites something off the menu that sounds totally complicated—and fattening.

I lean in, our hands still touching. "A water would've sufficed."

"Leni, this is one of my favorite places. I'm a regular. I'd love to take the lead tonight, if you'd trust me."

"You're just a regular ol' *regular*, aren't you? Here, the park, anywhere else you frequent that I should know about?"

Lane laughs, deep and addictive, toying with the buttons on his shirt with his free hand. "Let's just say when I moved here from Tuscarora, I really wanted to take it all in. And I have. Every bit of it. I love my hometown, but New York is so diverse and rich in culture . . . I can't seem to get enough, you know?"

Of course I know what he means. Most people feel the same. "I guess I'm just used to it. Not that I don't love it, too, but I probably don't take advantage of everything right under my nose because it's just always been here."

"Silly girl. You think too much."

"You know me so well already."

"And I know you're looking at the menu and worrying about what you'll eat. Don't think I didn't hear your little comment before."

"What comment?"

"When I told you to live a little you said it was easy for me to say."

Ah, so he did hear. "Guilty as charged." No use trying to deny it.

Lane takes the menu from my hand and tucks it underneath his. Leaning across the red tablecloth, he caresses my hands with his thumbs, tickling my palms with the rest of his digits. "I think you're beautiful, just the way you are. And before you go doubting what I say, you should know that I completely understand your struggle."

My straightened posture slumps as I flip him an *oh really* pout.

"Looks are deceiving, Madeline. I'm not the person you think I am."

Cryptic much? And there's that phrase again. "Oh yeah, then who exactly are you, Mr. Fancy Pants? Because what I see before me is a devastatingly good-looking man with a body that makes girls weak in the knees. And, in case you've forgotten, I've seen you in action—on the track. You're a machine and it shows with every sinewy groove of your muscled form. So, how, dear Lane, can you relate to *my* struggles? Because every molecule in my body is begging me to order the nachos supreme and the double enchilada special with extra guac, but I can't because that would ruin everything I've worked for up until this point. Including sitting here with you."

I expect that to render him speechless, but instead it pushes him to continue. "Like I said," he whispers, his face, his eyes, his lips, closer to mine than they've ever been, "looks can be deceiving." His fingertip taps the tip of my nose and then he retreats. "Now, if you want those nachos and the best enchilada in town, that's what you should have. I will never judge you, Leni. That much you can count on."

¡Ay caramba! with a side of guacamole. My snark has left the building. There's no comeback for what is the biggest turn on I've yet to experience in my life.

# chapter

# fifteen

LANE HAS PROVEN TO BE the king of surprises. Not only is it utterly flabbergasting that he can barely keep his hands and eyes off *me* throughout our meal, but every little thing about him makes me wonder if he's just too good to be true. *Screw it if he is. I have no intention of letting this one go for a while.*

We finish off the shared plate of fish tacos and a mango salad, which were ordered by Lane with special instructions to the chef to keep things light in the kitchen. My stomach is sated and my heart—that lonely sucker is bursting at the seams. I can't remember ever feeling this happy in the presence of a man. Not Alex, not Hudson, nobody. Putting all my eggs in one basket isn't usually my thing—especially since deciding to do me before doing anyone else—but if Lane asked me out again, or to be exclusive, or to marry him and have two point five kids and move to Schenectady—I'm there. And I haven't even kissed the guy, so that's saying a lot.

There's just something about him that is so addictive

and . . . dare I say, inspiring? Of course, there's the handsome packaging—perfect from head to toe—but it's so much more than that. When he speaks, words flow out of his mouth like poetic prose. His storytelling is passionate and each tale about his past or even his daily life brings every one of my senses to the exact place and moment in time he describes. It's an escape and it awakens an awareness I haven't had much experience with.

I like him. *A lot.* Now that I know him as more than just Mr. Fancy Pants, runner in the park, I'm definitely smitten. And from what I can tell through his dreamy eyes and the gentle nature of his touch—he likes me, too.

"Your smile is gorgeous, Leni. You need to do that more often." Lane pushes the empty plates aside and licks his lips as his eyes hone in on my mouth.

I nip at my bottom lip, feeling the weight of his stare boring into the tender flesh. "Then I need to hang around *you* more often. I haven't had such a nice day in a long time. Thank you, Lane."

His dimples appear and he winks, sending a jolt right to my lady parts. I squirm in my seat, fighting the urge to jump across the table and hump Lane right here at the restaurant. He must notice the heat that's risen to my cheeks because his own brighten in color and he glances down at his lap, surprising me yet again by his reserve when things start to cross the skinny line between like and lust.

When his eyes return to mine, he smiles and takes my breath away once more. "Is it horrible of me to say that I'm happy you bumped into that tree?"

The pitter pattering in my chest might actually be visible through my chunky chenille sweater. "Horrible or not, I don't care. I'm glad it happened, too."

We share a quiet moment, basking in the delight of our unusual first encounter. A growing need to kiss him swarms within me. Maybe even a need for much *more*. If the physical connection is anything in comparison to the way we've clicked thus far, the chemistry will be way beyond anything found on the periodic table.

"Check please!" I cry out when I spot our waiter, a desperate plea for his aid in ending this part of the night and allowing us to get on with the next.

The kind, older man obliges. Lane insists on taking care of the bill, and together we put our coats back on. The irony isn't lost on me. I'd rather be stripping away our layers of clothing, not adding more.

"Ready?" Lane asks, sticking out his arm and creating a place for me to hook our elbows together.

I gladly take his lead and latch on, my hand traveling down the length of his forearm and finding it's home in his hand. I hold on extra tight as we pass the jealous hostess from earlier and make our way back outside. *Adios, muchacha.*

The sky has darkened since we arrived, the temperature cooler than this afternoon. I snuggle closer to Lane and suggest, "Let's get a cab back to my place?"

A glint of apprehension washes over Lane's handsome features, but it doesn't take long for him to comply. And after a few chilly minutes of cuddling together on the busy corner of Kenmare Street, the taxi pulls up and my heart kicks into high gear because once we're at my place, I intend on escorting Lane directly into the bedroom.

"HOW LONG WILL YOU BE in Miami?" Lane asks after the cabbie takes our directions and we settle in for the fifteen-minute ride.

"About a week." I try to hide the disappointment in my voice. I was so excited about the trip just a few hours ago; now I wish I could pack Lane alongside my new tankini and bring him with me. "Gonna miss me while I'm gone?" The question oozes from my lips before I can stop it from happening. I regret it for a moment, but it's fleeting because Lane's response is something far better than what I was after.

"Oh, Leni." He turns so his back is flush with the car door, our eyes locked on each other. His warm hands cup my face as he tilts his head so our foreheads touch. I can feel his cool breath on my skin, and like the presence of a ghost it haunts me. *Kiss me, kiss me,* my brain chants on a repeat reel of longing. Lane's fingertips trail along my jawbone and his thumb caresses my practically panting lips. *Do it, do it, please, please do it.* I might burst into flames if he doesn't. Talk about your panties being on fire. If he postpones this any longer, I'll have to take matters into my own hands. I don't mind making the first move, but I'm in awe of his spellbinding touch and finding it impossible to react.

"Lane," I pant. Never have I wanted my lips to connect with someone else's more in my life. His name is a plea. No, a demand for him to take me in the back seat of this cab. My arms wrap themselves around his neck and my fingers inch into his stylishly tousled hair. I withdraw my forehead from his and angle to go in for the kill.

Thankfully, he responds to my desperate need and by the merciful grace of God, his lips press against mine. The tender friction is equal parts sweet and sensual. It takes my body a nanosecond to soar into overdrove and my lips part in invitation. Lane's tongue penetrates, a ribbon of silk dancing in my mouth. I love nothing more than a slow, romantic kiss, but— *fuck me*—I *need* more.

In a bold move, I claim his tongue and suck it into my mouth, my fingers meandering wildly in the perfect length of his hair.

Lane groans against my mouth, his hands traveling from my face, down my neck, to my arms. He pulls me to him so we're as close as two people can be without becoming one, and deepens the kiss.

I don't dare open my eyes, blocking out the driver and the fervent heat swirling through the car. *Why does our first kiss have to have a witness? Why can't we be alone? Why are my clothes still on? Can't this car go any faster?*

My brain is in overdrive and I beg it to shut the hell up so I can enjoy the heady touch and taste that is Lane. It takes me to a place where all of my insecurities about weight and size fade away. But then, of course, the dirty part of my mind goes right back to *size*, making me wonder if all this kissing has Lane as worked up as I am. *Why don't you check it out for yourself, Len? Cop a feel.*

*Shall I?* Our lips and tongues are still enjoying this back seat party and our hands have voyaged everywhere from the waist up, but—yeah, *I shall*. One hand anchors itself at the base of Lane's neck, eliciting another growl from him, the other scales his rock hard chest and abdomen on it's decent to his lap.

Without breaking contact, I take the plunge and palm meets peen. *Hello!* Size certainly does matter and his overwhelming thickness is rigid in my grip. Lane sucks in a breath when I squeeze his shaft through his jeans, and then the cabbie clears his throat. We've come to a stop and haven't even noticed, and here I am, all cat ate the canary—aka dick in the hand—and our driver's waiting for his fare.

I giggle from pure embarrassment and return my very full, very greedy hand to my own lap. My head falls against Lane's shoulder as he adjusts himself and rakes his hand though his just-made-out-in-the-backseat-of-a-cab hair. I expect him to reach into his wallet so we can hop out of here and straight into my bed, but when Lane speaks, I freeze. "Can you hang around a second? I'll be right back." His question is for the cabbie who nods with a sly smirk as he eyes me through the rearview mirror.

Lane opens the door and offers his hand to help me out.

I slap my palm to his, and he tugs me outside. Once on solid ground, he pulls me close and closes the door. The loud crash and squeak of the old hinges startle me into reality.

"You're not coming up?" I ask, my voice laced with incredulity.

Lane ushers me to the front of my apartment and backs me up against the wall. He cages me in his arms, one above my head for support against the building, the other hugged around my waist. His green eyes, no longer dark with desire, bore into mine as he explains, "Leni, I want more than anything to come upstairs and continue what we started back there."

"I'm sensing a but." A familiar pang of rejection steals my dignity.

He takes a deep breath and primes himself, but it's me who needs readying. "But it's not a good idea. I like you a lot and—"

"I like you a lot, too," I interrupt. Apparently he's taking the lead though, because he shushes me with a finger at my gaping lips. The touch ignites the passion that fueled our intense make-out session a few minutes ago. How things can go from frenzied to flat-out frozen is beyond me. *What did I do wrong?*

Lane tucks a piece of unruly hair behind my ear. "You're leaving in two days. You'll be gone a week. I'd like to see you when you get back."

Any other time I'd be chomping at the bit—*Sure thing, Lane. Let's do this again. Anytime, babe.* But I feel like I'm being dismissed and quite honestly, I'm confused.

My body stiffens underneath his touch. I have nowhere to go, no escape. I'm dying of self-consciousness inside. "I don't get it. What am I missing? I thought we were having a great time."

Lane looks over his shoulder to the waiting cab and raises his finger to indicate he'll be another minute. *A minute.* I'm only deserving of one more minute of his time to wrap up this crazy turn of events? Excuse me while I remove the tail—and vacant, throbbing need—from between my legs.

His warm lips meet the chilled skin of my cheek—such a step back from the progress we made with our lips—and he retreats with a shy smile. "There's no need to rush things. I told you I'm not the kind of guy you think I am. Can you trust me enough to accept that you did nothing wrong? You're beautiful and sexy and I really, really want you, but—"

There's that annoying word again. "But?" I ask, trying with all my might to stop my lip from trembling.

"But I'm not going anywhere. Let's take it slow. And if you'll allow it, I'd love to see you again when you get back."

That's it? No explanation? I'm still stumped, even if enamored by his proposition.

I can do one of two things. Walk away and sulk because I didn't get my way. Or, gracefully trust his hesitance as an *it's not you, it's me* situation.

While the old Leni would no doubt opt for scenario one, make a fool of herself, and then drown her sorrows in a gallon of Rocky Road, the new Leni has turned a new leaf. "Fine," I huff, my body slumping against the wall. I almost make a joke about how my trusty Lelo will have to finish what he started, but I think better of it and smile with poise. "I hate to see you go, but I'll love watching you leave." I wink, masking the devastation that has to be visible in my eyes.

Lane hovers against me and places a soft kiss on my lips. I want more. I want to pull him closer and get lost again, but I have to trust that he knows what he's doing. With one final peck on the tip of my nose, my hand falls from Lane's as he withdraws. "Thank you for a perfect date. It may not have ended the way you wanted it to, but this is far from over."

I smile, hoping this isn't a let down, just a hold up in our—whatever this is. I wave him off as he gets back into the cab, holding back the tears of rejection until he's out of sight.

# chapter

## sixteen

I CAN'T RELY ON HER as a shopping buddy, but Tatum wants to be front row center while I wallow on Misery Lane, pun totally intended.

She shows up at my place wielding a giant stuffed teddy bear that's almost the entire length of her five foot four frame. I can barely see her behind the massive thing, but there's no denying it's Tatum. I'd recognize those hot pink Uggs anywhere.

"Get in here, you idiot."

I pull her inside and she stumbles, the bear breaking her fall.

"I thought you had plans with Paul, number one. And number two, what's with the bear?"

Tatum seats our new furry friend on my oversized armchair and adjusts him, just so, until he's no longer lopsided. His inanimate, beady black eyes mock me and I hold myself back from punching the factory manufactured smile off his plush face.

"Paul fell asleep mid-Netflix so we never got to the *chill* part, and the bear is a comfort gesture because I know Rocky Road is off limits." Her eyes flicker with an idea. "Oh! That can be his name! Leni, this is Rocky Road. He's here to listen to your dilemma." Her voice is high pitched, saccharine. She over enunciates her words the way a mother would when speaking to her baby in goo-goo-ga-ga language. It doesn't make me feel any better. In fact, it pisses me off even more.

"Please don't make fun of this situation. This blows donkey balls, Tay. You shouldn't have come. I'm just gonna haul my ass to bed and forget this night ever happened!" I plop down next to Rocky Road and crane my arm around his neck. It's not a hug, it's a choke hold, but his warm, round body *is* kind of comforting so I ease up on the big fella.

"Start from the top and leave no stone unturned. I need all the deets to make sure I can give you the best friend advice you so rightly deserve." I almost expect her to whip out a pencil from behind her ear and a notepad from her back pocket. She doesn't have to, though. We've been down similar roads many a time, and Tatum is like my own personal therapist, minus the hefty copay.

"We had the best time." My heart thunders in my chest when I recall how effortlessly wonderful the entire day with Lane was. "We laughed while we shopped, and he actually helped me pick out a few things that I might not have found on my own. He carried my bags for me, waited patiently outside of dressing rooms, yayed and nayed when I asked for his opinion. It was surprisingly comfortable, considering we just met.

"Then after we were done, we walked over to La Esquina— hand in hand, the way a couple would. We sat at a quiet table; it was romantic, and candlelit, and all the things a girl hopes for in a first date setting. He never took his eyes off me; his hands, either. The connection was intense. I'm not just saying it, Tay. I felt it. From the tips of my fingers to the ends of my toes. His words mesmerized me and his touch made me weak. I haven't enjoyed a man like that since—since *never*.

"And before you think about mentioning Hudson, just don't. Hudson was a one-night stand, a Stella's-got-her-groove-back moment. Sure, it felt good, but it didn't feel *Lane* good." I sigh and deflate into the couch cushions, remembering just how good that feeling was. *Good, but gone.*

Tatum remains quiet, her wheels turning underneath her beachy blonde waves. Her silence means she's evaluating, trying my tragic love story on for size. I won't dare mess with her mojo and ask anything prematurely, so instead, I continue. This is the part that needs the most judgment, anyway.

"So, after dinner I was tired and my feet hurt a little from all the walking. I suggested we get a cab back to my place—and let me tell you, Tatum, there was no denying what I was getting at. It was an invitation to jump my bones and he had to know that when he accepted. The heat between us was the real deal Holyfield, even in the restaurant. If I weren't so worried I couldn't stuff my big ass *and* his together in a bathroom stall, I would've dragged him into the little niñita's room and had my way with him right there. So, we get in the cab and we're talking and flirting, and he's dimpling and I'm squirming, and one thing leads to another, and—Oh my God. The kiss. Earth shattering. Measured 9.5 on the Richter scale. Things got a little heated, his hands copped their feel and mine wound up in his lap—"

"You copped the cock. In the cab. You dirty, dirty whore. Continue."

"It was a nice cock, too, might I add. But! And this is a major *but*, this is where the goddamn cabbie stopped the car *and* our momentum, and rather than pay the dude and rush upstairs, Lane asked him to wait so he could say goodnight to me. The end. Good night. No night cap."

"Yeah, yeah, yeah. I get it . . . Do not pass go. Do not collect two hundred dollars. What did he say when you asked him *why?"* Tatum scootches to the edge of her seat and narrows her penetrating gaze. Damn, when did she become Dr. Fucking Ruth?

"That's the thing. He never really gave me the answer. He beat around the bush."

"Not your bush, unfortunately," she sneers.

"No, Captain Obvious, but he *did* pin me against the wall and he *did* tell me he wants me but also wants to take things slow." I take another long breath. Getting it out feels better, but I'm also biting my nails in anticipation of Tatum's analysis. She knows the male species better than any of my other friends. Ashley's been with Reynold and only Reynold since tenth grade. Jane and Mandy are into each other. Raven and the girls at work are all married with children and totally out of the wooing stage. That leaves Tatum. My lovely, wonderful, beautiful friend, who has been around the block a time or two. She's not exactly what you'd call a slut, but . . . okay, there's a very thin line here . . . but my point is that Tatum knows her dating shit and I'm scared to hear her achingly truthful advice about my flop with Lane.

My thumbnail is down to a jagged nub waiting for her to process. I picture her brainwaves working on overdrive, computing and calculating. She snaps her neck from side to side and then cracks her knuckles. The chick is ready for battle. This can't be good.

"Okay, from the way I see it . . . he seems . . . I don't know, Len. I hate to break this to you, but is there a possibility that Mr. Fancy Pants is, well, you know . . . *fabulous?*"

*Oh no she didn't.* "Gay!? You think he's gay?" I scream, jumping out of my seat and sending Rocky Road the bear tumbling to the floor.

Tatum rushes to rescue him and pulls him onto her lap where she can hide behind her accusations and his fuzziness. "Your story had a couple of red flags, Len. His love of shopping. The 'I'm not the kind of guy you think I am.' His hesitance to get down and dirty with you. I'm sorry, babes, but there is a strong possibility that Lane is playing for the other team. Call it a hunch or what have you, but—"

My brain becomes an internal cheerleader chanting, *DEFENSE—clap clap—DEFENSE—clap clap.* "So, basically what you're saying is that I'm *crazy* for thinking there was any kind of spark between us—I imagined it—*and* that a guy as good-looking and swoony as Lane can't possibly be attracted to someone like *me.*"

Rocky Road is tossed to the floor again as Tatum stands to make her point. "No, that's not what I said. He's not *not* attracted to you because of who *you* are, Leni. What I'm saying is, maybe he's just not attracted to women. Period."

This is a lot to take in. I mean, seriously. I've been through a lot of shit in my life with the opposite sex, but this is a first. I've never thrown myself at a gay guy, and I'd like to think I'm pretty keen on reading people and would have known if I set my sights on someone who wasn't into me. I replay every conversation, every tender touch, every dimple flash, the kiss that felt like fireworks inside my body. "It can't be. It simply can't be." My head falls into my hands as uncertainty plagues me. When you don't want to believe that something can be true, you find every excuse to have faith in the opposite. But I'm drained. From the accident, from the dieting, from the day with Lane, from this joke of a life.

Tatum's hand jolts me from my blubbering. "Hey, come on. Maybe I'm wrong. Maybe he's just shy, Leni. Maybe he doesn't know how to handle someone as fierce as you."

"Fierce?" I don't lift my head, I don't react, I just mumble the word, wondering what business it has describing someone like me.

"Look at me!" Tatum orders, her hands prying my own from the clutches of my tear sodden face.

I don't budge. I can't. I don't want to face her. I don't want to face *this*. I'm not up for convincing myself of his reasons for rejecting me. I can't force myself to believe that what I felt was nothing more than hopefulness because it was . . . *wonderful*. It was so goddamn wonderful to feel wanted by Lane and there was not one second of our time together when I was fat Leni. I was just *me*. And the thought that Lane liked me for me was simply . . . *wonderful*.

"Madeline Moore! Look at me! Now!" Tatum stomps her foot like an insolent child and then shakes my shoulders.

I can't ignore her forever and maybe if I just get on with this humiliation, I can move on and she will leave me alone to wallow in my misery. "What? What can you possibly say to make this any better?"

Tatum kneels in front of me, her hands on my knees, her eyes sparkling with optimism. I have been friends with this wacko a long, long time. She's been by my side for all of it—the good, the bad and the portly—I don't know what I'd do without her. And although I'd love to push her tiny frame and send her teetering over to join Rocky Road in the belly up position on my area rug, I don't have it in me to do anything but hug the bitch.

"Why do I love you? Please remind me?" I fling my arms around her neck and squeeze—maybe a little tighter than I should. *That's for making me think he's gay, bitch.*

"You trying to thank me, or kill me?" She breaks free of my hug/choke hold and sits in front of me, legs criss-crossed into a pretzel.

"I wish we had real rocky road right now," I admit with a sigh and wipe the remaining droplets from my soon-to-be-puffy eyes.

"Well, you have me instead, so deal. Slumber party?" Tatum's smile spreads wide across her flawless face, her eyebrows reaching her hairline.

It's been eons since we had a good old fashioned sleepover that didn't include puking and morning after hangovers. As much as I thought I wanted to be alone to overanalyze this whole Lane thing, a Tatum and Leni couch-campout including our time honored favorite and most quotable flick, *Mean Girls*, might just be what I need to recharge before my trip to Miami.

"DVD in place?" she asks, reaching for the remote.

"Of course."

Midway into Regina George getting her plastic ass fooled by the pre-train-wreck Lindsay Lohan, I sleepily surrender to the reality that I cannot allow a man's affections or rejections to define me. Before I slammed into that tree I was on the right track—the road to loving me. Gay or straight or what have you, I cannot give Lane, or any man, the power to doubt myself. Anyone with that influence, is just totally *fetch*.

# chapter

seventeen

MY PHONE BUZZES LOUDLY, SKIDDING across the side table in an effort to get my morning off to an aggravating beginning.

"Shut it up! Stop it! It's too early!" Tatum mumbles from underneath the blanket cocoon we shared in our toe-to-head position last night.

I rub the sleep out of my eyes and focus them on the cable box clock. "Not exactly that early, Tay. It's nine o'clock."

"Ungodly," says the woman who doesn't ever have to be at work before noon. She pulls the fleece throw over her head and curls herself into the fetal position. "Wake me in half an hour."

We stayed up to watch all of *Mean Girls* and then wound up chatting some more, way into the wee hours of the almost dawning new day. While I'm okay with less than eight hours of beauty rest, my best friend is a diva who can barely function on nine.

The phone vibrates again, reminding me that I already

ignored one incoming message. I stretch out the kinks in my back caused by uncomfortably squeezing on the couch with my restless sleeper of an overnight guest, and reach for the confounded thing that just won't stop buzzing. "Geez! Who are you and why are you so persistent?"

My eyes go wide and I gulp back a nice helping of stanky morning breath when I notice I have a few messages from Lane. Before swiping the screen to open them, I shake the shit out of Tatum. "It's him, Tay! It's him!"

A moan that could rival a lion's growl erupts from the fleece cocoon. "Who? Who the hell is so hell bent on waking me up?"

"Lane! Lane texted me—"

"And?" One eye pokes out of the blanket, waiting for my answer.

"I didn't look yet."

Tatum rockets into a sitting position and snatches the phone from my hand. Typing in the passcode I once told her in a drunken stupor—stupid me for not changing it—she scans through the texts. A beaming smile brightens her groggy features as she reads. "Definitely not gay, I'll tell ya that." She hands the phone back to me and then drops back onto the pillow.

I open the texts to see for myself what has Tatum convinced she was wrong. This is a day for the Guinness Book of World Records. My best friend rarely admits defeat. Between that victory and Lane's messages, my skin is tingling all over.

*Lane (8:30am): Hey, gorgeous. Did you open those beautiful big brown eyes yet? Wanna join me for a run?*

*Lane (8:48am): Either you're still asleep or ignoring me. If it's the latter, I need you to know that I hardly slept last night, thinking about how we left off. I'm sorry if I weirded out. It's not what you think. You definitely know how to drive a guy to the brink of insanity with that incredible mouth of yours.*

*Lane (9:12am): I'm not leaving until 10, so if you get this and feel up to it, put a guy out of his misery and text me back.*

"Oh my God! Praise the Lord!" I clutch the phone to my galloping heart and let my head fall back against the couch.

"Are you going to answer him or leave the guy hanging?" Tatum still hasn't emerged from the blanket, but I know she feels the deliberation oozing from my always indecisive body.

Biting my lip and bobbing my leg up and down like a jack hammer, I take a split second to ponder and then—*fuck it!* My fingers fly across the screen with more ambition than a backstage groupie after a rock concert.

*Me: Morning! I'll meet you at the benches by the fountain in twenty.*

I press send and within seconds—seconds that drip with the agony of anticipation—the three tiny dots appear in the bubble, mocking my eagerness.

*Lane: So you're not ignoring me?*

*Me: Nope, not today.*

*Lane: Good, because I was up all night thinking of a way to leave you with something to remember me by while you're away.*

That elicits a squeal and an uncontrollable burst of energy. "I gotta get ready. Get your ass up and out!" I pull the blanket off of Tatum with a strong tug that rolls her onto the floor. She comes nose-to-nose with Rocky Road and then looks up at me with a *what the fuck* expression.

"I take it you and your *beautiful big brown eyes* are meeting Lane for that run?"

"Uh huh!" I nod joyfully, folding the blanket.

"What else did he say?" Tatum rises into a sitting position. So does Rocky Road.

I'm not one to kiss and tell but—who am I kidding? "He said he was up all night thinking of a way to make me remember him while I'm in Miami. He was . . . flirting. I think." And just like that I'm back to reading in between the lines. I hand my phone over to Tatum again, showing her exactly what he said.

"Have I not taught you anything?" She shakes her head and hands the phone off.

"I was never an A student, you know this."

"Even though it kills me to say this—" She winces, her tongue hissing between her teeth as if whatever she's about to say is painful. "I was wrong."

I clamp my mouth shut with both hands, as to not spoil this moment of triumph.

"He likes you, Leni. For the record, I never doubted he *could*. I just thought—"

"You thought *wrong*. Wrong, wrong, wrongity wrong. Say it again, Tay. Savor it on your lips, cherish how it feels on your tongue. This might be the first and last time you ever experience it, you stubborn bitch!"

Never faltering or discounting my minute of glory, Tatum rises from the floor and searches for the bra she peeled off before we went to sleep. "I have to say, it's a great reason to be wrong. This is a good thing, babes. I'm really happy for you."

"I'm really happy for me, too." And I am. So happy that the kale smoothie I make myself for breakfast tastes more like an ice cream sundae with a cherry on top.

I TRY TO MAKE MYSELF look like I'm not a ball of nerves on the inside by acting professional on the outside. With my right foot propped on the bench for support, I fold my body in half and reach down to touch the tips of my toes. I repeat the same warm-up exercise with the opposite leg, until a pair of chilly hands at my waist startles me.

"Shit!" I shout, craning my neck to see who just got a handful of muffin top.

"Hey, you." Lane smiles, coming around to plant a kiss on my cheek.

The nerves from earlier send shockwaves through my body, and then slowly come to a simmer when I inhale a deep breath of Lane's manly scent.

"Hi." I can just see my face right now—a total goof. Warm and gooey and all crimson stained cheeks.

"You look adorable, as always," Lane scans me from head to toe and I can't help but relish in the lustful expression on his face. But, *adorable*? A puppy is adorable; a newborn baby is adorable. Whatevs, I'll take what I can get, considering last night Tatum had me convinced that the guy over there walking his dog is Lane's idea of adorable.

"Thanks. *You* look breathtaking, as always." He does. There's no better way to describe him. In his proximity the altitude seems higher, my lungs feel smaller. He has that effect over me all the damn time.

Lane ignores my compliment and takes my hand. "Ready? I want to show you something today."

I gladly accept his invitation, no words necessary, and we start on the path in the opposite direction of my normal route.

Lane is like the mayor of Central Park—everyone waves or gestures a greeting as he passes them. I recognize some familiar faces from my daily routine, but since this is a path I don't normally frequent, it's like a whole new world. The October sun is strong in spite of the subtle chill in the air. I'm glad I layered because with the sun beating down on us head-on I'll need to shed my Pink hoodie soon.

"So, about last night." Lane breaks the comfortable silence only filled with our footfalls. I find myself enjoying the steady pace between us, the fact he's simply beside me is enough. And then he brings this up as if I need a reminder of how I acted like a horny fool last night. Suddenly, my pits are sweating again and the hoodie has to go.

I unzip it, feeling self-conscious of the way my T-shirt clings to all the wrong places, and tie it around my waist to hide the worst of it. Without making eye contact, my focus still on the paved path, I reply, "Maybe we don't need to talk about it. Let's leave it alone and just start fresh. I'm embarrassed enough for throwing myself at you."

"There's nothing to be embarrassed about, Leni. In fact, if anyone should be embarrassed, it's me. I led you on and I feel like an ass."

*Did* he lead me on? I thought we were on the same page? Did he ask me out here to let me down easily? People don't usually flirt their way out of a hook-up. Or do they? I'm lost. It's a big, big sea, with so many fish, and I'm a tiny guppy getting washed up in the tide. I take a sip from my water bottle, unsure how to respond.

Lane slows up a bit, I follow suit but stagger a few steps to the right. As much as I adore being around this man, the mixed signals are making me feel schitzo. Sensing my confusion from the distance I've put between us, Lane takes my hand in his and brings it to his lips. The tiny token of affection sets my heart galloping again.

"I know you have this certain idea of what I'm about. It's easy to judge a book by it's cover and I guess at first glance I seem—"

"Hot!" I interrupt, giving him the boost of confidence he deserves. "You're smoking hot, Lane. How do you not see that? Are you blind?"

Lane chuckles, raking his fingers through his hair. His expression turns serious, though, when he straightens to answer me. "No, I'm not blind, but—let's just say I wasn't always this way."

The dude is a man of few words—I get this and I actually like it, but, Jesus H, he speaks in riddles and from what I've seen, he doesn't like to elaborate. If this is going anywhere, the cat will have to let go of this man's tongue. "Has anyone ever told you that you're as cryptic as the Da Vinci Code?"

"No, I can't say I've heard that one before." He cocks a brow and flashes one of his dimples.

"I don't want to pry or come off as some nosy Nellie, but I don't get it. I've struggled my whole life, I'm *still* struggling, and then I meet you—this gorgeous, fit, fun guy who seems to have everything going for him—and I can't help thinking that you either don't have a mirror or you're naïve because, Lane, I see how the girls look at you. Don't you see how *I* look at you?" I nudge his side. He jumps to the side. He's ticklish—fantastically adorable. "You got it going on, Mr. Sheffield. I promise you that much."

Lane takes it in, but I can tell it's not sinking in. I never imagined *I'd* have to convince *him* of his hotness. What a roller coaster of a role reversal. Is it a full moon or something?

"You must think I'm weird." From the corner of my eye, I notice he's biting his lip. This whole thing is so—flummoxing. It sincerely makes zero sense, but if anyone can understand what it's like to let your insecurities get the best of them, it's me.

"I think nothing of the sort. I think so much more. I want so much more." There I said it. I do not speak in riddles. I speak the truth. Here it is, come and get it.

"I do, too. I like you. You make me smile and laugh and not worry about being the guy everyone thinks I am. I can just be *me* around you and I love that."

There we go. We got a little something out of him. This is progress, slow going, but progress nonetheless.

Forgoing any more awkwardness of getting to know each other's flaws, we follow the bend in the road and continue on our way, discussing my upcoming trip. Lane's stride comes to a halt when we come up to one of the most picture perfect sights I've ever seen. It's funny how a piece of serenity like this can lie in the center of one of the busiest cities in the world. Bow Bridge at this time of year is simply breathtaking. The leaves have started to turn which adds to the bridge's vintage charm, and the water beneath its arch reflects the vibrant colors of the trees and the bright blue sky. "Oh my goodness, Lane. How beautiful!"

Sweaty and all, Lane pulls me closer to him and hooks an arm around my shoulders. My initial reaction is to back away so he doesn't get grossed out by my clamminess, but the autumn-painted view is too spectacular to experience without the pleasure of his arms enveloping me.

"Want to cross it?" His question is so metaphoric I nearly burst out in laughter.

"With you? I would gladly cross Bow Bridge, or any bridge for that matter. You know this is totally romantic, don't you?"

"Exactly what I was going for. I need to make up for being an idiot last night."

"It's forgotten, I swear it. Now that I know we're on the same page—wait, *are* we on the same page?" Riddles, by nature, are meant to be confusing. I haven't gotten a straight answer from Lane about what he expects from me. We need to make things clear so there's no more second guessing or jumping to conclusions. I don't need Tatum coming up with another cocka-mamie idea of why Lane might not be interested in me.

Strong, sinewy arms whirl my body around so that we're face to face. Lane dips down to place a chaste kiss on my wait-ing lips. Before I can deepen it by anchoring my fingers into his hair or tasting him with my tongue, he retreats and sets off to guide us across the bridge. "If your page includes many more candlelit dinners, and going at it in the back of cabs, then yes, babe, we are on the same page."

"Yeah?" I ask one more time for good measure.

"Yeah. I'm not about to let something this good slip away."

*Squee!* I nuzzle into his warmth, feeling closer to him than I ever have. "Good thing I don't plan on going anywhere."

"Except to Miami."

Damn, I nearly forgot. "You're so gonna miss me."

"And you're not?"

"I never said I wouldn't, and if I recall correctly, this morning you told me you would leave me with something to remember you by." I place one palm out, facing up. "It's time to pay up. Show me what you got."

"The bridge isn't enough?" He waves his hand, exhibiting the gorgeous scenery beneath our feet.

"Oh, no, no, no. I need something to keep me warm at night."

"It's hot in Miami," he jokes.

"Make it hotter," I whisper into his ear.

With that, at the peaked arc of the bridge, Lane takes my face in his hands and kisses me. Our lips meet softly and then his tongue breaches, caressing mine with chaotic longing. This kiss is full of urgency, desperate desire, and the answers to all of my looming questions. I don't care who or *what* sees us, I throw everything I have into this kiss. My body bends as his arches, his hand tugs at my ponytail while his tongue circles mine. I moan against his mouth, his name a faint whisper on my occupied tongue. After a dramatic, movie-like dip and some peppering of sweet kisses against my cheeks, neck, and shoulders, a few passersby erupt into applause, sending me into the safety of Lane's arms.

Mmm, he smells good. Almost as good as he tastes. I melt into his touch and whimper against his neck. "We put on quite a show, didn't we?"

He tucks a lock of loose hair behind my ears, still holding me close. "Any regrets?"

"Not one."

"Good, because once you're mine, you'll need to get used to me kissing you everywhere and anywhere I please."

*Would you look at that?* The man *can* be sexy and domineering. I like it. I love it. I want some more of it. I tangle my fingers with his and pull him into a slow stroll.

Once we've crossed to the other side of the bridge, he bends down to tie his unlaced shoe and I start to jog in place. "Come on. Let's finish our run so I can bask in the memory of our crowd pleasing kiss while I pack. Race ya home?"

Lane dusts off his pants as he stands, stealing another quick peck. "You're on."

# chapter
## eighteen

AS THE PLANE LANDS, ROLLING onto the runway of Miami International Airport, Will Smith's *Welcome to Miami* is the first thing that comes to mind. I'm in love with all things Latin culture, South Beach, and Gloria Estefan. I've never been, but I won't lie . . . this mama is ready to party in the city where the heat is on.

I try to shake Raven awake to soak up the tropical paradise of palm trees peacefully swaying in the wind. She's not budging. How she slept through the entire flight is beyond me. Then again she did say she was up all night with her son because he was sad she was leaving. I have no idea how she juggles so much and manages to keep it all together. I'm single, only in charge of me, and my life is almost always a hot mess. Swoony thoughts of Lane remind me that the messiness could very well be coming to an end. At least for now.

"Hey, chica! We're here! Wake up, Sleeping Beauty."

Raven grumbles something that barely sounds English

and finally opens her eyes when I poke her in the ribs. "Here already?"

"You were out five minutes after take off and snored the whole way down. Welcome to sunny Miami, babes."

"Shit. Sorry, I guess I'm not much of a travel buddy."

"Don't apologize. I'm glad you got some rest. I know how hard you've been working to iron out all the details. You're only human."

"If by human, you mean sleep deprived, then sure."

Raven and I grab our carry-ons from the overhead and amble off the plane and into the terminal. The rest of the team is on a later flight, so it's just me and her for a while.

"Hungry?" she asks, nodding in the direction of the chain restaurant to our left. "I can't believe they don't even give out in-flight peanuts anymore. The world's gone fucking mad, I tell ya."

I chuckle at her hangriness and pull a Kind bar from my purse. I came well prepared with low-cal munchies to avoid any unnecessary temptation. "Here. Feed your face. Wouldn't you rather get to the hotel so we can settle and scope things out?" And by scope things out I mean, get my tan on before the real work begins.

Raven snatches the granola bar from me and rips the wrapper open with her teeth. "You and your rabbit food lately." She noshes down on the *rabbit food* with a doubtful frown. "Eh, not as bad as I thought, although I'd die for a cheeseburger and chili fries."

"And I wouldn't?" I mumble. Raven can afford to eat that way. I certainly cannot.

She swallows another mouthful and nudges me with her Louis Vuitton travel bag. "I'm sorry. You've been so good and you look great and here I am being an unsupportive bitch. Pay no attention to my sleepy, grumpy, hungry ass."

I shoo away her ridiculousness. "Don't be crazy. I don't

expect you not to eat what you want because of me. If you want a burger and fries, let's go. I can grab a salad."

"In other words, more rabbit food." She gives me a wink and we continue toward the baggage carousel. "This is good for now. Plus, like you said, we should get to the hotel and make some headway before the rest of the crew gets here. I have a meeting with the photographer that I'd like you to sit in on."

*Say what? Have my ears not popped yet?* "Really?" I've always wanted more responsibility, duties that stretch beyond the studio. Just the idea of getting a behind the scenes experience with the photographer has me nearly skipping through the terminal.

"Really. I told you I wanted you as my right hand woman for this job. I wasn't kidding and I promise it won't be all work with no play. I managed to schedule some free time to shoot the shit by the pool and enjoy a few happy hours. You can't come to Miami and not live a little. Maybe you'll even meet a Cuban cutie, huh?"

I shake my head, laughing at Raven's incessant need to set me up. It's never worked in the past, and even though I'm feeling a little bit more confident these days, I have Lane on the brain.

"What's that look?"

Oops. She caught me, didn't she?

"Oh . . . nothing." I feign innocence but I can tell she sees right through the flush of my cheeks and the smile on my lips.

Raven darts in front of me when she notices her luggage circling around the carousel but that doesn't stop her from prying further. "Spill it, sister. What's going on with you? A new man?"

"New would imply that there was an old, and we both know I haven't been on a date in forever."

"What about that Hudson dude?"

"That was a hook-up; this was a date." I can't help myself. I want to talk about it. Gloat, brag, speak of nothing but the way

Lane made sure I would be thinking of him this whole trip.

"So, there *is* a man! I need a cocktail for this! Can it wait until we're back at the hotel and my hand is occupied by a filthy martini?"

"Yes. It can wait. There's not much to tell anyway." The lie detector determined *that* was a fib. In the grand scheme of things, the Lane stuff isn't a big deal. But it's been a long time since I felt this way, and I can barely contain the giddy emotions from spilling out of every pore, crevice, and orifice. I hope the shuttle to the hotel is a quick one.

BY THE TIME RAVEN'S SUCKED down her third dirty martini, I've only nursed one vodka-club. Once I gave her all the deets about Lane, she went on and on about how she had a great feeling about him and that he had to be the one. *Fate doesn't just make you bump into a tree and stumble into the arms of a hot nurse for nothing,* were her exact words.

I can't lie, her belief in the whole destiny thing and how it threw me and Lane together makes me more hopeful than it should. I'd toast to that, but the alcohol has taken its effect on my boss and it's time to cut her off before she winds up hung over and cranky before our big meeting tomorrow.

"'Nother . . . shplease?" She slopes to the side in the pool-side lounge, waving her empty glass at the approaching waitress.

I intervene, shaking my head and mouthing *no way* behind Raven's back. I knew she was three sheets to the wind when she started to share some TMI about the sexual fantasies she acts out with her husband. I love Raven, but I don't need those visuals.

The waitress nods in understanding and sets off to help the other non-inebriated hotel guests, leaving me to deal with this shit show.

"Hey, I think we should go back to the room and freshen up."

"Soon as she 'rings my drank."

I giggle at her drunkenness, allowing her a pass. With three kids and the demands of running a hectic business, who am I to deny her a little buzz? Standing and straightening out my sarong so I'm not revealing more than anyone cares to see, I collect our bags. "I'll have her send it up to the room. Come on. The other girls will be here soon."

"Fiiinneee," she drawls, sliding off the chair and flat onto her ass. Contagious giggles erupt from her, causing a few people to turn their heads.

"Shit, Rave!" I run to her side and scoop her up by her underarms. "You need a nap and a shower."

"I *need* a shmoke and a pancake. Or a bong and a blintz." This time her laughter pierces through the quiet oasis and causes me to bowl over myself.

"Okay, Austin Powers."

"Don't you mean, Goldmember?"

"Sure, whatever, you psycho."

She reaches out to grab hold of me for leverage and winds up grabbing a generous helping of my ass. "*Raven!*" I yelp when her grip closes in on my crack.

"Well, well, well. You've got a toit ass, Len. Toit like a tiger."

I don't bother scolding her because I'm certain she won't remember any of this later on.

GETTING RAVEN INTO THE ELEVATOR and up to the room is a death defying act of hilarity. Stumbles, stutters, and slurs, oh my! And not to mention the inappropriate leers at the young tattooed hottie who hopped in on the fifth floor only to quickly reroute his destination from the rooftop lounge to floor ten after three uncomfortable seconds of Raven's attempt at cougar life.

It doesn't take her long to drift into dreamland once she's stripped down to nothing but her tankini top and shoved onto the bed with her ass in the air.

I grab the spare blanket from the closet and toss it over her. "Nice, buns," I joke, even though I'm certain she has no idea she's unabashedly flashing me.

Peace sets in and for the first time since waking at the crack of dawn, exhaustion kicks in. But one buzz from my phone and the tiredness is quickly replaced by a flurry of exhilaration.

*Lane: Hey, beautiful. How's the Sunshine State?*

I shot him a quick text earlier to let him know I landed safely but was soon preoccupied with Raven and her antics. The fact he's checking up on me is so sweet it warms the chilliness in my bones brought on by the A/C pumping through our hotel room.

*Me: Good. Just got back from the pool. Cut it short because my boss is trashed.*

*Lane: Oh, boy.*

*Me: Yup. You can say that again.*

*Lane: Any big plans for tonight?*

*Me: Nah, I think Raven needs to sleep this off, and she asked me to join her for the meeting with the photographer tomorrow so I should rest up, too.*

*Lane: Look at you! That sounds awesome, Len.*

I take a moment to let that sink in. Is it just me or does everything seem to be falling into place lately? I'm not sure if that thrills me or scares the shit out of me. It's either a foretelling of good things to come for Madeline Moore *or* the proverbial 'other shoe' getting ready to drop and kick me in the ass. But I don't want to give those negative thoughts any power, so I continue texting my man (oh, the glorious sound of that) with my legs curled underneath me, cozy and content.

> *Me: Thanks! I'm definitely stoked. What's on your agenda for the day?*

> *Lane: Oh, nothing, just pining over this sweet thing that left me here all alone.*

Swoon. He misses me. This is good.

> *Me: You could always hop on a plane and join me . . .*

> *Lane: Don't tempt me.*

> *Me: What if I want to tempt you?*

> *Lane: Babe, if I could, I would. I'm working crazy hours this week so we'll just have to resort to the long distance thing on my down time. Looks like you'll have to tempt me with something else.*

Oh, really? Lane has a feisty side. Fantabulous. I only wish it hadn't come out *now*, while I'm thousands of miles away.

> *Me: Not fair! No teasing when I can't exactly do anything about it.*

> *Lane: Are you alone?*

*Whoa!* That's usually the way most sexting starts, isn't it? I've never done this. Do I have it in me? I mean, on the one hand, he's initiating and ever since that night in the cab—maybe even before—I've been dying for this side of Lane to come out and play. But even if Raven is passed out and ossified, the fear of the unknown and screwing this up gets the best of me.

*Me: Um . . . kind of.*

*Lane: Good enough. Still remember that kiss?*

*Me: Haven't stopped thinking about it.*

*Lane: Me either, but I'm in need of something . . . visual.*

*Me: Lane Sheffield are you asking me to send you a nudie shot? What kind of girl do you think I am?*

He doesn't need to answer that. I'm already snapping cleavage selfies like they're going out of style. His text comes in as I'm saving a pic that highlights just the right amount of moundage.

*Lane: The kind that has me all worked up after only a few dates. I can't tell you how much I regret not coming up to your apartment that night.*

Ah! The infamous rejection. I've been secretly hoping it haunted him. I'm not sure how to answer him, so instead I send over a tasteful money shot of the girls, accentuated by the gold and black netting of my swim suit.

The phone feels like a grenade in my shaky hands. Did I really just do that? *Yes, you whore, you did. You sent the dude a picture of your jugs and for all you know he'll post it on social media for the whole world to see.*

Regret floods me in nasty swells, but the vibration of my phone startles me out of my shame. I expect it to be another incoming text, but this time it's actually him. He's calling. *Shit!* What do I do?

I scurry to the bathroom and lock myself inside, as to not disturb Frank the Tank in there. I take a deep breath and pray for the heat tingling throughout me to calm the hell down. Clearing my throat, I answer in a sugary pitch, "Hello?"

"If you think I regretted my mistakes before, that picture

just solidified my you're-an-asshole-for-not-jumping-her-bones-when-you-could-have status. Leni, you are fucking hot."

Me? *Hot?* Bottle up and sell whatever the hell this guy is drinking because clearly it's giving him a distorted view of life. "It was nothing, but had I known this would get you so excited I would've flashed you a long time ago."

What can only be described as a frustrated growl comes through the phone, sending pulses of pleasure to my lady bits. "I won't survive this week, but know this, I don't make the same mistake twice."

*Well, that sounds delicious.* "So, should I expect a hot and heavy welcome home?" *Yes, please?*

"Expect the unexpected."

Oh, do I love that, because *that*, in a nutshell, is Lane. Someone who's been so guarded and timid, yet pleasantly surprising in all the right ways. As much as I'm tickled pink to be here because this trip means great things for my career, this week better fly on by so I can get home to whatever it is Lane has waiting for me.

# chapter

# nineteen

"WHY DIDN'T YOU STOP ME? You're fired!" Raven's fired me at least nine times this morning since waking with the hangover from hell. She pops four Advil tablets in her mouth and chases them down with a swig from her second cup of coffee.

I pull a bunch of bangle bracelets over my wrist as I move about the room, getting ready. "Hey, listen, it could've been worse. You had no intention of retiring the martini glass until I cut you off. Fire me if you must, but I think I deserve a raise for dealing with your shenanigans. You do know you tore off your bottoms, stripper style, as soon as you got up here and then proceeded to flash me with that tiny tush of yours."

Raven clicks her tongue and grabs her boobs, one in each hand. "James calls it pancake ass. And let's not even talk about the girls." She points to her boobs, shaking her head. "Minion number three wouldn't wean off the breast milk until he was a year old. I want a lift but James doesn't see the need for it. I guess he likes that they sag down to my knees and clap when I walk."

I break into a fit of giggles just thinking about it, but truth is, I'd give . . . well, my left tit, to have a body like hers. "Listen to James. He's a good man."

That seems to close out the tits and ass seminar for the day because Raven dashes around the room, filling her rolling studio with more brushes and products.

I sit at the edge of the bed to lace up my gladiator sandals, allowing the excitement of our meeting with the photographer to catch up with me. I've always dreamed of doing a fashion shoot, but a fashion shoot *and* a runway show—this is beyond amazing. "You do know I'm freaking out a little inside, right?"

"Why?" Raven doesn't look up from organizing her bags. She's in the zone—regardless of the hangover—and that frays my nerves even more.

"Because you know what you're doing and I don't. I've never really stepped outside that make-up artist box and thought about the infinite possibilities of the cosmetology world. What if I fuck up? What if the photographer thinks I'm a flake?"

"He won't think that, Leni, and you do know what you're doing. Why do you think I picked you?"

"Because I'm your friend?"

Raven stops what she's doing and glares at me. The stone cold look on her face kind of scares me. "When have I ever showed favoritism because of our friendship, number one? And number two, I'm friends with *all* my artists. Carol's my cousin, for God's sake. I chose you because of your talent. Because you have an eye for detail that no one else does. You're fresh and funky, yet classic and timeless all rolled into one. I also think you hide behind your insecurities and settle for what's in front of you when your gift would be so much better put to use out in the field, on projects like these.

"I picked you because you're the best candidate for this job and I think this is a great opportunity for you. I don't muddle my personal relationships with my career. So, even though you are a dear friend and you've seen me half naked, I will not let you sit here and doubt the reasons you're here with me on this trip. Are we clear?"

"Crystal." I nod. It's always been hard for me to accept a compliment—flaw number one hundred and ninety seven—but hearing someone I see as a role model say these things about me puts me in my place. "Thank you," I offer, needing her to know that being under her wing has been a godsend.

"Good. Now, finish getting ready and then help me pack the rest of this stuff so we can grab another coffee before our briefing with David.

"Yes, ma'am." I hop to it and thank my lucky stars that there are so many people who believe in me when I haven't been able to believe in myself.

DAVID'S PORTFOLIO IS BEYOND INCREDIBLE. It's so posh and glamorous my fingers itch to trace every outline of his work. This particular room in his studio is packed with racks of intricate clothing, both from the shoot I'll be working on and others. My eye is immediately drawn to a silk kimono that is simply exquisite. The mix of colors on the delicate fabric pops, making it something that I'd love to add to my wardrobe, if only I could afford it. I vaguely remember that ventures of this magnitude usually come with perks. I'm all set on the makeup goodies from our vendors, but a designer freebie would be really freaking sweet.

I try to stay up to speed with David and his assistant's photographer lingo, but my ears perk to attention as soon as he asks for Raven's input on a color palette for the shoot. He stands to roll one of the clothing racks over to us; the hangers clink against the metal rod, bringing the bold pieces to life.

"Here's the line. This season the designer is working with lots of bright neons. If we don't complement them the right way, taking into account all the different skin tones and hair colors of the models, the prints will wind up . . . unappetizing to the eye." I can tell from his tone that the color scheme is not his favorite. I tend to agree—neon reminds me of the 80's, but the trend is back and we'll have to make the best of it.

My fingers rove the patterns, the textures, the intricate weave work of one of the swimsuits. I immediately have an idea I would love to pitch. "Rave, I think . . ." I stand from my seat and head for the rolling studio. "Is it okay if I mess around a minute?"

Raven nods, a huge smile painting her fashionably made-up face. "Go for it."

Her obvious belief in me and her compliment from earlier give me a confidence I never knew I had the ability to embrace. Especially in a position like this. I have to admit it feels amazing, and for once I don't doubt myself or the creative vision begging to be seen outside the realm of my brain.

Raven and David sit at the table ironing out more details as I mess around with my tools. I play with and mix the colors on the back of my hand, but I soon run out of surface that's yet to be coated with vibrant shades. I flip open the vanity mirror attached to the case and wipe my own make-up off one of my eyes only to replace it with the shadows and liners I have in mind for the shoot.

My hands do their thing as if someone else is controlling them. A swipe of this here, a dab of that there—it's so much better on my face than it was on my hand. I take a step back, closing one eye to focus on the other. It pops, just like the designer's work, but I have to do the other eye for the full effect. I check over my shoulder to make sure no one's waiting on me and my perfectionism, and when I notice that David and Raven are still engrossed in their own conversation, I make quick work of duplicating what I've already done on the other side of my face.

"Done!" I shout a few minutes later, jumping out of my seat like I'm the winner of a race. I clutch my chest, take a breath, and do another once over, inspecting every angle of every feature. When I'm totally happy with the result, I spin around to show them my suggestion and my eyes land on a new face. She must have snuck in while I was in the zone.

"Who are you?" She starts to make her way toward me as if she's in a trance, mesmerized by me for some odd reason.

"I'm . . . uh . . . Leni Moore. I'm Raven's . . ." Her scrutiny is unnerving. I can't tell if she likes the makeup or hates it, and who is she, anyway?

Raven bounds to my rescue, forming the words that have escaped me. "Leni, this is Siobhan, the designer of the gorgeous line we're working with this week. Siobhan, this is Leni. She's one of the best girls on my team. I had her sit in because I knew this was exactly the kind of reaction her work would produce. It's stunning, isn't it?"

Siobhan Colbert. THE Siobhan Colbert. I cannot believe I'm in the same room, sharing the same air as one of the most influential designers of my time. I can't believe Raven didn't tell me this was the designer we were working for. I can't believe I'm—oh my God, I'm gonna pass out.

Siobhan examines my face, her head tilting for a better view, her fingers at my chin to angle me to her liking. "*She's stunning. David, darling, how have you not sunk your claws into her yet? This face is a work of art and I'm not just talking about the makeup, doll.*" Siobhan smiles, tapping me on the cheek.

I bring my own hand up to touch the skin she's just blessed with her own, in awe of what's transpired around me. *Someone pinch me. This is a dream, right?* I cannot believe Siobhan Colbert is talking about me and using those words. I'm fucking speechless, immobile, in shock.

Raven nudges me and I take an inhalation of air that feels like the first since I realized Siobhan is *Siobhan*. "Say something," she mumbles through clenched teeth.

Saying something would mean I'd have to form a coherent thought and string together words that don't make me sound like a complete fool. Panic strikes and I bite my lip, looking to Raven for guidance. Her eyes widen, a warning for me to be a big girl, the woman she trusted to do this job. I delve deep within, and finally say, "Thank you, Ms. Colbert. It's an honor to meet you. I absolutely love your work." Not too gushy, but right to the point. Kudos to me for not stuttering through that.

Siobhan darts over to David and wraps an arm around his neck. She lifts her hands up to her face and forms them into an open-palmed square, framing her line of vision—*me*. "Davey, she's walking and I want her dressed and prepped in an hour." With that, Siobhan whirls out of the room as if she was never actually there. Maybe she wasn't. Maybe it was all an illusion because I'm so confused I don't know what's reality and what my brain has fooled me to believe.

Raven grabs my arms and shakes me. "Did you hear that? Do you know what this means?"

I don't. I honestly have no clue what the hell just happened. "No. What does she mean *I'm walking?*"

"She wants you in the show, Leni. Have you ever modeled? Please tell me you're not a runway virgin." David's scribbling something into a large notepad and then passing it off to his sidekick who jets out of the room faster than I can say, "What the hell is going on? Can someone please fill me in?"

Raven's smile is so big I fear her deep, jovial laugh lines will stay that way permanently. She rubs my arms up and down and kisses me smack on the lips. *Hello!* "You, my gorgeous girl, just wowed Siobhan with everything that is you. I don't know how we'll pull this off in such a short amount of time, but you just booked your first gig as a model and I couldn't be prouder."

*Me?* A model? Is this chick on crack? Has the world gone completely mad? All eyes are on me, everything at a standstill. I have no idea how or why this has happened and I haven't a clue how to process it. So, I don't. I ignore the ogling of David, the bumbling of Raven, and the measuring tapes snaking my body in the hands of what must be the seamstresses on Siobhan's team. *Where'd these grabby hands come from?*

I haven't even agreed to this madness, but something tells me that an offer like this doesn't come along more than once. How does one deny her fashion icon hero something as simple as modeling her clothing? Yeah, simple, my left testicle. Right, I don't have a left testicle. Shit, the room's spinning. Please excuse me while I go crap myself.

# chapter

# twenty

"AND THEN SHE CALLED ME stunning. Me! Stunning! That word has never been uttered in conjunction with me. How is this happening? Is this real life?" I babble on and on to Tatum who is as much in shock as I am. Not for the same reasons, but simply because this is not the type of good fortune that ever comes my way.

"Have you told Lane yet? What did your mother say? Oh Em Gee, Ashley's probably shitting herself." Her bubbly reaction to my news gives me more reason to freak out.

"Would you come up for air? You're the first person I called and I don't have much time. I'm due back at the studio in less than an hour." I'm frantically shaving my legs and plucking at the stray hairs that have sprouted since my last bikini wax a week ago. I knew the pain of that shit was not in vain. Though I had imagined Lane would be getting the benefit of my grooming before Siobhan would.

"Tell me again how this happened. Slowly this time. I

need to soak it all in and live vicariously through you." Tatum's mouth runs a mile a minute. She might even be more excited than I am.

I perch my other leg on the ledge of the tub and switch the phone to speaker. "I told you . . . she loved what I did with the makeup and then she literally pointed at me and told me I was walking. At first I had no idea what the hell she meant, but after David—the photographer—gave me the run down, it all fell into place. She has a plus size line that is to die for, Tay. You know how much I hate bathing suits, right? Well, this . . . this thing is magical! I look slim and curvy and dare I say it, va-va-voom!" I can barely believe the words coming out of my mouth. Who is this woman who likes herself, and what has she done to the snarky bitch who hates what she sees in the mirror?

"Leni!" she squeals, her voice so high pitched I fear for the well-being of every dog within a five-mile radius of the hotel. "This is beyond amazing. This is epic. This is history in the making!"

"I know!" I squeak just as obnoxiously, because let's face it—this is pretty freaking clutch. "I don't have time to call Mom, Ashley *and* Lane. You think you can handle the ladies so I can share the big news with him?"

"Of course I can! Look at you all *have my people call your people* and shit. I can see it now. This is just another stepping stone in the direction of greatness!"

"Don't do that!" I scold. "Don't get me all hopeful. This is a one time, beginners luck kind of thing, Tatum. I'm still trying to wrap my head around what's so special about me. It's a lot to grasp."

"Oh! Shut it! Grasp this." I picture her flipping me the bird. "Own it, Leni! Own every last second of that shoot and prowl that catwalk like your life depends on it. I know confidence has never been your forte, but if someone as inspiring as Siobhan Colbert sees something in you, it's time to realize what I've been telling you for as long as I've known you."

"And what's that?" No, I'm not fishing for compliments. I just need the extra push from someone who knows every little detail down to my molecular make-up.

"Beauty comes in many shapes, sizes, and colors, Len. *You* are beautiful. You're modeling, for Pete's sake! If you need a label, this is it, babe! Every doubt you've ever had about yourself, every asshole who rejected you because they couldn't see past a few extra pounds, every girl who made you feel less than perfect because you weren't a size two—this is a big fuck you to all of them! It's a day of reckoning, goddamn it!"

Well, when she puts it that way. "Don't wake me up," I say on a sigh, and allow the joy of this moment to surge through me in a rush of victory. "I never want this feeling to end."

"It doesn't have to. Roll with it. The more you embrace your sexy, bad self, the easier it'll be for you to accept that this new you is really just the *old* you with a little extra *umph*."

Is she right? I mean, she has a point. I haven't exactly morphed into a supermodel overnight. It's not like I've lost a *ton* of weight or done much to change the way I look on the outside. The transformation, if any, has mostly been internal. A true learning experience. And this new gig is just the icing on the cake. *Mmmm, cake. Just one tiny peace of chocolate blackout to reward myself.* What? Old habits die hard.

After a promise to recount every detail of my day once it's done, I hang up with Tatum and set out to call Lane. Time is ticking away and as each second passes, my nerves unravel even more. Saying you'll do something is so much easier than actually following through. I may have sworn to Tatum—and myself—that I'll rock that runway like Heidi Klum but part of me is shitting a brick thinking my runway debut will be a lot more like Carrie Bradshaw's.

"Hello?" Lane answers right away, his voice stirring even more excitement.

"You sitting down?" A bit dramatic, but if Lane and I are going to be an item, he needs to get used to the whole package. Sarcasm and drama are par for the course. *Poor guy.*

"Actually, no, but—is everything okay?"

"Lane! It's more than okay!" I go on to tell him about everything and his enthusiasm vibrates through the phone, making me wish he were here to experience it with me. I've never had a guy to travel alongside the ups in my life. I've had plenty who were the cause of the downs or who had a part in kicking me while I was there hoping and praying for days like these, but this—this is something I've always wanted. *Did I miss a genie escape from his magical lamp somewhere?*

"I told you so! I knew you had this in you." I remember how he assumed I was a model when I told him about the fashion shoot a few days ago. Maybe it was his conviction that oozed out into the universe and caused karma to repay me in kind? Who the hell knows? Either way, I'll take it!

Suddenly the weight of it all consumes me. Happiness. Companionship. Success. I can't bear to mask my true feelings any longer. We're barely even dating, but I've come to like Lane—*a lot*—in this short amount of time. Above all else, he's been a friend during a really weird time in my life and I want him to know what I'm thinking. It can't hurt. "I'm so nervous, Lane. I really wish you were here," I blurt it out with zero remorse.

"I wish I were, too. I wasn't kidding when I said I'd pay serious dough to see you doing something like this, but work is—work—and I just can't get away right now." There's no denying he's genuine. Still sucks, though.

"I know and I'm sorry for laying any guilt on you. I have Raven, thank God, but a familiar face in the audience would've made it a little less terrifying."

"Don't you dare be scared, Leni. You have a fire in you that burns so brightly it makes me want to be around you all the time. I love that about you and you need to love it about you, too."

Has everyone gotten into my Joel Osteen books? What's with all the motivational pep-talks? Am I that much of a sad sack?

Never mind. There's no reason to dwell on why everyone's being so amazing. I'd rather relish in the fact I have so many supportive people in my life. "Thank you, Lane. That means more than you can know."

We spend a few more minutes on the phone, laughing and joking. It totally cools my jets and makes me a little less nervous about what's ahead. Lane encourages me to put my best foot forward and to enjoy myself during what could very well be a once in a lifetime experience. I hang up feeling truly blessed. My friends—new and old—have had my back all this time.

"LENI!" RAVEN RUSHES OVER TO me, heels clicking, with tears in her eyes. "You look fucking gorgeous!"

My legs are wobbly trunks of panic; I'm not sure I'll be able to prompt them to move when the time comes. Her tears incite more nerves and I lose it in the safety of her arms.

"This is crazy! I need more time! I don't think I can do this!"

Raven brings me closer, patting my hair-sprayed head and trying to calm me down. "Tell your nerves to fuck off. You can walk out there and puke all over the catwalk and no one will notice because you look absolutely incredible."

That gets me to laugh, but then I imagine myself hurling all over and my body erupts into overdrive again. "I'm not going to puke, am I? Oh my God, what if I fall? What if I—?"

"Stop it!" She pulls back and grasps my arms, staring into my heavily made-up eyes. "Do your best! This is an honor and you will accept it with grace and dignity."

"Rave, we're talking about me. When have I ever done anything with grace?"

She takes a beat and lifts her chin, jutting it out to make her point. "Always." A single tear rolls down her cheek and she swipes it away, coughing and sniffling to pretend it never happened. "Everything about you is graceful and dignified. I don't know why you can't see that, but we all do. So make us proud, Leni, and most of all . . . have fun!"

I hug her again, completely overwhelmed by a swell of accomplishment. How am I this lucky? If I never lose another pound, or kiss another guy, or walk another runway, this moment will be forever ingrained in my memory as one of genuine pride.

"Thank you," I say, choking back my own tears.

"You cry, I kill you," Marjorie from my studio waves her blush brush at me, shooing Raven away.

I laugh, taking the twenty-millionth deep breath of the day. The hustle and bustle of backstage is enough to momentarily distract me and put me in the right state of mind. *It's almost go time. Get your shit together.*

I take another look in the bulb-lined mirror and smooth a few strands of my styled hair. The girls from the studio—my friends, teammates, the women I was supposed to be working alongside on this project—dolled me up to perfection. David and Siobhan instructed them based on the example I showed them yesterday. The rest of the models—mostly thin and svelte—look almost *fake*. What you think is airbrushed or superimposed in magazines—it ain't, honey. These girls are *perfect*. And while I know I'm not, I won't allow that to take anything away from me today. I'm here, too. Siobhan saw the same thing in me that she saw in Blondie over there.

"Show time!" Someone with a clipboard and an ear piece scurries through the dressing room.

The girls who've done this before—aka everyone but me—
line up in the order they were assigned and I'm left lost somewhere between disbelief and delusion. *Is this really happening?*
"Yes, it is! Now, make me proud." I don't realize I said it out
loud until Raven slaps my ass and ushers me in line with the rest
of the models. *The rest of the models.* Seriously? I'm one of the
models. Holy mother hell!

I do as I'm told, inhaling and exhaling, shaking and swinging my arms, tapping my heeled feet against the floor. I squeeze
between model ten and twelve, being as I was allotted the elev-
enth spot, and the rest unfolds so quickly I'm in the wings before I can talk myself into anything other than walking.

The audience applauds as model ten makes her way back
down the runway and a backstage assistant pushes me forward.
With my heartbeat thundering in my ears, the pulsing of my
blood drowning out the crowd, and the commotion of everything all at once, I can almost swear I hear a jingly rattle accompanied by a shredding tear. Ah, whatever, there are so many
noises going on at once, I can't make sense of any of them. I
take direction, a man pointing to a mark on the stage, highlighted by a glaring spotlight. My legs start to do what they were
taught to do during the quick rehearsal and I plaster the most
convincing smile on my face as I ready myself for a real, live
catwalk.

One foot forward, one hand on my hip, one really, cold draft
wafting right around my ass. I can't look back to see where it's
coming from because that would be completely unprofession-
al, but I just know something isn't right. One glance to my left
and the look on her face—the girl that was in charge of sending
me out—says it all. Not that I have to examine her face to get
the picture, because hanging from her wrist full of dangly, obviously *sharp*, bangle bracelets is a huge, unmistakable chunk of
my bathing suit bottom. Which means—my right ass cheek is in

full view and indecently exposed for the entire fashion world to feast their eyes upon.

Face down, ass up . . . yeah, FML!

# chapter

## twenty-one

THINK FAST. I CAN EITHER stop the show like the amateur they already think I am or . . . the show must go on, right?

Everything floats around in slow motion. Stage lights, cameras, a rumbling audience, the low hush of backstage snickers—no doubt all the skinny minnies are having a field day with this back there.

But rather than allow my wardrobe malfunction and major WTF moment to steal my thunder, I channel the deepest, most neglected parts of me. Behind the bulge, beneath the self-doubt, right below the worst of my insecurities. *Own it*, they told me. I'm not about to destroy Siobhan's art or disappoint Raven. If not for me, I decide to do it for them.

With a sexy pout and a confident arch of my brow, I jut one hip out and trace the outline of my plus-sized but fierce figure. The audience seems to approve of my gutsy demonstration because their low murmurs are replaced with noticeable praise—and a catcall from Raven. This sparks a fire that's always been dormant inside, fueling me to kick it up a notch. I sensually slide my hands from my breasts, to the curve of my waist, down the swell of my hips, and bring them around to my rear. With one single hook of my index fingers in the remaining elastic of the swimsuit bottom, I bunch the fabric together and stick it right where the sun don't shine. This full-coverage, full-figured piece of art has just become a thong—improv at its best.

Without so much as a thought about the fact my cellulite riddled ass is on display for this whole room of spectators, I strut down the aisle with as much grace and dignity as one can muster with her bare cheeks swaying in the wind. I make it down to the end of the ramp and pose the way I was instructed. Surprisingly, it comes naturally and the amazement of actually going through with this floors me. Like almost literally floors me. As I swivel to make my way back, I nearly lose my footing, but when I catch Raven's proud-mama-gleam in her eyes at the front of the auditorium, I take another deep breath and continue on steady feet. *Sashay, shante. Shante, shante, shante.* RuPaul would be proud.

Once back at the start, I give a final pose and then walk off the stage as if that was not the most humiliating *and* exhilarating moment of my life. My ribcage is probably cursing my heart right now because it's beating so rapidly, it's on the verge of popping some serious vesselage. I notice that the girl with the bracelets has been replaced by a gawky young dude with no accessories to be seen, but I spot her in the corner, blowing her nose into a wad of tissues. I could walk away. I'll never see her again. But this isn't her fault and honestly, it could have gone so much worse. So what? My ass had its debut. If Kim Kardashian became famous for her big, naked ass all over a sex tape . . . the future is bright for Leni Moore. Maybe I'll get my own reality show, too. Andy Cohen, here I come! *Mazel!*

I accept the terrycloth robe handed to me by another backstage assistant and kick off the killer heels. Making my way to

Bracelet Girl, I look around the rest of the buzzing area. The show is almost halfway through and we're all due back on stage for a final curtain call. The models who walked before me are all off sipping cucumber water and getting touched up, but before I return for duty I'd like to talk to this poor girl.

"Hey," I say, approaching her.

She looks up and starts to blubber again. "Oh, no! I'm so sorry!" Her words are muffled by tissues, hands, crying, but her red-rimmed eyes hone in on me, pleading for mercy.

"Come on, now. There's no need to cry." I place a hand on her knee and smile. "I survived. The show went on without a hitch. It's nothing to get your panties in a bunch over." I force a laugh, hoping my jibe will lighten her mood.

"Is that supposed to be funny?" she cries.

"Well, yeah."

The girl—whose name I never actually got—jumps out of her chair and stalks off in a string of moans and wails. I'm left in utter shock as she disappears into a room behind a door, hidden by a row of racks, lined with hoards of clothes. "Well, then. Bye, Felicia." No skin off my back. Oh, wait. It actually kinda was.

"JESUS, RAVE. DID YOU CALL TMZ? I feel like a celebrity."

The mini after party at the auditorium was hard enough to take in. Everyone was congratulating me and pawing at me, and all the attention, although fabulous, was distinctly uncomfortable. I stayed as long as I could until the spotlight and questions became too much. While I pretty much had the time of my life, Dirty Dancing style, I left that party knowing today was the first and last day of my short lived modeling career. Been there, done that, came, saw, conquered. A model I am not cut out to be, and while everyone was trying to convince me otherwise, my mind was made up that I'd rather be behind the scenes than in them.

Once back at the hotel, I finally had a moment to check my phone. The calls and messages came flooding in in droves. First it was my family, then Tatum and Ashley. Lane not only called and left me the sweetest message, but he had flowers delivered to my room that had me giddy and gushy and over the moon. Then there was Hudson. I'm not exactly sure *how* he found out about my fashion shenanigans, but he did and he left a message, congratulating me with an invitation to dinner.

"How exactly did Hudson find out?" I ask, scrolling through the rest of the messages.

"A little something called *social media*." Raven sings and sips the glass of pink champagne sent to us from Siobhan herself, thanking me for *rocking the runway*, as she put it.

"What did you do?"

Raven downs the rest of her bubbly—I'm not sure how she can even look at alcohol let alone drink it after yesterday afternoon's booze fest by the pool. "I might have posted a montage of you."

"*Montage*? What is this, a Sweet Sixteen? Rave, it wasn't exactly my most shining moment." My ass tingles with the reminder of its shameful unveiling.

"The hell it wasn't! Leni, get over it. You were amazing, and even if you don't want to do it again, you did, and you deserve every bit of the praise you're getting." She cups her hand to her ear while I nose around her Facebook page. "I'm waiting for my thank you."

As I scan the pictures and read the comments from clients, friends, family, and strangers, my heart fills with something very foreign. Pride. I can count on like three fingers the moments in my life when I could look at myself in a picture and not want to cringe. I don't know whether it's the lighting or the make-up or that the moon is in retrograde, but . . ."Wow. I actually look pretty good."

Raven rushes over and plops down next to me on the edge

of the bed. "Not pretty good, gorgeous! And this is just with my iPhone camera. Can you imagine what the photographer's shots will look like?" She claps her hands and bounces up and down.

I shake my head, rolling my eyes at her childish excitement. "What am I going to do with you?"

She throws her arms around my shoulders and squeezes me. "The question, my dear friend, is what are we going to do with *you*?"

"Meaning?" Insert scowl here. Not her, too. The act of convincing people is utterly draining.

"I'm just saying that this is quite an accomplishment and you're not nearly as keyed up as I thought you'd be. A little confidence goes a long way."

What is she, the excitement police? "I didn't realize my feelings were being measured on some emotion meter." I don't mean to be curt, but until she's walked a day in my Chuck's, she shouldn't judge. I don't get my hopes up about things like this. This was a one time, one trick pony kind of deal. Luck, if you will. Not everyone is as accepting of the plumper peeps. Believe me, I know. I've had my fair share of ridicule, and just because one person happened to find me and my size appealing, doesn't mean the world has suddenly changed its view on the topic.

My flippant comment seemingly offends Raven so she walks back to the mini bar and refills her glass. "I would ask what's up your ass, but after the show, I know the answer to that."

"Ha. Ha. Very funny. Let's drop it. I want to call Lane and thank him for the flowers, anyway."

"I'll drop it after you admit that you're wrong." Raven's my friend, but she's also my boss. I never thought to tread lightly around her because we have a great relationship, but even though I'm trying to curb myself, I can't help but be annoyed by her insistence.

"Wrong? What could I possibly be wrong about?"

She slams the glass down and beelines it to me in one long stride. With her finger in the air, she reminds me a little too much of my mother right now. "You! You're wrong about *you* and this ridiculous image you have of yourself. It's got to stop. It's not good for you or your career, Leni. You hold yourself back because of your insecurities. You don't think I see it? Because I do. Stop worrying about what you can be by losing weight or changing your appearance. Focus on who you are *now!*"

I don't know how our celebration turned into a screaming match. One minute we're laughing and toasting and the next I'm being schooled. All because I don't want to model again? Getting up there and agreeing to what I did was one of the scariest moments in my life, and while it all turned out okay in the end, one wrinkle in time does not erase a lifetime of misgivings. How the hell does she know what goes on in my head on a daily basis? She doesn't! "It's so easy for someone like you to say, Miss Size Two, Successful Business Owner, Married with Three Gorgeous Kids. What can you possibly know about hating what you see in the mirror? About failure?"

Raven's determination never wanes. Her face is red and splotchy with heat, her hands tight at her sides. I ready myself for another lesson in self-worth brought to you by Raven Lee, but a calmness washes over her and she laughs, condescendingly. "If you think you're the only woman in the world with insecurities, then you're out of your mind. We all have them, regardless of how pretty, skinny, or rich one might be." Raven starts to unbutton her blouse and I blanch. Am I losing it? First champagne, then a fight, now a strip tease?

"Raven, what are you—"

She sheds her shirt and drops it to the floor, her beautifully slim figure covered only in a lacy push-up bra and a fitted pencil skirt. My eyes immediately fixate on her belly. While it's flatter than mine will ever be, it's marred from sternum to belly button and beyond with deep, white stretch marks and loose, inelastic skin. I would've never guessed that was hiding behind such a poised woman.

I pick up the shirt from the floor and drape it around her shoulders, urging her to redress. "You didn't have to show me that," I say, feeling bad that she had to expose this part of herself to prove a point.

"I know I didn't but I wanted to, and while my war wounds of motherhood might be the only visible thing that make me hate the mirror, there are so many other things about me that I wish I could change, too. I was a gawky kid with braces and frizzy hair. I was bullied in junior high because of that. I grew out of it, and later I met James and the rest is history, but you don't think that scrawny, ugly duckling doesn't still live inside me?"

I bite my lip, unsure how to answer.

Raven buttons her blouse and then pulls her trendy, pink-tipped hair back in a ponytail. "She'll always be a part of me and I'm actually happy about it, because it humbles me. It reminds me that shit like that does not define a human being."

I nod as I witness one of my role models shrug off the vulnerability she just shared with me. *Grace and dignity,* that takes guts. Modeling for the first time with your junk exposed takes guts. After her revelation, I admire her even more for laying into me for being whiney about my weight all these years. But rather than continuing this Debbie Downer duo deal, I walk over to the bar, pour myself a glass of champagne, top off Raven's, and bring it to her.

"Toast?" I ask, hoping to let the heaviness of the last few minutes pass without any malice.

"To?"

I think long and hard about what to say. It should be sweet, empowering, something to show her that what she said sank in.

But that's not me and Raven wants me to be *me*. I lift my glass and clink it against hers. With a nod of my head and a subtle wink, I say, "To ugly ducklings and fat chicks."

Raven giggles and then snorts as the exasperation from earlier disappears from her face. "I'll drink to that."

And just like that, we pull a P!nk, raising a glass in honor of the underdog. *Misfits aren't misfits among other misfits.* Thank you, Barry Manilow, for your words of wisdom . . . it looks like we made it.

# chapter

## twenty-two

THE HAPPENINGS OF THE REST of my week in Miami are insightful and overall . . . fun. Along with Raven, the other girls from the studio and I have plenty of downtime to relax and catch some rays and even get out to a trendy, Latin hot-spot one night. Drinks, dancing, letting loose . . . it's a blast. But the highlight of the trip; however, is not the runway show or even the photo shoot, but rather that in ten minutes I'll be landing at JFK, one step closer to home and my normal routine. And Lane, of course.

I missed him while I was gone and even though working on this project was an eye-opening experience *and* a giant step in the direction of expanding my career, I hated going through it all without having someone to share it. Silly, because Lane and I managed to talk every night so it was as if he were right there beside me for all the ups and downs of the wild ride. We grew closer while spilling our guts over late night chats and intermittent texts that, now that I look through them, could make a porn star blush. And while there's no doubt that absence makes the heart grow fonder, the distance mixed with the flirting also has us desperately deprived of the other. It's crazy what can happen over long distance phone calls and the span of seven lonely days. Crazy and pretty damn amazing.

As the plane descends, I imagine being welcomed home by Lane, the way he promised me he would. He's my ride home from the airport, so I dig into my purse for a few frills to freshen up. I haven't seen him in seven days, and while the sun gave my skin a nice bronzed glow and my hair a few extra highlights, I'm positive my jeans are tighter than they were when I left. All that overindulging and no time to work out—I can't think about it now. No use in crying over a few unwanted pounds when you have a hottie like Lane as the sole member of your welcoming committee. If I'm being honest, it's not necessarily the actual welcome home I'm looking forward to. It's what comes after. That's where the real promise lies. *Skin on skin.* I had him swear on all that's good and holy.

"I'll never get used to landing, either." Raven squeezes my wrist. She must've noticed my squirming.

"Mmm hmm." I go along with it. She doesn't need to know that I'm all hot and bothered thinking about how Lane and I will be spending the night.

By the time I've said my goodbyes to the girls and grabbed my bags from the luggage carousel, my heart has become the focal point of my entire being. Fluttering, then galloping. Skipping, then palpitating. I have never been more excited to see someone in my life. Rolling the bags behind me, I check my phone to see if Lane's texted. Sure enough, the first thing that pops up from three minutes ago is an "I'm here," from the boy who has my heart up in arms.

If I knew how, I'd back handspring my way through the terminal and out the door to get to my handsome chariot driver as quickly as possible. But I'm me and we all know I have no business even pretending that's a possibility, so I settle for a fast-paced stride with a shit-eating grin on my face.

When our eyes lock, Lane immediately throws his door open and comes around the front of his car. I'm not even sure it's his car—who owns a car in the city—but who cares? He's here and that's all that matters. "Hi!" I beam, dropping my bags dramatically and spreading my arms for a hug.

Lane forgoes my open armed invitation and grabs my face in his hands. "Hi, gorgeous. I missed you." His lips find mine as if they've been searching a lifetime and I kiss him right there, the way I want to, without reservation, as if we're alone.

We're soon interrupted by a security guard who clearly has no respect for the art of love in bloom and orders Lane to move the car. After one more soft kiss and a look that melts whatever's left of my insides, he grabs my luggage, loads it in the trunk, and we get into our respective seats as driver and passenger. I touch my fingers to my lips, relishing in the feeling of *home*.

Call me bananas. Call the whole thing a bit much. But then I'll call you a wench, because I don't care how it seems—too fast, too forward, too whatever—this is exactly right. Timing and all. My heart's waited a long time to feel this good and I'm allowing her this moment of glory.

"How was the flight?" Lane snaps his seat belt and puts the car in drive, signaling before he pulls out of the apparently illegal spot.

"Flight was great. Trip was great. Everything was great." Which I hope translates to: enough small talk. Get me home so I can have my way with you.

Lane leans over the console and wraps his hand around mine, sending another pulsing ache to my lady bits. "You better step on it," I demand.

"Hasty, much?"

"No, another word that starts with h and ends with y."

Recognition washes the smirk right off his face and one of his dimples sinks into the pinkish tint of his clean-shaven cheek.

I bring my hand to touch it, needing to feel the heat radiate off of him. "You can't kiss me like that and think my lips won't snitch to the rest of my body about what they're missing." In a sensual trail that could very well risk our lives, my hand travels from his face to his lap. *Hello, down there. Nice to make your acquaintance again. It's about time we get to know each other a lot better.* I squeeze a hefty helping of hardness and order, "Home. Now. I don't care how many laws you have to break to make this happen in a timely fashion, but do it."

Lane's hearty laugh reverberates through my core. Hilarity overpowers longing and my hand flies to my mouth to mask the unattractive guffaw that escapes me. Looking back on the moments with Lane thus far, big and small, significant and inconsequential, this has to be my favorite. I don't know if it's that we became more comfortable with each other through the phone calls, or if it's just a natural progression of things, but the happiness trapped inside this car could cause spontaneous combustion. And I'm not just talking about shattering windows and crushing metal. Can you have an orgasm from sheer happiness? Is that possible?

Traffic cooperates for a change and we find ourselves hand-in-hand as we pull up to the curb outside my apartment. "Aren't you going to park it?" I gesture behind me with my thumb, in the direction of the parking garage down the street.

"Nope." The word echoes through the car with a deafening pop.

"Not this again! You can't be serious." If disappointment and fury gave birth to a human, she'd be Leni Moore.

Lane's strong hand caresses my fiery cheek. "Calm down, gorgeous. It's my friend's car. I borrowed it so I could pick you up. He should be here any minute to take it back."

Relief triumphs overreaction. "I thought you were chickening out again," I admit, the air returning to my lungs, with zero traces of rage.

"I wouldn't dream of it." He leans in and kisses the tip of my nose. It's so endearing, yet so sexy, my body goes into another tizzy.

"Let me grab my bag and air out the apartment while you wait for your friend. I need the little girl's room, too."

Lane kisses the palm of my hand and nods me on.

When I step out of the car, I take another look at Lane and smile. Happiness is an understatement for what's overcome me. I offer him a wink and spin around to head upstairs. Out of the corner of my eye, a tall, handsome man catches my attention. From afar he looks familiar but as he nears and throws his hand up to wave—at me—my uterus contracts and a wave of nausea nearly knocks me off my wobbly feet.

"Leni!" he calls, picking up the pace.

There's no mistaking him now. No turning back, no jumping into the safe haven of the car with Lane, no pretending I didn't see him. "Hudson? What are you doing here?"

# chapter

## twenty-three

"I TRIED GETTING IN TOUCH with you, but you never returned my calls. I really wanted to see you." Hudson's sharp features and perfectly-styled hair do not match the vulnerable tone of his deep voice. His dark eyes measure me, only me, with a fondness I wish I could reciprocate. It's not that I'm not insanely attracted to Hudson or that I didn't enjoy our . . . time . . . together. He's gorgeous. Stunning, even. More so than I remembered. But to my left, in his friend's car, probably wondering who the hell this strange man is, I have all I've ever wanted in a man.

Backing away from his towering stature, a pang of guilt stings me from the inside out. I've never been on this side of things. I've always been the reject*ed*, not the reject*er*. This blows donkey balls. "Hudson, this really isn't a good time." I cringe as the words leave my mouth, lingering in the air with an aftershock akin to a slap in the face. I feel like such an ass. An insensitive ass, at that. He came all this way and I *have* been avoiding him, but for good reason. I thought our fun together was over. I never imagined he'd want more.

An uncomfortable moment of realization flashes before us, as Hudson becomes aware of Lane waiting in the car. "Who's that?" he asks with the malice of a jealous boyfriend.

Cool your jets, bro. When did one roll in the hay become reasonable proof of ownership? Thumbing in the direction of the very patient man in the driver's seat of the Honda, I respond a little more tersely than I'd like. "*That* is Lane. My boyfriend." The word comes out like profanity. Considering it's the first time I've ever spoken it in relation to Lane, it's a letdown. Not how I envisioned it. This better not be an omen.

Hudson lets out a deep sigh and his rigid posture slackens. Guess I'm not the only one feeling a bit defeated. "Shit. I had no idea, Leni. I'm sorry."

"Sorry for?" Why's he apologizing? This is *my* mess. A simple response to one of his texts would've freed me of this whole crappy situation.

"Well, this is kind of awkward, no?" He smirks, pointing to Lane with a cagy glint in his eyes. He leans closer and whispers. "The guy you cheated on your boyfriend with shows up unannounced, at your apartment, while he's here, no less. I really didn't mean to cause any trouble."

"Oh! No, no, no. It's not like that at all," I start to explain myself, waving my hands and shaking my head. Before I can set things straight and let Hudson know that I don't have a cheating bone in my larger than life body, Lane exits the Honda.

"Everything all right, here?" I'm not sure what finally prompts Lane to come out of the car, but my guess is curiosity. Hudson's proximity, his body language, the hushed conversation. This isn't exactly painting a pretty picture.

Hudson becomes a tight-lipped coward, leaving all the 'splaining to me. I can't exactly blame him.

Lane makes his way around to the two of us, honing in on

Hudson. He doesn't ask again, but I sense a "what's going on here" coming on, so I apprehensively think fast.

"Lane this is Hudson. Hudson this is Lane. My boyfriend." This time the word has a tender ring to it. I grab Lane's hand and squeeze it tight, hoping to infuse my genuine feelings for him through osmosis.

His fingers tighten around mine and his gait stiffens. "Nice to meet you?" It's a question, rather than a sincere statement, but Lane extends his free hand to shake Hudson's nonetheless.

"Ditto." Hudson reacts with a snappy punch and then his eyes dart to mine. "I guess I'll be going now. I was just passing by and thought I'd visit my, um . . . friend." He's careful with his words but not his tone. It's riddled with artificiality. I stop myself from kicking him right in the shin.

After a moment of deliberation, Lane bends to place a quick kiss on my cheek and then gives Hudson a sideways grin. "I'd ask your *friend* to come up, but you and I have lots of catching up to do."

Is friend a new dirty word? Whatever. Who cares? Lane is claiming what's his and Hudson knows his role. "No worries. I'm on my way to Stone Street to . . . meet someone." I don't miss the sharp arch in Hudson's thick brow and the mention of the place he and I hooked up. *Bastard.*

After an amicable goodbye, Hudson nods in Lane's direction. Before he walks off exuding the same sexy confidence that drew me to him in the first place, he ends our little debacle by saying, "It was good to see you, Leni, and nice to meet you, Lane. Be good."

I look over my shoulder as he strides away, scowling at his final words. *Be good?* "I'm better than good, thank you very much. In fact, I'm grand!"

I don't realize I've said it out loud until Lane's arm is draped around my shoulder. "Total mood killer, huh?"

He can say that again, but I'll be damned if I'm about to let my ex-one-night-stand put a damper on getting busy with my new boyfriend. "Only if you allow it to be."

Lane shakes his head and dips in for a sweet kiss. "Just go on up. John should be here any second. I'll bring your bags, too."

For a moment I worry he'll fly the coop just to avoid talking about Hudson. "You are coming up, right?"

Lane chuckles, pulling his jacket closed when a gust of chilly fall air breezes by. "I promised you, didn't I?"

With my bottom lip between my teeth I look up at him through half mast lids, tilting my head.

He taps my ass, ushering me to the door. "Go on. My promise holds."

I prance up the steps and put the key in the lock. The door swings open, welcoming me with the familiar scent of home. I glance over my shoulder to check on Lane one last time, and I'm not sure if it's just me or the melancholy moonlight, but I can sense apprehension beneath those drawn in dimples.

LANE'S FRIEND TAKES A LITTLE longer than expected, but I use it to my advantage by washing up and slipping into something super sexy.

Leni Moore has never done lingerie, but after the swimsuit shock heard 'round the world—okay, heard 'round *some* of Miami—I found my inner sex goddess. And dayum do I like her. She's a feisty thing I wish I had met a long time ago.

Putting on the finishing touches of my get-up, I adjust the lace trimmed thigh highs and smooth my hands over the silky nylon. What I see in the mirror surprises me. Not because the image is a teensy bit slimmer than before, or because I'm wearing something straight out of a *Hips and Curves* magazine. No, what I see is a girl—a *woman*—who after years of body image issues has finally come to terms with her curves. Don't get me wrong, Lane's affections are responsible in part, but with all the pep-talking and ego-boosting, oh, and let's not forget the Joel Osteen messages, I actually don't hate what I see. In fact, it's quite the opposite. I'm digging it. Junk in the trunk and all.

"Hello?" Lane's singsong entrance into the apartment startles me out of my mirror miracle.

I dip my hands into my bra to plump the girls one more time—as if any part of me needs further plumping—and position myself on the bed. Again, I've never done this before. The sexy seductress act. But I have my eye on the prize and with the boost of confidence inspired by Lane's promise, I look and feel every bit the part.

"In here, babe." I realize how cliché it sounds, so I giggle. All humor, however, is erased from the moment when Lane enters the bedroom.

"Wow." His words match his stupefied expression. Call it what you may, but putting that look on any man's face is damn near spectacular. *Hashtag: winning!*

Enjoying the angst filled silence, I curl my finger in invitation for Lane to join me.

In one fell swoop, my dashing stallion kicks off his shoes, peels off his socks, and practically nosedives onto the bed. His body hovers over mine as he takes me in. All of me. I should feel vulnerable under his gaze—he's perfect and I'm far from it—but I don't. I feel worshiped. That glorious insight sends a rush of shivers over my exposed body.

"Gorgeous. Absolutely gorgeous." His words are lyrics to an unsung song I've always wished to hear. I savor his appreciation of my body, committing this moment to memory.

Lane's kisses pepper my neck; his hot tongue licks my collarbone and teases my skin. I anchor my fingers in his hair, thrust my hips against his, and moan out his name, "Oh, Lane."

Instead of inciting him to push further, he stops. My skin misses his lips as soon as they're gone. "What's the matter?"

Lane rolls off of me and rests his head on the pillow beside mine.

The room is silent save for my panting, and I'm pretty sure the butterflies in my belly have become ravenous beasts, ready to gnaw away at my anxiousness.

"Old boyfriend?" he asks, catching me off guard. I don't register the meaning of his question right away.

Then it hits me that he's curious about Hudson. I shimmy closer to him, turning on my side. With one hand propped under my head, I rest the other on his chest. There is no reason under the sun that Hudson's name should come up in the throes of passion with Lane, but honesty is the best policy, so I'll let him have it so we can get back to the main event. "No, because I don't have any old boyfriends. Unless you consider that one from college, who really was never my boyfriend."

Lane closes his eyes and keeps them shut for a long beat. When he opens them, he stares straight up at my popcorn ceiling. "Then, what was all that tension down there?"

Chocolate fudge! Seriously? I felt zero tension. Maybe a tiny wave of awkwardness, but that's all she wrote on that. "There's nothing to worry about, Lane. I promise."

Lane says nothing, but disbelief is written all over his face. That alone sinks my battleship.

I'm not sure why this is an issue. There's really nothing to tell; no lies to weave. And let's remember . . . these are seriously foreign waters for me. I've never been in a real relationship, let alone had to defend myself against a jealous boyfriend, a one-night stand, or *any* kind of man for that matter. I don't know what's going on of late, but I don't think I'm in Kansas anymore and . . . Auntie Em, I wanna go home!

I pull him closer and try to make eye contact. "He's no one, Lane. We hooked up *once* a while back and that's all you need to know." I blurt it out, ripping off the Band-Aid. Maybe I sound a tad frustrated, but that's only because this whole Hudson thing is a non-issue. And I am most certainly frustrated. One minute we're rounding home plate and the next I'm being called out at third.

"How long ago?"

I contain my eye roll and answer him honestly. "A few weeks ago. Before you." There. More truth. But it doesn't have the effect I was hoping for.

Wilted and motionless, Lane looks like a deflated balloon. He's one second away from petering out in a whirl of air-leaking shrills around the room. He doesn't, of course, but I almost wish he would do *some*thing because his quietness worries me.

"I'm laying it all out here, Lane. I have nothing to hide. Can you please say something?"

He shoots up into a sitting position and says the last thing I want him to say. I've been rejected more times than I can count. I should be used to it. But for some reason the five words that spill from Lane's mouth rip open every old wound and pour salt all over them.

"I think I should go."

# chapter

## twenty-four

"THE HELL YOU SHOULD!" I blurt it out like a woman scorned . . . *and* left high and dry.

Lane is quick to ignore my outburst and he hasn't fled yet, so that's one point for the home team.

I join him at the head of the bed, scooting closer but not *too* close. Apparently the more I throw myself at him the more he retreats. I'm beginning to think I have cooties or a bad case of BO. "Wanna tell me what's going on?" I whisper, careful not to let my true emotions—rage, rejection, remorse—come shining through.

"Nothing. Forget it. I'm just . . . tired."

*Sullen much?* He sounds like a middle-aged housewife making excuses not to get down and dirty. I want to reach over and shake him by his muscular shoulders because if that's not the brush off of the century, I'm not sure what is. If anything can come of this could-be relationship with Lane, he'll have to start peeling away those thick layers so I can get to know him for more than the cute, sweet guy who saved me from the big, bad tree.

"Lane, you can talk to me about anything." I look down through hooded lids, arranging the duvet so it covers my exposed nooks and crannies. Before I can tell my inner sex goddess to pour herself a nice warm glass of shut the hell up, Lane's eyes find mine. They're a less lively shade of green than I'm used to. "Is it me? Do I not do it for you?" I can't figure out what has Lane so averse to slipping into the sheets with me. The only logical solution is that he doesn't find me physically attractive. Sure, it's easy to promise things over texts or phone calls, but it might very well be that once he actually *sees* me—every last curvy ounce of me—the blood doesn't pump to the right places the way it should. At the harrowing realization, I bring my hands up to my eyes as if that can shield me from the truth.

"Oh, no," Lane interrupts my self-loathing before I have the chance to vocalize my thoughts. "This has nothing to do with you, Leni. I know what you're thinking, but you didn't do anything wrong. This is all me."

"How am I supposed to believe that? Every time we get close to being together, you freeze up. It's okay if you're not sexually attracted to me. I'll understand." I won't understand. I mean, I'll have to, but I really won't be okay with a letdown like this. *Rocky Road, I'm coming for you!*

Strong hands grasp my wrists, pulling my splayed hands from my eyes. "Look at me," Lane orders.

But I don't open my eyes. I'm not ready to face this. A few minutes ago I was certain this man and I had something special blooming, now all hope is lost. I know intimacy isn't everything in a relationship but I've waited forever to feel wanted the way I thought Lane wanted me; the way Hudson had no issue wanting me.

*Wait!*

*Hudson!*

My eyes pop open. "Does this have anything to do with him?"

"Who?" It's a faint whisper, as if he can toss it under the bed and leave it unnoticed.

"Oh no, you don't! Don't play shy. I'm sitting next to you, practically down to my birthday suit, willing, able, panting, and almost begging. If I can do *this*, you can find the balls to tell me if Hudson has anything to do with why you stopped."

Lane blanches at my frankness, but I don't care. I want answers, not assumptions. We all know that old saying about those pesky things . . . and *I* already feel very much like a big ol' ass.

"Of course it does, Leni." He jumps out of the bed and starts to pace around my bedroom. "If Hudson Blackman is the kind of guy you're used to, how am I supposed to—"

"Whoa, whoa, whoa. Back the hell up." Without so much as a thought to how he knows Hudson's last name when I never caught it or to how little I'm wearing, I toss the blanket off and follow Lane in his march around the perimeter of my bed. "The kind of guy I'm used to? I'm not used to *any* kind of guy. I told you that!"

"You said the two of you hooked up. That means you've slept with him, no?"

"Yes! Once. And if you're looking for my entire sexual history, before my extremely inconsequential one-night-stand with Hudson, there was a guy named Tony that I was seeing for all of two seconds until he decided his fat ass was too good for *my* fat ass. And before Tony there was Alex from college, and that's a story for another day of humiliation. But why does any of that matter? And how do you know Hudson's last name? I thought you liked *me*. You know I like *you*. So, before I jump to any more ridiculous conclusions can you *please* tell me what the hell your major malfunction is, dude, because I simply do not *comprende!*" I'm out of breath and completely void of reasons why Lane is so hell bent on the Hudson thing. I haven't been with enough guys to know how they tick, but Lane's acting more like an insecure girl than the adorable, athletic, appealing man I met at the park.

"You mean to tell me you didn't know that *the* Hudson Blackman is trying to woo *my* girl?"

*The?* As in, important? "What are you talking about, Lane? He's just some random guy I met at a bar. Am I missing something?"

He plops back onto the bed and let's out a huffy laugh laced with contempt. "Hudson Blackman is the sole heir to his land developing tycoon grandfather, Ronald Blackman's fortune. You really didn't know this?"

"Are you calling me a gold digger?" I mean, of course I didn't know. If I had, I might have actually returned Hudson's calls. *Tycoon? Fortune?* Damn! I should've cashed in before I sent him away with his silver spoon between his legs. But I digress, and that totally negates my rejection of Lane's claim. "Never mind that. The better question is how do *you* know this?"

"Uh, I read the newspaper."

"Great. So now I'm a gold digger *and* a dumbass. Nice, Lane. This is going oh, so well."

Lane shakes his head and raises his hands before him. "Would you just let me finish?" His tone is clipped.

"First fight before the first fuck. We're batting a thousand." Yeah, I'm flippant, but I was promised one thing and wound up with something totally different—including a handful of bogus insults.

"Leni." Lane rises and begins pacing again. "I only brought it up because I really like you and the idea of dating you while one of the city's wealthiest and most eligible bachelors is also in the running . . . I'm not into competition, and I don't have a private jet to take you to and from our dates."

Okay. Now I kinda get it. Lane feels inferior to Hudson. There's a word I've gotten to know on a first name basis. Any insecurity is a curse, so I can totally relate to Lane's issue with

Hudson, but he has to know I would never compare them. Even though the esteemed heir's eligibility, his good looks, and his heaping pile of dough might sound like something to compete against—they're not. This newfound info about *the* Hudson Blackman doesn't change how I feel about Lane. I need to make him see his.

Lane rests at the window, looking out to the busy street below. I come up behind him—keeping my distance as not to scare off the timid lamb I once thought was a rugged lion. Funny, because that alone should turn me off. But it doesn't. It intrigues me. There are so many sides to Lane Sheffield I've yet to discover because I was too busy trying to get in his pants. *Note to self: get more of a background on the men you sleep with before you actually set to screwing them.*

Placing my hands on the shoulders of the man who charmed my mind, body, and soul in the short amount of time I've known him, I urge him to face me. I should be pissed, hurt, utterly baffled, but I'm not. I'm apologetic for trying to move things faster than necessary. That whole idiom about putting the cart before the horse makes so much sense now. "I'm sorry, Lane."

He looks at me with wide eyes, his mouth dangling open like a guppy. "Are you seriously apologizing to me? Leni, you should be kicking me out for acting like such a pussy."

The irony of the situation isn't lost on me, but rather than make this more awkward than it already is, I choose humor—it always prevails. "Yes, I'm apologizing for being hasty and not getting to know more about *you* before I tried to get to know *him.*" I point to his groin and his eyes follow my line of sight. He gives his junk a quick pat and then returns his gaze to me with a boyish grin.

"You're something else, you know that? I shouldn't have reacted that way about Blackman. Who you've spent your time with in the past is none of my business."

Lane rests against the window sill and I nestle between his legs, wrapping my arms around his neck. We stare into each other's eyes in silence. Recognizing his lack of self confidence with this whole situation, I tilt my head and pout. "How about we make a new promise to each other?"

Lane clips my chin between two deft fingers and smiles. "What's that, gorgeous?"

"Well, two, okay?"

Lane nods and waits for me to speak.

"Number one, no more Hudson talk. Rich, poor, hand-some, or homely, I don't want *him*. I want *you*."

"Deal." I'm glad he doesn't elaborate. There's no need to question it. I'm sure, so he should be, too.

"Good."

"What's number two?" he asks, his nerves seemingly less frayed than before.

I'm not gonna lie; it totally pains me to say this because I want more than anything to take this relationship to the next level. But seeing firsthand that Lane has obvious insecurities, it's time to steer things in a direction other than south of the waistline.

"How about we forget about sex for a while and just get to know each other better?"

Lane's eyes light up—the dull green from earlier revived with a livelier shade of sparkling emerald. "You mean—you're not pissed? I haven't totally screwed this up?"

"Oh, you didn't screw anything. Let's get that straight."

"Ha, ha, ha. You're such a smartass." That earns me a play-ful tap on my already heated cheek.

"And proud of it. You think you can handle that?"

"I know I can. The question is, how much longer are we talking, here?" He leans in, grazing his lips against my jawline and then nibbles at my earlobe. His tender touch causes all ra-tional thought to fly out the window.

"Hey!" I back away, leaving Lane with a sinful gleam in his darkened eyes. "You're the one with the giant red stop sign in his hands," I remind him to make sure he knows where I stand. "Wait. Don't wait. I'm cool with whatever, but I'm definitely not okay with mixed signals. So, decide."

Lane growls, obviously frustrated. "I guess seeing Blackman here messed with my mojo. I think we need a do over."

"Then a do over it is. There's more to a relationship than sex, even if I'm pretty sure I could've rocked your world tonight."

Lane circles his arms around my waist and returns his warm lips to my ear. His embrace is a perfect combo of friendly and passionate, and it feels just right.

Except for the chilly draft wafting itself around my thonged ass.

"Um, Lane." I mumble into his neck, where I can feel his quickening pulse.

"Yeah, babe?"

"I think I'm gonna change into a pair of comfy sweats."

He takes a step back and examines me once again. His dimples appear when he smiles and licks his lips. "I'm such as ass. I can't believe I'm about to pass this up."

I make my way to my dresser to grab a pair of pants. Closing the drawer with my hip, I assure him, "You're not passing it up, just putting it aside for a better day." It's the only way I can look at it without wanting to slap that sexy grin off his even sexier face.

"Thank you for understanding."

"Of course." I wink and head for the bathroom. "I'll be right out."

"Hey? You think I can I raid your fridge while I wait? I'm suddenly starved."

*Yeah, so am I, but not for food.* Rather than dwell on my hunger, I give in, "Have at it, but there's not much there. I was gone a week, remember?"

Lane laughs, ignoring my obvious jibe. "How about I order some take-out? Pizza? Chinese? Burgers?"

"Um . . . again, I was away all week. I think I should stick to something diet friendly if I ever plan on wearing this sexy contraption again. You know, for when the time is right."

His eyes wander, taking in what he's decided to leave untouched for the time being. I can sense a glint of regret, and that's more than enough to show me it won't be this way forever. "Leni, tonight calls for comfort food. We can go back to working out tomorrow. I promise—and this one I'll keep." He crosses his heart with his index finger, holding his other hand up in honor of his vow.

My insides melt into gooey goodness at the innocence Lane possesses. "You're a hard man to say no to. What am I going to do about that?"

He rushes over to me and pulls me close. Lips on lips, nose to nose, fingers tangled with fingers, Lane embraces me again and says, "Just keep saying yes. That's all I ask."

# chapter

## twenty-five

"ASH, IF I DIDN'T KNOW better, I'd think he's trying to plump me up!" I stare at myself in the three-way mirror, wondering how I managed to go back to feeling—and looking—like I'm back to square one.

"You're exaggerating. You look great." Ashley fusses with the dress while the seamstress works on my hem.

I don't want to stress her out with the wedding getting so close, so I drop the subject to touch on something far more pressing. "So, can you believe the whole Hudson Blackman thing? How did we not know who he is?"

Immediately following the catastrophe at my apartment, I found myself dwelling on my lack of current events knowledge. In other words, I wanted the scoop on Hudson Blackman so I did some digging. Turns out, Lane was right. Hudson's worth millions, and while he is most definitely out of my league in *more* than a million ways, the fact still remains that he *was* interested in me. "I still can't wrap my head around it. Why would a guy like him want someone like me?"

"We're back to this again?" Ashley whines, practically stomping her foot.

I throw my arms up, earning a scowl from the elderly Italian seamstress. "I'm sorry. I know I'm a total PITA, but I don't get it. Nowhere in any of the pictures in the rag mags is he seen with a woman my size. He's usually photographed alone, but on the rare occasion he does have a chick on his arm, she is so far my opposite she might as well be from Mars."

"I think you mean Venus."

"Oh, whatever. You know what I'm talking about. Why, Ash? Even Tatum's speechless about the whole thing. Someone of his wealth and power shouldn't be single *or* chubby chasing."

Ashley's hands fly to her hips, her diamond sparkling when the light filters in from the window and catches it just right. "Would you stop it, already! I don't like when you talk this way about yourself."

"You mean, when I tell the truth?" I laugh. "Face it, Ash, this is me. I can diet, work out, starve, but I'll never be a size two and guess what, I'm finally okay with that. So, if I can poke fun at my weight, just shut up and let me roll with it. I promise I'm not fishing for compliments. Just explanations."

She closes her eyes and lets out a long sigh before shaking her head. "Why are you harping on this? Are you regretting your decision? Do you want Hudson instead of Lane? Is it about his money?"

"Ouch. Now *that* kinda stings."

"Well, you did say honesty. So tell me. What gives?" She sits on the stool just outside the dressing room curtain and makes herself comfortable.

"Maybe I just don't know how to be happy because, for once, I'm *so happy* with every aspect of my life, it's scary. Myself, my career, Lane. It all feels so good, I wonder if I'm setting myself up for failure." Admitting that feels like a brick's been lifted from my chest.

"And this has what to do with Hudson?"

"Nothing, really. I guess the attention from him and now Lane is just a lot to swallow."

Ashley giggles, bringing her hands to her lips. "You said swallow."

"Seriously?"

Her giggles turn into cackles and my body starts to shake with her infectious amusement.

"Ouch!" I shout when the seamstress pricks me with a pin right in my calf. I look down but she doesn't offer an apology, save for the Italian curse words I recognize from my days with my crazy great-grandma.

"So, you still haven't told me. Is he your plus one?" Ashley composes herself as she bobs her knee up and down.

"Who? Lane?"

"No, Donald Trump. Of course, Lane. He is your boyfriend now, right?"

"That he is." I beam, remembering last night when he spent the evening at my place and whispered sweet nothings in my ear until we fell asleep in each other's arms. With our clothes on. *This waiting thing is getting harder by the day and it's only been five.* But all that aside, things are going much better than I could've imagined.

"Okay, so he's coming to the wedding, then. I'll adjust the seating chart." She claps her hands and wiggles on the stool.

"Someone's excited."

"And it shouldn't be me. I already found the man of my dreams. Maybe Lane's yours."

Could he be? Is it too soon to tell? I mean, I'm happy and for me that's a huge deal. The notion that I haven't seriously stressed about my weight since before Miami says a whole lot about how Lane has changed me for the better. Couple that with how great he treats me and how wonderfully we get along, without even sleeping together yet—"You know what? Yeah. All that's left to do is catch the bouquet. You think you can hook a sista up?"

A smile brightens her already bride-to-be glow. "I'll see what I can do, but watch out for Tatum. She might trample anyone who gets in the way of her being next."

"Things with her and Paul are so weird right now, I don't know if she's focused on marriage so much anymore."

"That sucks. Trouble in paradise?"

I step down from the pedestal when the seamstress tells me she's done and head for Ashley with my back toward her so she can unzip me. "Who knows. I never get a straight answer. Maybe we should hook her up with Hudson. One of us should benefit from his inheritance."

"Leni!"

"What? He's loaded! I may not be a gold digger, but Tatum has a not so subtle tendency to check a guy's net worth before she gives him the time of day."

Ashley snickers. "Get Hudson off your brain. It's trouble. Lane sounds like a good guy."

"He totally does, doesn't he?" Giddiness overcomes me and all thoughts of Hudson and his oodles of cash vanish into thin air.

"Now, chop, chop. Get yourself dressed. We have cake tasting next." She draws the curtain closed and leaves me to change.

"Doesn't my brother want to be part of any of the planning?"

"Let's get one thing straight. I love your brother, but he's useless and couldn't care less if we even have a cake."

I shimmy into my jeans, and pull the zipper closed. "Then you've come to the right Moore sibling because me and cake—we're tight like that."

"THESE JEANS ARE TIGHT!" I whine louder than I intended, hating Ashley for talking me into that tenth sample of wedding cake.

"So, wear something else. Like a skirt. I love your legs." Lane calls from the living room where he's waiting for me to get dressed so we can meet up with the Cake Nazi and my brother. *He* should be the one squeezing *his* ass into ill-fitting jeans after all the tasting *he* should've been forced to do today.

I throw the once skinny jeans to the floor and rummage through my closet. Lane's suggestion is adorable, but it's chilly outside and a skirt would mean tights and tights would mean Spanx and what I really want is to be comfortable. With no other outfit options in the forefront of my mind, I grunt and groan, and consider cancelling our plans. Suddenly throwing on my bathrobe to watch a movie on the couch with Lane sounds mighty tempting. But then I remember how excited he was when I told him I wanted him to meet Reynold and Ashley. That came after his enthusiasm over being asked to be my date for the wedding. The guy is meant to be a boyfriend; I can tell you that much. So far, I've yet to find anything he doesn't want to do as a couple or any excuse not to appease me. He's wonderful, and it's not merely because he looks at me like I'm the only woman in the world. It's because I'm my best me around him. I don't think I've ever been my best me before.

"Need any help in there?" he calls again, forcing me to pick something out in a pinch.

"No! I'll be right out. Just a slight wardrobe malfunction."

I overhear him chuckle, probably remembering my runway story, and the sound travels through my apartment and spreads to my own lips. Another Lane induced smile dances across my face and I realize that I'm being stupid over a pair of freaking pants. "Screw it!" I say to myself, heading for my dresser. "Trusty old black stretch pants, it is."

As I pull them up over my silky shaven legs, the reason

they're actually called *stretch pants* becomes evident when I tug the tight, black spandex over my thighs. "Mother hell! You too! Just two weeks ago you fit like a glove. A loose one. Fucking Ashley and that cake!"

"Talking to yourself again?" Lane appears in the doorway, propped against the frame with an expression only a girlfriend could love.

"Get out of here, Mr. Impatient."

He strides into my room, ignoring my request for him to leave, and kneels in front of me, where I'm playing tug of war with my pants. "Allow me?" I should be embarrassed because I'm only half-clothed, but I'm not. His eyes calm me, his tone hypnotizes me, and his hands soothe me into submission.

Luckily, I had enough sense to put on a top I liked before fighting with the bottoms. But I'm pretty flustered from rushing and tugging, and I'm trying to get the guy to sleep with me one of these days, not run for the hills. If any man can survive the wrath of me and my closet feuds, he's a sure keeper. And right now, with Lane's hands traveling up my now clammy legs as he guides the stretch pants over the parts of my body I hate most—I cannot believe he's still smiling like that. Like he likes what he sees. Like I'm still the most beautiful girl in the world. Like he wants me.

"What?" I ask, when his eyes find mine and the silence becomes too painful to bear.

"I know I'm supposed to be putting these on, but I think I'd rather take them off." Tonight, Lane wears confidence almost as well as he wears that tightly fitted button down. But we've been down this road before and we have dinner plans.

I place my hands over his, where they've so fittingly stopped right before my crotch, and I shake my head. "I know you don't want this yet, so let's just get me suited up and go meet my brother."

"Do you always mention your brother when another guy's

between your legs?"

"Ew, and no." I shove Lane's hands away to get back to the original plan, but before I can slide the pants up any further, Lane is pushing me onto the bed.

He hovers over me with dark eyes, and then buries his face into the spot of my neck where I just spritzed an extra dab of perfume. "What are you doing? I thought you wanted to wait until you were more comfortable."

"I never said I was uncomfortable with *your* body. Now, don't take this the wrong way, but, *shhh*." He hums against my skin as his hands meander, working my pants—and panties—totally down my legs and to the floor.

I could be my regular big-mouthed self and argue that he was the one who started this no sex policy in the first place, but I'll be damned if his *shhh* hasn't totally shushed me. And his fingers . . . those magical fingers have found their way to the sensitive skin around my navel and they're teasing, exploring, lower, lower—"Oh, yes!" He finds the Mecca of womankind and I moan rather prematurely. I've been imagining this exact moment for as long as I can remember. Way before Lane became my boyfriend, prior to the tree, maybe even the first day I laid eyes on him on the runner's track.

Needing to kiss him, I dig my fingers into Lane's hair and force his face to mine. I kiss him like my life depends on it and it totally does because now that he's started this, I might just die if he doesn't continue. His tongue slides with mine and then darts in and out of my mouth with deliberate, torturous strokes that match the pace of his fingers down below.

"Lane," I cry, when he enters another long digit into my warmth and sends me into a frenzy of stimulation. I buck against his hand and with each harmonizing thrust, Lane's smile grows wide against my lips.

"You like this?" he asks, as if he has to. He'd have to be deaf, dumb, and blind not to know what he's doing to me.

"Yes!" I whimper, appreciating that men like that sort of affirmation in that kind of tone—it keeps them going, and he *must* keep going. But he doesn't. He stops. He jolts up and retreats, his fingers and lips leaving me hollow and aching for his touch again. This time, if he leaves me high and dry, I might deck him right in the balls. *He ain't using them anyway.*

Faster than I can think about why he's torturing me, he slithers down my body. His hands grasp my thighs to unclench them and his tongue finds a different set of lips to enjoy. "Holy hell!" I shout when he delves between my legs and makes up for every bad thought that just crossed my mind. *No high and dry for you tonight, Leni-poo!* I almost fist pump the air, but the heavenly sensations brought on by Lane's wonderfully skilled tongue have turned all thought processes to mush. I'm stupid right now. Absolutely senseless. *What a fantastic feeling.*

Lane's tongue stiffens as it beautifully violates me and then, and if it's not enough that he's heightening every one of my senses with the literal flick of a tongue, his thumb finds my clit and circles it until the throbbing vibrates from that one tiny spot to my entire body.

"Yes! Lane! Yes!" I unravel beneath him, thrashing my arms against the bed with each potent wave of paradise. "We need to cancel dinner. Now." I shouldn't be greedy, but I most definitely need more of wherever the hell *that* came from.

Lane slowly inches up my motionless yet still trembling body, and then rests beside me on the bed. With one hand over my galloping heart, and the other sweeping tousled hair from my face, my boyfriend whispers the most reassuring words I've ever heard. "Baby, we'll go to dinner and I'll make sure to save room for dessert." He licks his lips so sensually, so methodically, that I wonder where shy, reserved Lane has gone. Doesn't matter, though, because I've come to appreciate all sides of Lane and I'm hoping to explore every delicious part of him as my zero-calorie dessert later on.

# chapter

## twenty-six

"WHY DOES IT SEEM LIKE you're in such a rush? Got somewhere else you'd rather be?" Reynold playfully but forcefully elbows me in the arm, knocking me closer to Lane. When my body grazes his again a warm rush of memory engulfs me.

I ignore my annoying brother and face Lane, who's all smiles now that I've almost landed in his lap again. I right myself in my chair and then crane my neck to lean in for a chaste but direct kiss. "I know exactly where I want to be." I whisper so only Lane can hear.

"None of that." Ashley waves her hand in front of me. "You're making me really jealous."

"It was your dumb idea." Reynold looks down at his plate of half-eaten steak, sulking.

Jealous? They're getting married, for Pete's sake. Why would she be jealous of me and Lane? "What am I missing?" I ask, darting my concentration between the two lovebirds.

Lane rests his hand over mine on the table and squeezes.

"PDA not your thing?"

"*Pfft!*" I laugh, almost showering the rest of the table with my mouthful of wine. "I think Reynold and Ashley *invented* PDA. Thank God my parents love her, because they've seen more of her itty bitty body than any in-laws should ever have to!"

Lane laughs, triggering his dimples to attention. He takes another long pull from his beer and then rests his elbows on the table, propping his face on his fists. "Huh, interesting. I'd love to hear this."

I have many first hand accounts and no issue sharing with the table. "Well, first there was the time that my father saw Ashley's—"

"Yeah, yeah, yeah." Ashley interrupts. "If we're sharing war stories, Lane, I have quite a few doozies in my arsenal that will make your girlfriend's runway issue look like a regular walk in the park."

I perk to attention. "You wouldn't dare." Embarrassing moments from my past flash before me like some comical blooper real of a sitcom.

Ashley tilts her head and grins. "Don't give me a reason." She then turns to Lane and winks. "If you ever want an inside scoop, you know who to call."

Lane nods his head and accepts Ashley's sneaky offer. "Definitely. Now, what is it that has your groom-to-be looking so—unattended to?" Maybe it's some guy code thing or just Reynold's blank stare, but come to think of it, Reynold does seem kind of distant. I've never really brought a guy around him so maybe this is weird for him. I might have been laying it on too thick with the kissing and flirting and—*shit*—I really hope he didn't overhear me bragging to Ashley about what happened back at the apartment before we met up.

Reynold finishes chewing a mouthful of blood-dripping-rare Porterhouse and nods his head up and down while glowering at Ashley.

*Trouble in paradise this close to the wedding?*

Before I can bust a nut over an imaginary lover's quarrel between my second favorite couple in the universe, Ashley sips her dirty martini and deadpans. "Rey and I stopped having sex a month ago so the wedding night can be really special."

Reynold drops his fork and knife with a loud clanking of silverware against porcelain. He leans back against his chair and huffs. "I don't know where she got this ridiculous idea—some stupid wedding blog or something—but, dude," he turns to Lane for support, "I'm freaking dying. No man should have to go this long without touching his girl. It's unhealthy. It's—it's—it's not like she can unpop her cherry and magically become a virgin again overnight. I don't get it. Do you?"

Lane laughs and shakes his head. He better be speechless because he's put me through the same sexless hell since we became a couple.

Even still, I'm not about to hash that out with him over dinner with my brother. I bite my lip and shut my trap. Ashley's had some eccentric ideas in the past, but this one takes the cake. I never thought I'd be able to relate to my brother on a level like this, but I totally get it. I mean, thank God I got a little something something tonight, but I'm dying to have sex with Lane and the only thing stopping us is him.

Ashley breaks the silence, throwing her hands on her hips. "Well, it doesn't matter how stupid you think it is. We've gone this long, and we can last another two weeks. It's not the end of the world."

"Says you!" Reynold laughs. "I'm a man in my twenties. This is my prime. I need sex from my woman. Every night. It's a stress reliever and this wedding crap has me completely stressed."

"Oh my God, Reynold. Are you serious? *You're* stressed? You've barely lifted a finger to do one thing. Your sister picked out our wedding cake today!"

"I knew you were going to throw that in my face! I just knew it! Someone has to pay for that cake, you know, and I'm busting my ass with extra shifts to give you the wedding you want."

"Whoa, hold up! Are you saying I don't work? Because last I checked I brought in a decent paycheck, too. I don't know why you're bringing this up now, when we still have to . . ."

The two of them go on and on, ignoring Lane and me as we look at each other and shrug. Luckily, the restaurant isn't too crowded and Ashley and Reynold aren't overly loud. But they are noisy and heated enough to forget that they have us as an audience.

"Is this serious?" Lane asks, spreading his lips into a tight, straight line.

"Absolutely not. That PDA you asked about—they'll be pawing at each other again in ten minutes."

"You did *not* just go there, Reynold Moore! I already told you the groomsmen will not be wearing ruffled tuxedos. This isn't a joke. This is supposed to be the happiest day of my life!" Ashley's neck is redder than the Bolognese sauce on her chicken as she throws her napkin across the table and it lands in my brother's face.

"Nice shot," Lane mumbles, but the two wedding crazed nuts are so enthralled in their argument they don't even hear him. He leans closer to me and whispers in my ear, "Is it safe to leave, or will they kill each other?"

"Nah. And honestly, I don't want to be a witness to it, so—"

"Wanna blow this popsicle stand?"

"Totally."

We throw down enough money to cover our portion of the bill and slink out of the restaurant without so much as a "see ya later" from Ashley and Reynold. What may seem like a shitty sisterly thing to do is actually in everyone's best interest. If I had intervened, someone would have reamed me, and if we stuck around, Lane would have gotten a little too much family drama for my taste.

Once outside, Lane pulls me close as we make our way down the street. "So, is it safe to say you're the *normal* Moore?"

"Ha! Define normal."

Laughter rolls through him but his gentle touch never wavers. His hand travels from where it's wrapped around my shoulder to down around my waist. "Believe it or not, I've seen worse. My brothers are kind of rowdy and Leo's wife makes Ashley look like a pushover."

"You never really talk about them. You must miss everyone back in Tuscarora."

"Meh." He shrugs against my frame as we stride along the street without a care in the world. Out of nowhere, he leans in and pecks my cheek. "I like it here a lot better."

A giddy warmth tingles within and even though our dinner was cut short and I was sure we'd be rushing home for that dessert he promised earlier, I'm eager to hear more and enjoy this beautiful fall evening. "Come on." I prod. "Tell me more about where you came from."

"There's not much to tell. It's nothing like New York, at all."

"Funny, because when I picture Illinois I think of Chicago which seems to be exactly like New York."

"Not where I'm from, babe. It's a *whole* different ball game. You'd be quite a sight on my grandparents' farm."

"Hey! You think I'm too city to handle a little barnyard livin'?"

He throws his hands up in defense and flashes the dimples. Even if I wanted to be mad at him for discounting my country bumpkin skills, those things make all sensibility melt into a puddle of mush. "Let's just say, I think of you as *refined*—your beautiful hands do not belong anywhere near cow manure or pig slop."

"Wow. So you're talking the real deal. Very interesting." Call me small minded, but I never got around to doing my Tuscarora research to learn how the other half live. Besides, I'm too taken aback by his compliment. "And refined? I'm not quite sure that's an adjective that's ever been used in the same sentence with my name."

"I can think of a lot of adjectives you've probably never used to describe yourself."

Placing a hand over my pitter pattering heart, I smile thinking of all the lovely ways Lane reminds me that I'm beautiful. "I'd love to let you throw some out there, but we're talking about you, remember?"

"How could I forget?" He half groans, half huffs. Either way, I can tell he doesn't like being the topic of conversation.

"Lane, you're so closed off. Either you were an axe murderer back in Illinois or you're even more timid than you let on. I like hearing about you. You know everything there is to know about me and I still feel as if you're an enigma."

"An enigma is interesting. I'm definitely not an axe murderer, and although I have a tendency to be shy, I don't feel that way around you. It basically leads me back to my first point. There's not much to tell."

*Bullshit.* Someone like Lane who left his humble beginnings and his entire family to move to a big city, start a career, and is sinfully good looking and sweet to boot . . ."You're full of it. Everything about you interests me, from the top of your just-fucked hair to the tips of your runner's toes." At this point in our mindless walk, we're stopped at a corner, so I nudge him as we wait for the crosswalk signal to count down. He bumps me back, prompting me to lean in and steal an innocent kiss. I may not have gotten much out of him, but I'm still happy to have him by my side. "I guess this is the purpose of a relationship. Getting to know each other? Peeling away layers?"

"I guess so. Although I don't have much to go on."

Now, *there's* something. "Are you telling me you've never been in a serious relationship?"

"Would that surprise you?"

"Um, yeah!" I pause between easy strides, facing Lane with disbelief written all over my face. *"I've* never been in a serious relationship that didn't include a dare or a dick, but that's just me. But *you?* Lane, that can't be. There's no ex from Tuscarora who's daydreaming by some willow tree, pining over you? No hot nursing student who ever asked you to help her study her anatomy notes? And what about Jenny from the block? The first time you mentioned her you seemed a little—I don't know, scorned? I assumed you two had something going on at one point and you just didn't want to mention it."

Lane snorts through his nose and then spins me back toward the street ahead. He hooks his arm with mine and we continue walking while we talk. Maybe being stationary made him feel as if all eyes were on him. "I can't believe you caught that with Jenny. I guess I don't wear a poker face as well as I thought I did."

"So there *was* something?"

Lane hesitates.

"Babe, you can tell me. I don't judge. You let me tell you all about Alex. It's the past. We all have one."

Letting out another long sigh, Lane starts, "We went on a few dates after we met on the track."

"Do you meet all your lady friends on the track?" I joke, arching a brow.

"I'm there a lot, what can I say? But it's really not like that. You're completely different. You know that, right?" His expression turns serious and there's really no need. He doesn't have to convince me that he's not some Central Park stalker who preys on women in yoga pants.

"I know, I know. Continue."

He shrugs, placating me. "You're holding out for a let-down. There's no story to tell. In the end, we didn't have much in common besides the track. She wasn't the girl I thought she was when I first met her. It's why I trust that beauty is only skin deep. Sometimes the outside just doesn't match the inside."

"And vice versa," I add, knowing precisely what he's getting at.

"Exactly. And as far as any other relationships you might want to know about, there was never anyone special. No one who I clicked with. Not like you." He kisses the top of my head and that gooey feeling returns.

So, maybe Lane isn't a riddle to solve. Perhaps he doesn't have notches on his bedpost to brag about. Maybe he is the gentleman he's demonstrated to be, on all accounts. And it may very well be that as gorgeous and sexy as he is, he's as inexperienced as I am when it comes to this relationship thing.

I mull over those theories as we cross the street and step onto another that's lined with lively bars and pubs, and what looks like lots of fun waiting to be had.

Lane stops in front of one, and turns to me. "Now that I've endured a round of twenty questions with Madeline Moore, what do you say we grab a drink?" He points to a bar with strings of vintage Edison bulbs hanging from their awning to the streetlamp at the curb. A familiar song seeps out into the night through wood-paned windows. The sound is as tempting as Lane's invitation.

"Oh my God, I love this song!" I look up to the stars and smile, swaying back and forth with Lane's hands in mine.

"I've never heard it."

At that, I pull him by the hand and into the music just as it reaches the chorus—my favorite part. "If you like me, you're going to have to get to know the Lumineers. Come on, Fancy Pants. Buy me a drink and Karaoke Girl will sing you a song."

# chapter

## twenty-seven

A WEEK AFTER I SERENADED my man and kind of made a fool out of myself with one too many beers, I'm freaking out over how little time is left to get everything done for Ashley and Reynold's wedding.

"Len, did Ashley give you the final headcount for who's getting what done the morning of the wedding?" Raven shouts from her office into the salon where my fingers are ready to fall off from weaving the intricate braids this kid requested for her Sweet Sixteen.

"No, not yet. I'll get on that today," I yell back, careful not to unclench my fingers or skip a row of plaiting in her silky, golden hair.

My brain loops in circles as I contemplate all the things I need to 'get on' before the week is up. And nowhere on my list of to-do items is my boyfriend. He's pulled twelve hour shifts four times in the last seven days, and I haven't had a minute to breathe myself. But I'll be damned if the looming list of untied loose ends will interfere with us hanging out tonight. He's invited me to his apartment for a home cooked meal and a relaxing night in. Since I haven't been to his place yet and I need a night of nothing *but* Lane, I'm chomping at the bit. Unfortunately, relaxing isn't in the cards for this maid-of-honor. Favor wrapping, hair accessory making, and church program printing are just the tip of my wedding task iceberg. Lane just might become acquainted with my glue gun tonight. *Real romantic.*

"Ouch!" The girl in my chair hisses when I pull a little too hard on her hair.

"Oops. Sorry, hun." I'm so distracted I don't know how I even got as far as I did without scalping the poor girl.

I go back to my obsessing without so much as another uncomfortable tug and the rest of the day flies by, leaving me wishing for another hour to get more done before I head out. Tomorrow's another day with a full schedule, so I lock up my station, tidy up as best as I can, and make my way to Raven's office to say goodnight.

"Knock knock," I say, since there's not actually a door but a curtain separating her space from the salon.

"Come in."

I plop down on the chair adjacent to her mess of a desk and rest my head against the wall with a long sigh.

"What's the matter?"

"Too much to do, so little time."

"Wedding crap?"

"Uh-huh."

"Last I checked, you weren't the one getting married, babe."

I perk to attention and scowl. "I don't need reminding, thank you very much."

She clicks her tongue, shaking her head. "Seriously, though. Why is it all on you?"

"Because it was a rush and my brother is a dumbass. I can't fault Ashley for that."

"Tru dat." She barely looks up from her scheduling notebook, her glasses slipping down her nose. She's busy, too. She doesn't need me complaining about trivial nonsense, so I just get on with it so I can get on with me.

"While you have the book open, Ashley got back to me. Five for hair and makeup, three just for hair. I'm going to get here early that day to do my Mom and Ashley, but you think you can get Marjorie to come in to do me up?" Other than myself, Marjorie's the only girl I trust with my face. I can probably just do it myself, but with all the running around I've been doing, it'll be nice to be pampered for a change.

"You got it." She scribbles it down in the margin and pauses with her pencil in the air. "Lyla for hair?"

"Yes! Perfect. Seacrest out." I stand, feeling the tiredness in my bones, and pull my bag onto my shoulder.

"You okay?" Raven doesn't have to look up to show her concern.

"Yes, just stressed, but I feel stupid for saying that knowing how much you manage to do with all you have on your plate, so don't mind me." Seriously, she's like Superwoman. I'm considering a crash course in all things Raven the Great.

"You'll get it done, Len. You always do. Now, go treat yourself to some TLC with Lane. You're cranky because you haven't seen him all week. He'll be the cure for your woes."

I pat her on the back as I walk out. "Thanks for listening to me bitch and complain all week."

"And this time, drug the boy if you have to. You need to get laid."

I give her a thumbs up, laughing as I walk to my car. I haven't even had time to obsess over *not* getting laid. That's how you know I've been preoccupied. But Raven's like my own personal Confucius—always insightful, minus the roofie suggestion. Hopefully all I need to refuel is waiting for me on the other side of town.

LANE'S APARTMENT IS A TWENTY-MINUTE train ride from the salon. Rather than go home in the opposite direction and waste more time away from Lane, I packed a change of fresh clothes and something for tomorrow, in case I wind up staying over. The idea of finally getting a glimpse of Lane's personal life without having to pry has me eager to get off this overheated subway and into his arms. Of course, I'm just excited for the change of pace since we're always at my place or out.

When I mentioned it to Tatum, she thought it odd that I'd yet to be invited to his apartment, but that's Tatum. Especially now that she and Paul are kaput. Two years on and off and everything you could imagine in between were draining for *me*— and I wasn't even in the relationship. Paul wasn't necessarily a bad guy, just not the guy for Tatum. She deserves to be happy, not to settle. And that's exactly what she was doing with Paul.

Tatum swears she's okay, ready to move on, time to sow more wild oats, but I still owe her the best friend shoulder to cry on if that's what she wants to do. Before leaving the salon, I texted her a quick message asking if she needs me tonight. To my surprise, she made plans with some co-workers for dinner and drinks. Body's not even cold yet, and I have no doubt her bed won't be for too long, either. *Good for her.*

By the time I'm off the train and walking toward Lane's apartment, all thoughts of Tatum and her love life are far gone. It's been a whole seven days since I've last seen him and to say I feel deprived is putting it mildly. I miss him. A lot. And even though we speak every day, it's not the same as seeing those adorable dimples in person or having his lips against mine.

For the first time in forever, I know how it feels to have everything I want. Don't get me wrong, there are a million and one superficial things I could think of that I wouldn't dare deny if they were handed to me on a silver platter. But—none of that matters. Even the ten pounds I put back on since coming home from Miami. *Pounds, shmounds. Who cares?* I'm still keeping up with Jane and Mandy's workout routine and I haven't gone to hell in a hand basket with my old eating habits, but—I don't know—it's not my sole focus anymore. They say when you're happy in a relationship you gain weight. If that's the case, I should be morbidly obese, but I'll settle for what I am right now because it's still better than where I was a few months ago.

Rounding a corner, I pull out my phone to text Lane that I'm outside. When I look up, he's already there, waiting for me with an ear to ear grin. I contemplate pulling a dramatic stunt like tossing my bags to the ground and running into his arms, but he's at my side faster than I expect.

"Hey, babe. I'm so happy to see you." He kisses me smack on the lips. No wasting time, no pause to let me reply, just lips on lips and oh, does it feel so good. I let the heavy overnight bag fall from my grip and wrap my arms around his neck.

"They say absence makes the heart grow fonder," I mumble against his lips and melt into his touch. He has one hand burrowed in my hair, the other pulling me against him from my waist.

"Fond. Me. Very." Our foreheads rest against the other's, our inhales and exhales releasing in time.

I breathe is his musky man scent and then kiss him again, this time nipping his bottom lip between my teeth. "You. Mine. Now."

Lane laughs, smooching my neck and then leaning down to grab the duffel I dropped during our sweet reunion. "Come on up. It's cold out here."

"Is it?" I joke because it's actually quite chilly, but the truth is I'm an inferno inside. It could be ten below out here and I'd still be on fire from the way Lane makes me feel.

With his free hand, Lane tangles his fingers with mine and guides me down the street to a green side door next to a storefront. It's a small, rundown looking bookstore that I find absolutely charming compared to the oversized commerciality of places like Barnes &Noble.

"Have you ever been in there?" I ask, wishing it weren't closed so I could peruse the shelves just for fun.

"Only to pay my rent."

I pout, looking over my shoulder as Lane leads me up a dark stairway. "Shame. It looks adorable."

"Really? Looks kind of old to me."

I wag my finger back and forth. "Remember, looks can be deceiving, Mr. Sheffield. It's what's inside that matters, and I'm sure that old, dilapidated bookstore is full of more quality literature than Amazon can shake a stick at."

"Yeah?" Lane turns the knob on a wood-paneled door, wedging it open and smirking at me. "You think Amazon wants to shake a stick at the secret back room full of porn, too?"

"Oh." I utter. Even I don't have a witty reply for that one.

Lane's laugh rolls through his entire body, his shoulders rising and falling. He places a soft kiss on the tip of my nose and walks into the one-room space. "We can still go tomorrow if you want. They open at nine. Maybe you'll find something you like, after all."

"Nah, I'll pass. But—" I step into the tiny apartment and even though I'm dying to look around the entire studio, my senses are assaulted by the most delicious smell. "Oh my God! Lane did you make Thai food? Tell me you can't actually *cook* Thai food because Thai food is my favorite. And it's so delicious and savory and so . . . Thai."

"That's an awful lot of Thais in one sentence."

I tilt my head and smile. "Seriously, though? Did you really cook my favorite meal or—this is takeout, right? You can't be this perfect, Lane. Something's gotta give." I rush over to the two-person table, set with mismatched dishes and flickering votive candles. It's flush against one wall of the little kitchen and covered with plated food that smells and looks divine.

Lane comes up behind me and slips his hands into the front pockets of my jeans. I lean into him, and welcome his sweet, tickly whispers in my ear. "Well, I'm far from perfect, but I did in fact cook your favorite meal."

I spin around and throw my arms around his neck again. "The way to my heart is totally through my stomach, but you knew that already and if *I* didn't know any better, I'd think you're on some weird mission to fatten me up."

"No such mission exists, Leni. I just like making you happy—however I can."

"I would've been happy with celery sticks just to be here with you." I nuzzle into the warm space where his neck curves into his shoulder, slyly eyeing the rest of the apartment. I'm trying to get a glimpse of where Lane has made his home, and although I'm eager to get the two-cent tour, my mouth is watering from the dinner he's prepared.

"Can we dig in before I eat your arm?" My stomach growls and the sound somehow reaches Lane's ears.

"I'm glad you brought your appetite." He laughs, pulling back from our embrace to stare into my eyes. His are a deep, intensified emerald—aroused. I'm not sure if it's all this kissing, the food talk, or just an effect I have over him whenever we're together. Either way, I gaze back and feel myself falling.

I've never been here before. *In love.* For a brief time back in college I thought I was with Alex, but that was more of a crazy crush than the real thing. This? Lane. The whole entire thing—I'm pretty sure it's the real thing. It has to be. I haven't even had sex with the dude and already I'm hoping to have his babies one day.

# chapter

# twenty-eight

"WHERE'D YOU LEARN TO COOK like that, Lane? And if you tell me you googled it, I'm gonna kill you." I literally lick my lips of any remaining peanut curry sauce and take a breath to expand my lungs and very full belly.

"Then I'm safe from your threats. I took a course when I moved to New York. Part of my whole embracing my new surroundings thing."

"You're a man of many talents, aren't you?"

"I guess you could say that, but I never really honed in on one. I . . . dabble . . . in a little bit of everything."

The way he says dabble makes me giggle. I lean over the table, which doesn't take much effort since it's almost as small as a shoe box, and trace the pad of my finger along the thick veins in his hand. "What else are you hiding from me?"

Lane withdraws from my touch and stands from the table, taking our plates to the sink. I swear I sense a trace of nervousness on his part, but it's not enough to mention and spoil an already amazing night. I've come to the realization that Lane doesn't like to talk about himself, and when I put the spotlight on him he flees from the situation. I'm not sure if he's just modest or if there's something more pressing underneath there. Either way, I'm not about to make him uncomfortable after he just fed me the best meal I've had in God knows how long.

"Let me help you with that," I say, pushing my chair from the table and bringing a platter over to the sink.

"You don't have to. I don't mind." Lane smiles over his shoulder, his hands already sudsy.

I kiss his cheek and swipe a handful of foamy bubbles while he's not looking, only to plop them on to the tip of his nose.

I laugh and back away, but Lane's slippery hands drop the fork he was cleaning and he hurls straight for me. "Oh, you're gonna get it!" He shakes the bubbles from his face, a single, thick drop of water sliding down his nose as he comes after me.

"Not if you can't catch me," I tease. I *so* want him to catch me, wet hands and all, but part of the fun is the thrill of the chase and playing hard to get. I'll entertain that game and lead him right to the sofa, which I'm pretty sure serves as his bed since I don't see one anywhere in sight.

"You little . . ." Lane dodges between a chair and an end table, but I dart past him and wind up tripping over a stack of books on the floor, face first over the arm of the couch.

"Ouch," I grumble, wincing at the pain of stubbing my toe.

"Shit! You okay?" Lane comes up behind me, wet hands at my shoulders, pulling me up from my face plant.

Eye to eye, I examine the moment. It's a mix of hilarity and passion—two things that make my heart pump wilder than anything else. Except chocolate, of course. The water's still running from the faucet, Lane's face is wet from my bubble assault, and his soaked hands have dampened my shirt to the point of wanting to strip it off. A rush of varying foolish emotions catch me off guard and I find myself ready to confess the deepest parts of my soul.

"Lane, I think—"

He doesn't let me finish, though. His lips crash to mine and with no time to gauge what's about to happen, it's as if he read my mind and understands this shirt needs to get the hell out of our way.

Lips, hands, breaths, moans. It happens so quickly, I don't know how to make sense of it all. The water is still flowing from the kitchen faucet, a strange but soothing background music to our heated embrace. If that's what you want to call it. This is no sweet, love making prelude. This is raw and carnal and *finally* happening.

Lane's in control, his tongue still navigating my mouth as if he's steering my body to do what it's told. I have no complaints, no inhibitions, not even as he slides my jeans down my thick thighs and undresses me down to a bra and panty set I secretly hoped would get his approval tonight.

Without breaking our kiss, Lane's damp hands explore my entire body. "So beautiful," he groans as his fingers grab and caress every inch of my exposed skin.

Okay, so I do have one teensy complaint. Lane's clothes. They're still on and that's an issue. We need to get rid of those pesky things so we can finish what we started before he changes his mind again. I reach between us, where our bodies are grinding, creating a punishing but wonderful friction. In one motion, I unzip his pants and then hook my fingers into the waist of his jeans and boxers, working them over his round but rock-hard ass. Lane aids me in ridding him of the obstructions, swiftly standing and pulling everything down the rest of the way. I try to steal a peek of his goods, but before I can ogle, he returns to his rightful place between my legs.

"Your shirt," I point out, wanting the skin-on-skin contact in the worst way.

My efforts to strip him down go ignored as time stands still and whooshes past us in equal measure. Bra, panties, socks, box-ers—all gone. At one point I hear a foil wrapper and feel Lane sheathing himself against my thigh, all while his lips trail ardent kisses along exposed bits of my skin.

There's no time to question or second guess or to even speak for that matter. And you know what? I don't care! I've been trying to make this happen for a while now and I'm not about to set us back for a stupid shirt, even if I do wish I could feel Lane's muscular arms and washboard abs writhing against me while we make love.

Nibbling on Lane's lower lip, I reach below and stroke him. I bring his tip against me and urge him to come inside for the party. With one hard thrust, Lane enters me, tingles engulf my body, and my head falls back with a moan. "Yes!" I dig my fin-gers into his backside, pulling him toward me, meeting each plunge, rocking my hips with his. It's intense and hot and every-thing I've been praying for.

Minutes, hours, or maybe days elapse around us as we lose ourselves in each other. In a mess of tangled hair and sweat-soaked skin, my body turns stiff and then limp as an orgasm of magical magnitude rolls through me. I'm pretty sure a unicorn just died for that, because all I can see is an explosion of rain-bows and sparkly fairy dust as Lane pushes inside me once more and releases a string of curse words I've never heard him utter before.

I laugh when he collapses on top of me, wrapping my arms around him and relishing in our after-sex panting. Catching my breath and burrowing my fingers into Lane's tousled hair, I al-most whisper the words that are dying to escape me. Again. But again, my confession is interrupted. This time it's the crash of a dish and a splatter of water against the tile floor of the kitchen.

"Shit!" Lane jumps up and discreetly removes the condom with his back turned toward me. In a mad dash, he manages to find his boxers and slip them back on, and then he springs to the chaos in the kitchen.

I find my own undergarments, both tossed onto the floor in a heap of crumpled lace, and run to join him.

"Oh no!" I cry, assessing the situation. A sea of sudsy water is overflowing from the sink; an unwashed dish rolls with the current of the water and cascades toward the floor.

Lane dives to catch the plate before it meets its fate with the tile, and then quickly shuts off the faucet.

The kitchen is a mess. Lane is drenched from head to toe. I'm standing in a puddle of water in nothing but a skimpy bra and thong. There's really nothing funny about the situation, but I couldn't contain my laughter if you paid me.

Lane spins around in slow motion and gawks. "You think this is funny?"

I take a second out of my laughing fit to study Lane and for a split instant, I think he's actually mad. Until he grabs me by the waist with sopping wet hands and pulls me down to the floor to join him in the lake that has now formed beneath us.

"Stop! No!" I try to break free of his grip, but it's too late. I'm covered in water and flailing around is just making me wetter. "You jerk! You didn't have to do that."

"This is all your fault in the first place." Lane pins me down underneath him, straddling me, as he scoops big handfuls of water from the floor and splashes me.

"My fault?" I ask with tight-lidded eyes, trying to shield my face from the onslaught of dishwater.

"If you hadn't made me chase you, we wouldn't have wound up so . . . preoccupied."

"Are you complaining about the last twenty minutes? Because I'm pretty sure that was the best twenty minutes of my life. Earth shattering, mind blowing, amazing." I buck my hips to grind against Lane's already stiff bulge. "In fact, I'm ready for more. Right here. Soap suds and all."

All levity vanishes from his face as his eyes turn dark again.

"Right here?"

"Right here," I deadpan.

It doesn't take much convincing before Lane's pawing at me again. We're slick from the water, our bodies slithering against each other with lubricated ease. Except of course, for the damn shirt again. It clings to his chest and the heaviness of the soaked cotton slaps against my bare stomach each time Lane rubs against me.

This time, I take control. My fingers creep down his arms and back, gripping the hem of his ruined shirt. Lane is preoccupied with my tit in his mouth so I seize the opportunity and yank the shirt over his chest, stopping when I can't get it over his neck.

"Off. Now," I demand.

Lane pauses as he hovers over me, and then takes a deep breath. He rises from his hunched position and slowly peels the shirt off. I watch him in awe, dying to uncover what I know has to be a model-like physique.

What I notice first is his face—apprehensive, vulnerable, exposed. What I see next, makes me curious.

"What's that?" I ask, bluntly. His abdomen is scattered with five deep scars. One rests under his sternum, the others just at the side of his stomach, and another long, jagged line mars his belly button down to his groin.

"War wounds."

*War wounds?* What war? Did I miss something? My dumb-founded expression must say it all.

Lane dismounts me and sits up. I adjust my bra so the girls aren't sloppily spilling out all over the place and then sit up as well, pulling my knees to my chest.

"I told you I'm not who you think I am. I didn't want you to find out this way and I meant to tell you sooner, but I started to think it didn't matter. *None* of this matters when I'm with you. Not the past, not the insecurities, not a single thing. I should've

just told you while we were running one day, or during one of
our get-to-know each other chats about how we grew up. But I
was scared you'd see me differently once you knew."

I have no idea what he's talking about or how his scars have
anything to do with why I'd see him differently. Maybe my brain
is on overload from the unicorn killing sex or from the chill
seeping into my bones from being cold, wet, and almost naked
on Lane's kitchen floor. Either way, I'm clueless. "Dude, what
are you talking about? I'm lost."

Lane stands and sloshes past me to the bathroom. He's back
before he's actually gone, being that the apartment is so small.
When he returns he's holding two towels and a picture frame
in his hands. He offers me a plush towel, I gladly accept, and we
both drape the downy, white cotton around our shoulders.

He sits back down and hands me the black rimmed frame.
The three young men in the photograph are strangers to me.
They're young teenagers on a camping trip. A red tent and a
bonfire give that away, and the gooey marshmallows pierced
with wooden sticks in each of their hands solidify it. The boy in
the middle—all chunky and mowhawked—looks oddly familiar
even though I've never seen him before.

I examine the picture, wondering what this has to do with
Lane or why he's showing it to me now and then I detect an
unmistakable trait on the boy in the middle that sends my chin
to the floor.

*Dimples.* Those adorable dimples.

"Is this you?" I point to the chubby-cheeked, overweight
boy sporting a sweaty, flushed brow and then I take another
long glance at his scars. I've seen these before. I know what they
mean. He's had Lap Band and he didn't tell me?

"Yes, Leni. That's me. I hope this doesn't change anything."

Having plenty of experience coping with my own struggles, my own letdowns, my own insecurities, this *shouldn't*
change one damn thing. He's still the same Lane—kind, caring,

sexy, perfect—only he's not.

He lied to me.

He kept this a secret as if it were something to be ashamed of. If he's that embarrassed to keep this part of him from me, how am I supposed to feel about myself? The weight is a thing of the past for Lane, but it's very much a part of *my* existing makeup *today*.

Hurt strangles me, erasing the happiness that's taken place since I collided with that tree and let Lane into my life. Into my heart. The three letter f word that has haunted me my entire life has just tainted the best thing that's ever happened to me. Like every other obstacle in my life, I can choose to let it define me or work through it. But in this moment, smothered with deception and uncertainty, I wish I'd fade away.

# chapter

## twenty-nine

A RUSH OF OLD HURT and pent up humiliation surge through me. My first instinct is to run. My second is to cry. Guess what I do?

"Why are you crying, Leni? Look at me." Lane tries to pry my hands from my eyes, but I don't budge.

"You—you, lied!"

All I can think about is Alex. *He's not Alex.* I tell myself that over and over again. But lies *are* lies. No matter how big or small, when you find out someone you trusted, cared about, maybe even loved isn't who they said they are—it's a stinging slap in the face.

*"Alex, you're already in, bro. All bets are off. You can give up the act and dump the chubby chick to finally get your hands on one of the Deltas we've got lined up for you." Ty, Alex's fraternity brother, punches him in the arm and cackles.*

*Alex stumbles sideways and my hand is knocked loose from his grip. My heart feels like it's bottoming out in my chest and slamming* around my rib cage like a dropped bouncing ball.

I look at Alex, hoping his face will wear the same confusion as mine. I had to have heard wrong. I had to. Because the alternative would be—No! I won't go there. Not until I know the truth. But what I'm met with leaves me with little hope.

Alex's eyes go wide and my ears ring to the point of buzzing deafness at the degrading poison Ty's vomited out of his vile mouth.

"Shut up, asshole," Alex mumbles, shooing Ty away. If that's not a dead giveaway, I don't know what is. He's guilty. If not by the mortified glare in his eyes or the way he's warding Ty off like he has some disease, it's conclusive by the pallid complexion on his face.

"How could you?" I cry, my lip trembling, my eyes so full of tears I can barely make out the small crowd of people who've formed around us. Five of whom are burly jerks who belong to the same brotherhood Alex has been hoping to become a member of since we started seeing each at the beginning of the semester. The same assholes who have always looked at me as if I have a third eye or who snickered behind my back when Alex and I walked past them on campus.

I should've known that any guy who wanted to be part of a clan run by cruel, arrogant, jerkoffs would become one himself. Or maybe he's been just like them the entire time and I was too blinded by his charming good looks and hauntingly blue eyes to care. No, I can't even blame Alex for this. I was blinded by my own self-doubt. I thought losing a little weight would make the world a better place to live, but I was wrong. It just made it more bearable. And I allowed myself to believe that everything was perfect because for once I had the guy I wanted.

"It's not what you think, Leni." Alex pulls me off to the side, away from all the gawking eyes, where we're secluded from everyone else. Funny, now that I think of it, we always met up in some secretive way; alone in my dorm room, at a table in the furthest corner of a pub, the most desolate section of the school library.

"Don't you dare play me for more of a fool than you already have. It's exactly what I think. You're a liar and an asshole and I'm just some stupid, pathetic, fat girl, borrowing someone else's made-for-society

*image for my fifteen minutes of fame. Only this isn't the kind of rec-*
*ognition I was looking for, Alex. This is—this is cruelty! I've never felt*
*so low, so humiliated, so . . ." I bring my hands to my face and sob.*
*Alex doesn't comfort me. He doesn't reach out to coax me or tell me*
*I'm wrong for thinking those things about myself or for believing Ty's*
*words without giving him a chance to tell me they're untrue. Instead,*
*he backs away like a coward and gives me an insincere explanation*
*that leaves me wishing the ground would swallow me up and help me*
*disappear for good.*

*"I'm sorry, Leni. I did what they told me to do. I didn't mean to*
*hurt you."*

"Please stop crying, Leni. I didn't mean to hurt you." Lane
can't have any clue how that phrase burns a hole in the very
marrow of my being.

I want to look at him, tell him I just need time to process
this, to hear him out and make him understand my reaction is
about me, not about him or who he once was.

But I can't do it. Not again. Just like with Alex, I feel the
man I've gotten to know and *love* is a phony. He's been hiding
something from me all this time and that something just so happens to be the one thing I've been obsessing over for the last
twenty some odd years.

I'd like to think I've finally found a way to dull the fixation.
I've learned to ignore the Alexes and the frat boys, the rude
comments that fly from people's tongues, lashing me without
remorse, my own embarrassment staring at me from the reflection in a mirror. Once I accepted me for me, I was finally able to
wear my flaws for the world to see, even when I tried to cover
them or compensate in other ways. I am who I am; I'm a heavy
girl. There's no hiding my personal imperfections because
they're as plain as the nose on my face. But Lane masked his
weight issue, clearly embarrassed by the person he used to be. If
he's this afraid to be himself in front of a person who thinks the
world of him, I'm terrified to know how he truly sees me.

With Lane hovering and oblivious to the root of my emotions, I cry until my body shakes. I feel betrayed by his secret. I feel inferior. I'll never be good enough. *Oh my God!* Is he only dating me because I'm all he thinks he deserves?

"This explains everything!" Sadness suddenly mutates into anger, especially with that asshole Alex in the back of my mind. I muster the energy to stand and push past Lane, shoving the picture frame into his chest.

He drops it on the counter and runs after me into the living area, where I use the towel to wipe away any excess dampness so I can put my clothes back on and get the hell out of here.

"What the hell are you talking about?" Lane's frantic. Confused. He sidesteps me to block my path to the door. To my escape.

I'm not sure I can take any more humiliation—*thank God he never gave me the chance to tell him I love him*—but I swivel to face him after I pull my shirt back over my head. "This is why you're with someone like me, isn't it? I couldn't figure it out, but now it's painfully obvious."

He speechlessly tries to interrupt me, but I continue to spew my feelings so I can get rid of the pit in my stomach. I've never stood up for myself with a guy. I've never had the upper hand. But this time—I'm not going down without fighting for *myself.* "I never understood why a guy as perfect as you would want me. I mean, let's face it, someone who looks like *you* does not belong with someone who looks like me. Unless, of course, you still have the chunkster mentality. And you know what? I've heard of this before. Except it's usually the other way around. Sometimes when a guy morphs from loser to hot shot, he winds up becoming a cocky son of a bitch and forgets all about his humble beginnings. It happened with Reynold for a while—if you saw pictures of him growing up, you wouldn't even recognize him—but it was just a phase. He smartened up and realized his dick wasn't made of gold just because he grew out of the ugly duckling stage.

"But *you*? You're the worst kind of fraud! A wolf in sheep's clothing. You chose someone like me because you don't think you can do better. You want a perfect girl like Jenny or her sister Karen because, well, who doesn't? But you're so hung up on your own insecurities that you clung to me because I'm all you can relate to. A fat girl for a former fat guy. I'm such an idiot! I fell for a man who only likes me because he's too weak to like himself."

My words come out in hysterics. I'm not even sure they make sense once they're spoken. But I know how I feel. This is Alex all over again. I feel used. I feel that Lane chose me by default. Because he doesn't feel worthy of anything better. And although I can see he's hurt and confused and completely blindsided by my rant, I can't do this to myself. I need to choose *me*.

I'm tired of being the butt of the joke. I'm so damn worn-out from worrying about what other people think of me, especially since I've finally succeeded in loving the skin I'm in.

That all comes crashing down when I realize that so much of my journey toward self-love had to do with how happy Lane made me. I want to believe that without Lane, or *any* man, I can still be as confident with myself as I was an hour ago. But I'll never know unless I'm faced with it and as Joel would say, *be a victor, not a victim*.

I will no longer be a victim of my flaws.

"I have to go," I announce, bee-lining for the hook where I hung my coat and left my bags.

"Go? You can't just leave, Leni. I don't even understand half of what you said. Sit down. You're not letting me talk. There's so much I want to tell you!" Lane has unshed tears in his eyes. I know how he feels. *Rejected*. I've been in his boat over and over again and sank to the depths of despair each and every time. But this time . . . I have to swim to safety.

"I can't believe you're reacting this way. This makes no

sense. Why won't you let me explain?" It's a choked plea for me to hear him out. But I can't. Not today. I can't see past being lied to, duped, and possibly used. Not when I've been here before.

I zip my coat and tug my bag over my shoulder. I turn to Lane, tears streaming down my face without avail; crying for me, for him, for what could have been. I was so close to ultimate happiness. I thought I'd finally found it all. I guess Lane was right—looks can be deceiving. And so is the fucking heart.

Rather than allowing him to feel less than perfect because of an imperfect past he can't erase, I leave him with one final thought before I go. "I'm sorry, Lane. This isn't about the person you used to be. I could never fault you for that. I just can't talk about this right now. I can't dredge up all these old feelings that make me feel like shit."

"What old feelings?" Lane manages to smile through his anguish. "Silly girl, how can I help you if you won't let me talk?"

"Not now. Please, Lane, just let me go."

Lane's mouth drops open with unspoken words. I'm sure there's a mountain of information he wants to share, so much I'll be able to relate to once I can hear it with my heart and not be clouded by the pain of my own past.

I'VE NEVER BEEN ON THE giving end of a broken heart, but after five days of sending Lane's calls to voicemail and an entire box of donuts, I succumb to the daunting fact that being responsible for this kind of hurt sucks. Hairy donkey balls.

"Why don't you just hear him out?" Tatum lowers the speed on the elliptical so we can chat. I haven't been to the park for fear of running into him, and I'm pretty sure my best friend dragged me to the gym with her today because she's worried I might eat myself into oblivion. Either way, I'm winning. Right?

"I don't want to. I know that makes me sound like a terrible person, but I'm not ready."

"Ready for what? To be an adult?"

If I could knock her off the moving machine without bringing negative attention our way, I totally would. "Yeah, Tatum. That's it. I'm the one acting like a child because I decided to get out of yet another situation that made me feel like shit."

"Remind me how not listening to what he has to say *isn't* childish? Come on, Leni. That's bullshit! I've known you long enough to be able to tell you the truth. The biggest problem in all relationships is miscommunication. How can you just walk away from him without letting him tell his side of the story? You jumped to conclusions. You don't even know if your accusations are valid. He's not Alex. This is apples and oranges, babe."

She's right, my actions are based on assumptions. Call it pride, or instinct, or plain old stubbornness—but I can't face him right now. I *won't* face him right now. I'm focused on my brother's wedding and shedding a few extra pounds in the next week.

"I don't want to talk about it right now." I up the pace on my own machine to drown out Tatum's lecture and sweat away my worries.

By the time we've worked the circuit of fancy contraptions and free weights, I'm a little less down on myself and the pain of missing Lane, and everything looming around us is just a dull ache. I'm ready to brave the day as best as I can, until . . . I spot Hudson at the far end of the gym, purchasing a smoothie.

"Fuck a duck! Let's get out of here!" I tug Tatum by the arm to hurry her along, but my efforts aren't fast enough because Hudson spots me and makes eye contact.

"And that right there proves my point!" Tatum throws her hand to her hip and shakes her head.

I wave, painting on the fakest smile I can muster, and Hudson pays the cashier and starts our way. "What are you talking about?" I ask, through gritted teeth.

"Hudson fucking Blackman lights up every time he sees you, and you're concerned that Lane picked you as some pity prize? You're freaking mental, Leni. All these years of feeling sorry for yourself burned some valuable brain cells."

"Why, I've never!" I'm way more pissed at Tatum than I'm letting on but I have to be on my best behavior because the most eligible bachelor in all of Manhattan is approaching and I'll be damned if he thinks he has any kind of effect over me.

"Hey, Leni. I didn't know you go to this gym."

"She doesn't," Tatum speaks for me. "She used my visitor's pass today because she usually runs at the park with her boyfriend but she's currently—"

I elbow her in the ribs and she doesn't get a chance to finish her sentence. "It was cold this morning. I hate bundling up to work out. Decided to check out Tatum's place since my membership at the sports club is coming to an end." Lies. All lies. But he doesn't need to know that I'm avoiding any place where Lane might track me down.

"Ah. Well, it's nice to see you again. I hope you join so I get to see . . . *more* of you." Hudson smiles, his eyes following the bead of sweat that's trickling down my cleavage.

When I realize what he's doing, I quickly dab myself with the towel around my shoulders. "You too, Hudson. Have a nice day." I start to walk past him, Tatum following next to me, but he calls out my name.

"Yeah?" I huff, frustrated with the entire situation. Why? I don't know. Just add Hudson and his advances to the list of things that agitate me lately.

"Any relation to Reynold Moore?"

I tilt my head and scrunch my face. "Yes. He's my brother. Why?"

Hudson laughs through his nose, nodding his head. "I'll be at his wedding next weekend."

"Um . . . why?" It falls out of my mouth, unapologetically.

His brow arches when he sees he's hit a nerve. "Business. I like to attend at least one event before I legally acquire the property. The Moore wedding just so happens to be next on the calendar."

"Huh?" Tatum asks, clearly baffled.

"You're buying the winery?" I'm just as perplexed.

"Why do you seem so shocked? I own many different businesses, Leni, including restaurants and wineries all over the tri-state area."

I scratch my head, totally cliché, wondering how in the world the stars pulled off this alignment. "Well, if this isn't a coincidence, I don't know what the hell is."

"Some call it coincidence, I prefer to label it *kismet.*" The word slides off his tongue in a condescending nature.

*Oh, label my ass, would ya?* This has nothing to do with fate, or luck, *or* fucking kismet! The world truly has something against me at the moment and I'm about to show it I'm all outta fucks to give. "Then I guess I'll see you there." I whip around, my ponytail lashing in the wind, and storm toward the locker room without looking back.

"Save me a dance!" Hudson calls out. I don't have to see him to know he's smirking as if he's already won me over.

Truth is, I'm not his to win.

I'm not sure if anything in my life is a victory these days. I should be flattered by Hudson's unwavering interest. I should be proud of myself for jumping back on the workout wagon when all I want is to inhale another box of donuts. What I really should do is return Lane's phone calls and give my pride a swift kick in the ass.

"Well, this should be interesting," Tatum puts a stop to my pitiful pondering with a devilish dance around the locker room.

I click my tongue and shoo her away. "It'll be no such thing." Even I don't believe that. I'm just fooling myself into thinking that everything's hunky dory. Being in the same room with a flirtatious Hudson while missing Lane isn't a recipe for unexpected drama. Right?

# chapter

# thirty

ADMITTING I'M WRONG IS NOT my strong suit. Then again, neither is facing the music.

Growing up, I had an unhealthy fear of thunderstorms. At the onset of even the tiniest rumble from the heavens, I dodged for my bed and tucked myself underneath the biggest blanket I could find. Sometimes I rocked and cried until my mother had to pry me out of bed and hold me in her arms. As I got older the fear remained, but Mom explained that burying myself under the covers wouldn't make the storm go away any faster. When it was ready to pass, it would pass on its own. Eventually, I learned that hiding from my fear got me nowhere, and in time I was okay with joining the rest of civilization outside the comfort of my cocoon whenever lightening cracked through the sky.

Right now, my scary storm is this mess with Lane. I use the term *mess* lightly because, let's face it, this is so much more than a little snafu. I'm hurt. He's hurt. There's a whole shit load of hurt mulling around, I'm not even sure who's to blame anymore, and I kinda want my mommy to make it all better.

I fucked up. I know I did. I overreacted, I didn't allow him to explain himself, and now I feel even worse than I did when I thought Lane was using me as some fat boy fetish.

Problem *now* is that I'm too proud to go crawling back. Don't get me wrong, I'm still mad he lied, but the crux of our issue is my failure to hear him out. If I were Lane, I would count my blessings and move on to the next chubby chick. *She* would deserve him. *She* wouldn't doubt him for a few scars that he kept secret. *She* would understand that she isn't the only person in the world who got the shitty end of the stick when it comes to metabolic genes. *She* would have a date to her brother's wedding tomorrow night.

I have to text him. I want to text him. This has gone on long enough, and if I don't do something about it now, I might never get the chance to make up for what I've done.

Who knows? It might be too late. Lane's already gone a few days without trying to reach me so I suspect he's given up, and if he has—well, so be it. I made the bed and now I have to lie in it.

With a deep breath and a nagging suspicion that I haven't a shot in hell to redeem myself, I steady the phone in my trembling hands and type a message to Lane.

At first, my mind is blank, void of the proper way to gracefully beg for Lane's forgiveness. But once I've chewed the skin off my bottom lip and can taste the blood on my tongue, I decide to man up.

"Ah, fuck it. What've I got to lose?" I'm talking to myself again, but crazy is as crazy does and this entire situation is nothing short of cray cray.

> *Me: Hey. I'm sorry I haven't answered any of your calls or responded to your texts. I guess I'm just sorry for everything in general. Can we meet up Sunday, after the wedding is over*

*and done with? I'd like to talk. That is, of course, if you don't hate me.*

I press send and wait in agony for the three little dots to appear, indicating that Lane's responding. But I get nothing. There's no way to tell if he's even read the damn thing. I shake the phone, turn it off and then back on, and stare it at a some more, while subliminally channeling the wavelength gods.

Twenty minutes later and zilch, nada, no dice. I guess I got what I deserve in the end. The cold shoulder. Serves me right for getting all holier-than-thou on him. Unfortunately, there's nothing left to do but get some beauty sleep so I can put on my best face for the big day tomorrow.

It's not Ashley and Reynold's fault that I'm a train wreck. There's no reason to spoil their special day, even if I am so miserable that the thought of giving my maid-of-honor speech— it's totally kick ass, by the way—makes me want to gag.

Love is not patient, or kind. Love is fucking stupid.

ASHLEY IS A MESS. A beautiful mess, nonetheless, but her nerves have been through the roof all morning. The one advantageous of a jittery bride: distraction. Tending to Ash has kept my mind off what to do next, but Lane is still at the forefront of my thoughts.

Before I headed over to Ashley's parents' place this morning, I awoke to a vague text from Lane in response to my apologetic message from last night. It simply read, *I don't hate you.*

I took that as a good sign; a great one, actually. But what good is him not hating me if he's not willing to talk it out and give me a chance to grovel at his feet? Ashley shrieks from behind the bathroom door, where she's been holed up for a good fifteen minutes taking a shower, "Leni!"

I jump off the bed, dive for the door, and press my ear to it.

"Yes, dear?"

"I need you." It's a muffled whine.

"I'm right here, babe. What's up?"

"No, I *need* you. Like, *in* here. Now."

"Ash, I love you and all and you're totally the sister I never had, but save the peep show for later when you get freaky with my brother." The thought has me cringing, but her scream straightens me right up.

"Madeline! Get your ass in here!"

"Okay, okay." I don't want to mess with the bride on her big day, even though we're running behind schedule and should've been at the studio twenty minutes ago, so I bite my tongue and barge into the bathroom.

"Holy parting of the Red Sea! What the hell did you do? Murder someone while you were in the shower? I left you alone for ten minutes, Norman Bates—are you okay?" I rush over to her when I see the puddle of blood on the white tile floor.

She releases an exasperated sigh. "I'm fine, but my wedding night and the honeymoon is ruined and I don't have a single pad or tampon anywhere. Do you think you can send someone out to get some?"

There's no one to send. Her mother is already at the studio with my mother, her dad is with the guys at my parents' house, and the only one left is little ol' me. "This is why I told you a one-woman bridal party was not a good idea."

"Leni." Ashley tilts her head and scowls, wrapping the blood stained towel even tighter around her damp body.

"Your mother doesn't have anything lying around?" I rummage through the medicine cabinet and then under the sink.

"Don't you think I already looked? She went through menopause forever ago. There's nothing here."

I stand up and commence pacing. "Okay, okay. Let's think. Where are your underwear?" I scan the large bathroom and find a pile of neatly stacked clothes on a vanity bench.

I go to get them, but Ashley interrupts with another squeal, "No! We can't use those. They're my something blue. I don't want to ruin them." Ashley has tears in her eyes and a trail of blood leaking down her leg. If I didn't love her so much, I'd be totally grossed out.

"All right. Calm down. What to do. What to do." I tap my finger against my fidgeting lips, praying for a miracle.

"Give me yours," Ashley blurts out, an idea flashing across her worried face.

"Huh?"

"Your underwear. Give 'em to me. I'll wrap some toilet paper around them and we can grab what we need from the store on the way to the studio. Come on. Strip. Now, Len."

At first I'm quite appalled, but on second thought . . . this probably qualifies as something a maid-of-honor is expected to do when the bride is suddenly cursed with a visit from Aunt Flo the morning of her wedding.

"You're lucky they're clean." Without further thought, I remove my sweats and shimmy the white cotton down my legs.

"They won't be for long," Ashley sings, reaching out with grabby hands.

"You realize how disgusting this whole ordeal is, don't you?" Turning as Ashley drops the towel to get dressed, I put my own pants back on and uncontrollable giggles escape me.

"This is *so* not funny."

"It kind of is." I snort. "Just think, this will be some story for your grandkids."

"What? That their grandmother got the period of all periods and it ruined the happiest day of her life?"

"No, that their Great Aunt Leni came to the rescue and shared her granny panties with Granny Ashley in her time of desperation. And this day is *not* ruined. It didn't even start yet." I'm quick to make that point so Ashley doesn't let this minor setback spoil how happy she's supposed to be. How happy she's *been* up until this very moment.

After we're both dressed, I turn to her and notice that despite her having to ride the crimson wave on the most important day of her existence, she's glowing. If there was ever a person who knows how to make lemonade when life hands you lemons, it's Ashley. I freaking love this girl. "You look beautiful, you know?" I smile with pride.

"Beautiful? I'm a mess!" With no makeup, her hair thrown into a messy bun, and wedding-day nerves written across her flawless face, she's still the picture of perfection. My brother finally did something right when he met this girl and made her his. I can't imagine being his wife will be easy or that putting up with the entire Moore clan will be a walk in the park, but I thank my lucky stars every day that Ashley is a part of my life. And today she becomes a real-deal part of my family.

"You ready to get hitched, chica?" Before I get all emotional and allow the waterworks to get the best of me, I hook my arm in Ashley's and usher her out of the bathroom.

"Ready as I'll ever be."

I kiss her cheek and hug her close with one arm around her shoulder. "But first . . . let's plug you up."

"Only me." She brings her hand up to cover her eyes and shakes her head.

"Ash, have you met me and my shitty luck? The day of my wedding—if that day ever actually comes—I'll probably be blessed with a face full of zits, wind up with a nasty bout of explosive diarrhea, and even if it's the middle of the summer, there'll be a blizzard. Mark my words."

Ashley clicks her tongue, dismissing my negativity. "Oh, ye hath little faith, Leni. Your day will be perfect, because it's what you deserve. And speaking of *your* day, don't think I've been too preoccupied with this wedding to forget about what's going on with you and Lane. Once we get me some cooter corks, you've got lots of explaining to do. I'm not complaining about the wasted plate, but my maid-of-honor should have a hot date at her side tonight and I intend to get to the bottom of this before I walk down the aisle. So, while you make me pretty and keep me calm, I want to hear every last detail, including why you've been holding onto your phone like it's the Holy Grail all morning."

Leave it to this girl to bring everything to light on a day when all attention should be on her and her alone.

"Will you marry *me* instead of Reynold? I have a total girl crush on you, Ash." I wink, playfully nudging her arm.

"I'm flattered, but you and I both know that you and your heart belong with Lane. I'm as sure of you two as I am of me and Reynold. You'll see."

*Hope.* That funny four letter word sneaks up on me and spreads like wildfire. Ashley doesn't have a crystal ball and she certainly can't tell the future, but if I can just steal half of her optimism, all hope for me and Lane is definitely not lost.

# chapter

# thirty-one

JESUS, TALK ABOUT A BLUBBERING fool.

It started when Reynold nearly lost it the first time he saw Ashley as she walked down the aisle. He cried like a baby, which caused a domino effect of emotions amongst me, Mom, Dad and the rest of the guests with compassionate, beating hearts. Then, their hand-written vows to each other were so deeply heartfelt that my stomach coiled in knots at the fear that something this amazing might never come my way. I had him, but stupid me, I let him go, and no matter how happy I am for my baby brother and Ashley, I was feeling sorry for myself as they shared their first kiss as husband and wife.

But by the time the ceremony and cocktail hour are over, I'm enjoying myself the way any maid-of-honor should—in the damn bathroom, helping the bride pee.

"Are you done yet?" I ask from underneath three layers of crinoline.

"Yup. Just hold it up two more seconds while I switch out

my thingie so I don't die from TSS and make your brother a widower on our wedding night."

"I'm pretty sure TSS is a myth." I roll my eyes and turn the other way. She may be my sister now, but I didn't sign up for this shit. Tampon-changing and ass-wiping for a grown woman— not exactly my cup of tea, but that's what I'm here for.

When Ashley is done in the bathroom, she joins her husband off to the side where they prepare to be introduced to their guests and I make my way into the reception area to scope things out. For a wedding of this magnitude that was planned over only a few short months, everything is stunning.

The flowers Ashley chose are more elegant than anything I've ever seen in pictures of exotic, far-away gardens. The crystal chandeliers and diamond studded candles decorating the rustic space give it a vintage touch that's to die for. And the DJ— one of Rey's friends from college who travels around the world selling out venues of all types—could probably give Avicii and David Guetta a run for their money, if you ask me. I've only heard a taste of what he can do at the cocktail hour and already my feet are begging for more.

Securing my speech in the handy dandy pocket of my gown, I size up the place cards. I already know I'm sharing a table with my parents, grandparents, and Tatum, but when I notice Lane's name in calligraphy next to mine on the embossed stationary, I'm instantly bummed.

I could've sworn she told me she was fixing that. Maybe this is her way of digging the knife even deeper into the wound. That wound that no one wants to heal more than my sister-in-law. The wound that I wish would stop throbbing for the next six hours. I only want to have a good time and deal with this tomorrow. Is that too much to ask?

"Miss Moore?" A tap on my shoulder breaks me from my Lane spell.

"Yes?"

A tuxedoed man with white gloves and an ear piece flashes a genuine smile. "We're lining up the parents and the bridal party. The DJ will announce you shortly."

I nod and follow his outstretched hand to where everyone is huddled around the bride and groom. As I make my way over, a whistled catcall catches my attention and I make the mistake of peering over my shoulder.

*Hudson.*

"Mr. Wrong Place at the Wrong Time," I mumble to myself before waving curtly. I'm not sure why he gets under my skin the way he does. I guess I'm more on edge since my breakup with Lane, but as handsome, rich, and eligible as Hudson is, he's not the guy I want.

Hudson nods and waves back with a pompous smolder, but keeps his distance when his eyes reach beyond me to the line of people being organized by the maître d'. My heart grows heavy and my body tenses when I realize he'll be watching me all night and will no doubt discover that I'm here alone.

I grunt as I find the best man, our cousin Sally Boy, "This blows big, smelly, co—"

"Nice mouth. You kiss your mother with it?" Sal jokes, slicking back his enormous coif.

"Nice hair. You get any girls with it?"

Sally Boy bobs back and forth like Rocky Balboa pumping himself up for a fight. "Leni, babes, I actually have a date. Last I checked, *you* were going stag—again."

He may be dumber than a box of rocks, but he isn't wrong. "Yeah, whatever. Fuck off." There's nothing left to say, so I don't. I hook my arm in his and swallow my pride. As soon as I walk into that room, I'm beelining it to the bar. I plan on consuming enough alcohol to tranquilize a horse.

SALLY BOY'S DATE, JENNA, HAPPENS to be a great dance partner. She, Tatum, and I are killing it on the dance floor, and I'm not sure if it's the DJ's brilliant remixes or the bartender's promise to keep them flowing that have me feeling like an oversized combo of J. Lo, Beyoncé, and Madonna.

Jenna throws her arms above her head, bumping and grinding in my dance space. "Did anyone ever tell you that you could be—"

"If you say a plus-sized model she's going to impale you with her Valentinos," Tatum is quick to say exactly what's on my mind, but truth is, after all I've been through—short-lived, plus-size modeling career behind me—Jenna's would-be compliment doesn't piss me off the way something like that used to.

I laugh it off and continue fist pumping to the beat of the music.

"I'm sorry," Jenna shouts into my ear. "You're totally hot. I hope you know that."

I pull back from Jenna, ready to slap a sloppy but appreciative kiss on her cotton candy colored lips, but I'm met with a pair of warm, thick hands on my bare shoulders.

"She *is* totally hot, isn't she?"

Jenna looks like she's seen a ghost. No, scratch that. Jenna looks as though she's just laid eyes on Manhattan's most eligible bachelor. *Poor Sally Boy.*

I don't even have to turn around to know it's him. "You're a wedding crasher now?" I ask flippantly, continuing to dance with Jenna. Tatum is at the bar—again—probably ordering another round of shots. I have no desire to get tangled up in anything Hudson related tonight, but I'm pretty sure he didn't get the memo because Hudson spins me around and pulls me against his expensive suit.

My body traitorously submits to his and my limbs turn to mush when he says, "As of an hour ago, I own the place. I'm pretty sure I can do whatever I want."

*Gulp. Why does he have to be so arrogant? It's so goddamn sexy.* "Congratulations, but you owning the place doesn't mean you can dictate who I dance with."

"Do you know that for sure? Did you see the contracts? I might have made a special provision, just for tonight."

I wouldn't put it past him, but still. I was having fun with the girls. Dancing with Hudson or even talking to him feels like I'm cheating on the boyfriend I don't even have anymore.

Ignoring his dominant hands at my waist, I look up into his eyes to tell him I'm saving all my dances for someone else, but doing so is a huge mistake. Those eyes. So inviting. So captivating. So dilated.

And don't get me started on the DJ. He's switched things up from a booty slapping beat to a cheek-to-cheek melody as if he's luring me into the arms of this stubborn man.

"Why are you doing this to me?" I practically mewl. I'd like to think my legs are weak from the workout they've been getting on the dance floor, but unfortunately my boogieing is not the cause of their Jell-O like state. Not only is Hudson the total package, but he's a phenomenal dancer. Before I know it, my body is molded to his and my feet are following his lead.

"I'm not doing anything, Leni. I'm just here."

"It seems like you're always exactly where you shouldn't be."

"I'm an opportunist."

"No, you're obnoxious."

He pulls back from our embrace and brings his hand to his heart. He's trying to make it seem I've insulted him, but his smirk tells a different tale. "Why are you fighting this so hard? I don't see your man anywhere around. Either he let you down and dateless for your brother's wedding for some other selfish reason or he's not in the picture anymore."

I try with all my dwindling might not to answer him with a visual reaction. Instead of giving him the satisfaction he's looking for, I lie. "He had to fly back home for a family emergency. Believe me, he wants nothing more than to be here with me."

Hudson scans me from head to toe. I'll never get used to the way he eats me up with his eyes and then digests what he sees like I'm an extravagant, five course meal. "He's really missing out."

I'm flattered that Hudson finds someone as ordinary as I am so attractive and that he's gone to such great lengths to be in the same room as me, but it only makes me long for Lane that much more. I look down at our feet, in time, in sync, in such close proximity and the loss of Lane hits me like a ton of bricks all over again. "It's me who's missing out."

"Fuck! You love the dude, don't you?" Hudson stops swaying to the music and tips my chin up with his finger.

I take a deep breath and nod. "Yes. I really do. I love him." It's the first time the words have left my mouth and touched the air. It feels good to say them, only it sucks they're not spoken to the right person.

"I'm sorry I've been so annoying." Hudson's usually cavalier demeanor softens and for the first time since the night we hooked up, I see a boyish charm that makes me hope we can be friends.

I gently rub his arm and then veer him off the dance floor. "Don't be silly. You have no idea how your fruitless efforts have boosted my ego. People come into our lives for all different reasons. Your purpose has been served, my friend."

Hudson arches a brow and straightens his already well-placed tie. "Well, before you dismiss me . . . how about a celebratory shot?" He places one hand at my back and motions to the bar with the other.

I follow his lead and ask, "What exactly are we celebrating?"

"This is a wedding, isn't it?"

"Ah-duh." I feel kind of stupid, come to think of it. I was so wrapped up in my own love triangle of sorts that I nearly forgot why we're here in the first place.

Finally, at ease with the whole Hudson thing, I allow myself to relax and go with the flow. "Come on. I'll introduce you to my family. They're probably wondering who the debonair stranger dancing with the perpetual single girl is."

"I'd say let's give them something to talk about, but since your heart belongs to someone else, I'll behave."

I laugh as we approach the bar and a very tipsy Tatum to find that a line of shots has already been poured for a slew of us.

"Looky wha' the caz dragged in," Tatum slurs.

"Hello, again," Hudson smiles and nods at her, and then reaches for his tequila. "Don Julio, correct?" he asks the bartender, with a boss-man attitude.

"Yes, sir." News must travel fast. I guess the staff has already been informed that Hudson's the new suit calling the shots around here.

Hudson raises his glass and we all follow his lead. "To happiness!" Before he brings the glass to his lips he shoots me a wink that holds a different meaning than any of the others that have come before it.

"To happiness," I repeat, raising my glass and then gulping it down in one smooth swallow.

Everyone who's toasted slams their empties down on the bar and scurries for a lemon slice to chase away the burn of the alcohol. A familiar favorite, mixed with the beat of yet another favorite, swirls from the speakers. "No way! I love this song!" I throw my hands in the air and wince from the fire in my chest, but accept it for what it is. A natural, God given reaction to living life to the fullest. To having fun. To being happy.

The instant flood of emotions sends me into Hudson's arms for an impulsive, thank-you-for-being-a-friend hug. I close my eyes and wrap my arms around him. The visceral smile that paints my lips can't be mistaken for anything other than a moment of unabashed joy. There's just one thing missing. I wish Lane was here to experience it with me.

*Be careful what you wish for, Leni.*

When I open my eyes I'm stunned still. I'm not sure if it's an apparition, a joke, or a figment of my warped imagination but Lane is freaking here. At the wedding. In a tuxedo. Looking at me. In Hudson's arms.

# chapter

## thirty-two

"SHIT! SHIT! SHIT!" I CURSE, pushing off Hudson's chest and backing away from our embrace. Our extremely platonic embrace. An embrace that from the eyes of a scorned boyfriend probably looks anything *but* platonic, and very, very guilty.

"What's the matter?" Hudson asks and then catches my line of vision. He turns and sees Lane frozen in the doorway with his hands in his pockets as if he's deciding whether or not he's welcome. "Oh."

"Yeah. Oh."

"I thought he had a family emergency?"

"Uh. About that. I lied." I ignore Hudson's confusion and set my sights on Lane.

He's tense, his jaw visibly clenching even from this distance. With one more disappointed glance our way, he turns and starts in the opposite direction.

"I have to go to him." I don't bother with an explanation or an excuse. I refuse to let more miscommunication or assumptions screw this up.

As I hurry through the crowd of clueless relatives and random guests, it feels as though I'm running in slow motion and can't get to Lane fast enough. Like in those terrifying dreams where you're trying your absolute hardest to get away from something but you're eerily motionless. Only this time, I want my fears to catch up with me and allow me to stare them right in the face. Fears. Hopes. Wounds. Desires. Lane encompasses them all and I've never been more ready to confront them than I am in this moment.

"Lane! Wait!" I call out when I enter the vestibule. His back is toward me, already one foot out the door to the garden where the cocktail hour was held. I'm so tired of seeing this version of him—leaving. It's time he knows how badly I want him to stay. For good.

"Please, Lane. Don't go." This time he stops walking but still doesn't turn to face me.

I walk over to him, catching my breath and gathering some modicum of composure. Reaching out to touch him, I think twice and retreat. "I'm so happy you're here."

"Really? Are you? Because it certainly didn't look that way." His shoulders gracefully rise and fall with long, deep breaths.

"I know what it looked like, but—" I won't do this to his back. Face to face. Truth. That's how this has to be done. "Please look at me," I plead, placing a quivering hand on his shoulder.

This gets him to turn to me, but the pain on his face makes me wish he hadn't. "You are such a hypocrite. You find out I'm not perfect so you run to someone who is."

His words sting, but I deserve them. Even though they're the furthest thing from the truth. I peer down at my peep-toe shoes and summon the courage to do this right without sticking my big toe in the kisser. "Will you come outside with me and let me explain?"

"Why should I?" he snaps. "You didn't give me the decency

to explain myself when you jumped to conclusions and let your emotions run high. Maybe this isn't worth it, Leni. Maybe the two of us just aren't meant to be. It seems we do more leaving and lying than anything else."

It's a sad reality, but it doesn't have to be this way. "You're right. I don't deserve the chance to explain myself. I probably don't even deserve *you*, but if you give me a chance, I can make this right. All of it. That's all I want."

His eyes flutter and then close. His nostrils flare as he inhales and then releases a weighty breath. He opens his mouth to speak but clamps it shut as his eyes go wide.

"Is everything all right out here, Leni?"

I spin around to find Hudson eye-balling Lane as he rocks back and forth on the heels of his Ferragamos.

"Blackman. Perfect timing, as always." Lane rakes his fingers through his hair and huffs.

I wave a dismissive hand and shake my head. "We're fine. Could you please leave us alone to talk?" I don't want to be a jerk now that Hudson and I have finally come to an understanding, but his presence is making matters worse and there's already enough evidence to persecute me in the court of She's Fucked.

Hudson must sense my frustration because he nods and offers, "Of course. If you'd like some privacy, there's an unoccupied bridal suite back that way." He smiles at me but it fades slightly when he returns his gaze to Lane.

I mouth a silent *thank you* and turn to Lane for approval.

"Fine," he finally says, his features relaxing as he takes stock of the amicable vibe between Hudson and me.

"The room's yours for as long as you need it." Hudson gestures in the direction of the suite. "Would you like me to let someone know where you are so they don't worry?"

"Just tell Tatum that Lane is here. She'll understand." I offer a tight smile, grab Lane by the hand, and start walking.

When Hudson is out of earshot, Lane asks, "Why is he

offering up the room like he owns the joint?"

"Well, he kind of does. He bought the place today. That's why he's here."

"You mean—he's not here with you?"

"Nope. I told you it's not what you think."

"I'm so damn confused. I've never been more confu—"

"I tend to have that effect on people. Come on. This must be it. I'll explain everything."

TEN MINUTES AFTER I'VE GIVEN him the entire rundown about Hudson, Lane is out of the dark and way more open to hearing me out. "When I saw you with him, you don't know what that did to me. I had to pull it together or I would've made a very unnecessary scene in front of your whole family. Luckily my temper isn't as bad as what I thought I saw."

"That's one of the things I love about you," I admit, palming Lane's clean-shaven cheek in my hand. I fear he'll back away from my touch, but he doesn't and that sparks a hope inside me that was snuffed out a few days ago.

Cupping his hand over mine, Lane's eyes drift over my body and then return to mine. "I've missed you so much. I know it's only been days, but when you left, and then didn't answer my calls, I didn't know what to do."

"I'm so sorry I reacted the way I did. It's my own fault for letting my past get the best of me. I know now that my insecurities are my own worst enemy. You couldn't have known that and you did nothing wrong. I'm the only one at fault here and I'll apologize a million times if I have to just to prove how much—" I can't hold the words back anymore. I have to tell him. He needs to know. "I love you, Lane."

His eyes flicker with something beautiful. I know. He knows. I'm certain from that look alone that he's in love with me, too. But I can't expect him to jump back into the way things were before I screwed everything up with my issues.

Lane swallows a large, visible lump. For a moment I expect him to succumb to the moment and pick up where we left off, but his gaze trails off to the far end of the room and my stomach sinks when he doesn't repeat the same phrase. "How can you love me when you don't know all of me?"

*Oh, Lane. Why did I ever walk away from you?* "I *want* to know all of you. I'll never turn my back on you again. I ran for the wrong reasons. Not because of what I saw or who you are."

"Who I *was*," he corrects.

It's obvious we're more alike than we even know. If anyone understands how painful it is to hold on to a version of yourself that's defined you for the better part of your life, it's me. By some tiny miracle, I've finally found a way to accept who I am. I'd love to be the person to help Lane along that journey, too. "Tell me about him. I'm ready to hear all about it. Because, Lane, no matter what those scars mean or who you were in the past, I am in love with the man you are right now. And I don't know how or why you chose me, but if you give me another chance to be yours, I'll never question it again."

His acceptance is wordless, his forgiveness is a kiss, and his confession of love is his embrace. Lane's mouth crashes against mine and his hands tug at the loose curls dangling from my up-do. I almost—*almost*—forgot how perfect our lips move together. No one and nothing can convince me that this man was not made for me and I for him. Not even the secrets he kept from me about his scars.

"I love you, too, Leni," he whispers against my lips and brings his hands to my face. "I'm sorry I didn't tell you sooner about the surgery and my weight loss. I was so wrapped up in falling for you that I almost forgot I ever had those skeletons in my closest. I wasn't lying when I told you that you make all of that disappear.

"Before you walked out, I was certain that if I'd met you back in Tuscarora you would've loved me for me, even at my heaviest, before the Lap Band. You have no idea how I wish I had known you when I was eighteen. Things might have been different, but—I don't know. I wasn't happy for a long time.

"My weight was an issue all through adolescence. And the kids weren't nice. I was picked on, name-called, stereotyped; think of the worst and that's what I went through. The whole ordeal prevented me from living the teenage-boy dream. Sports, dates, popularity. I wish I could do it all over. See myself differently and not let any of that negativity get in the way of being *normal*." Lane looks down at the ground for a split second and then returns his eyes to mine. Empathy isn't always a good thing. I feel as if I'm reliving a lot of my own childhood by listening to him. I don't say anything because I sense there's more he'd like to finally get off his chest.

"I can't say there was one particular breaking point that pushed me to making my decision. It was more a culmination of everything I'd gone through and not being strong enough to deal with the ridicule anymore. I was ashamed of the weight. I wanted it gone. Quick and easy. I couldn't be stuck inside a body that was hindering me from being the *real* person hiding beneath the fat all those years. Maybe if I'd known you then, you could've helped me do things differently, but in the long run, I'm happy with my decision. And I'm happy that our paths crossed when they did because you made me believe that the person I am on the inside has nothing to do with the person I am on the outside."

"You do know that had we met all those years ago we'd both be larger than life, and not in a good way. I'm a pretty bad influence when it comes to food."

Lane laughs through his nose and then licks his lips as he brushes a strand of hair off my face. "You're nothing but an amazing influence, Leni. You fill me with a happiness I never thought I'd find."

It seems so simple when he says it that way, but on paper I still feel like we're the mismatched couple of the century. "But you're so healthy and fit, and from the outside you'd never know you used to be heavy. I still can't wrap my head around why you want to be with me. Don't you think you can do better?"

With a strong grip on my shoulders, Lane stares into my eyes with purpose. "I can't possibly do better when I already have the best. When I look at you, I see a gorgeous, funny, talented woman with a heart of gold and the purest of love to give. And no matter what you believe, I never settled when it came to you. You're crazy to ever think I could love you by default."

This erases any doubts I once had but also makes me feel terrible for running away when he needed me most. "I'm so sorry I dredged up old hurts. My reaction was callous and I'll never forgive myself for walking out on you the way I did. I have a tendency to blame my weight on everything that goes wrong in my life, if you haven't noticed that yet."

Lane shakes his head and rolls his eyes. "That needs to stop. Now. I can't have my girlfriend thinking of herself as anything other than the knockout she is. I say we chalk this whole thing up to one big misunderstanding and forget it ever happened. I'm ready to leave the past where it belongs and move on. What do you think?"

*What do I think?* I think I'm getting off too easy, but mama didn't raise no fool. I'll take it! "I think that sounds even better than McDonald's announcing their all-day breakfast menu."

"That good, huh?" Lane laughs, pulling me against him. "Can you promise me something?"

"Anything," I say, certain that no request from Lane is too much to fulfill.

"No more lies. No more secrets. And definitely no more of that *I'm not good enough for you* crap. You could never be someone's consolation prize, babe. You're the first place trophy.

Every, single bit of you."

The meaning behind that is not lost on me, especially when his hand travels down the curve of my spine and grabs a big chunk of my booty.

"All of me, huh? You sure about that? I have a tendency to teeter back and forth more than Oprah did in the 90's."

"I'm positive." He smiles. "You're stronger than your insecurities, Leni. I guess that's something we both have to keep reminding each other."

*Well, I'll be.* "Did Ashley get to you with her Joel Osteen obsession?"

"Joel who?"

"Never mind." I smack a kiss on his delectable lips and let my cares evaporate into nothingness as two lost souls get lost in each other. I don't care if it's divine intervention or Mercury in retrograde, Lane plus me equals perfection.

A knock on the door disrupts our reunion, forcing me to remember where we are. "Who is it?" I call out as Lane wipes away any evidence from my lips.

"It's Mr. and Mrs. Moore. Can we come in?" Hearing Ashley announce it that way brings this whole wonderful day into perspective.

"Just a minute," I answer, looking at Lane.

"I guess we should let them in. It is *their* wedding, after all." Lane flashes his dimples and straightens his very dapper bow tie. I could just eat him up. *Famous last words for a chubby chick.*

"Yeah. I guess we should, even if I'd totally blow this taco stand in a heartbeat to finally be alone with you again."

Lane sweetly pecks the tip of my nose. "Leni, we have the rest of our lives to spend together. Tonight we celebrate the beginning of *their* happily ever after."

My eyes light up and my heart somersaults in my chest at the sound of his charming implication. "Are you insinuating that you and I will get a happily ever after, too?"

"When you spend a lifetime hoping to feel half of what I feel for you, you kind of know when it's the real deal. I can't promise perfection, and we certainly know a lot about imperfections, but baby, you're worth the wait."

I nuzzle against Lane and the warmth of our blossoming love surrounds me. "Hey. Was that a fat pun?"

"Huh. I didn't think of it that way, but yeah, sure. That weight, too."

Lane stands to open the door and takes my hand in his. "Hey, maybe we should pay a visit to that tree tomorrow. Carve *Leni and Lane forever* in it, or something."

"I'm down for that. It's a special tree, isn't it?"

"The special-est. And it's ours." I tighten my grip around his hand and pull him close.

"And you're mine."

"You bet your cute ass I am. Every single inch of me."

# *epilogue*

## *one year later*

IF YOU'RE LOOKING FOR THE part where Lane proposed, we got married, had two point five kids, rescued a Golden Retriever on doggie death row, and I lost fifty pounds . . . keep looking, honey. It ain't here.

Since the night of my brother's wedding, everything pretty much stayed the same. Well, for me, at least.

Ashley and Reynold bought a beautiful home in New Jersey. My parents followed shortly after, settling two towns over in a fifty-five and over development when they found out they'd soon be grandparents to the second coming of Christ. Tatum and I nicknamed my unborn niece or nephew that when Rey and my overbearing mother went absolutely overboard with anything having to do with the baby. In fact, Tatum shouldn't talk because shortly after she started dating Hudson, she convinced him to pull some of his multi-million-dollar land development strings to erect a state-of-the art playground and custom treehouse on the four acres of land surrounding my brother's new mini-mansion. The kid isn't even born yet and it already needs for nothing. Uncle Lane and I plan on spoiling the kid rotten, too.

After we said our I love yous and put the past behind us, Lane and I continued to get to know each other, flaws and all, and my weight yo-yoed back and forth so much it gave me whiplash. Turns out, when a woman is truly happy and in love, she tends to eat more, work out less, and pack on a few extra pounds. Whatevs. It's all good because it also turns out that when a woman is truly happy and in love, none of those things mean diddly squat.

Not to worry, though, I haven't completely gone to hell in a hand basket with my old habits. I've managed to make Jane and Mandy a permanent fixture in my life, even if they've given up on me at least twenty times in the last year. Those two charge a pretty penny for their notorious training sessions. I'd like to think I'm getting my money's worth by giving them a run for it.

And speaking of running, Lane and I still do it often. In fact, after we moved in together and I got used to his haphazard schedule at the hospital, we decided to dedicate at least three mornings a week to the place where we first met and collided head on with our beautiful fate.

"Hey! Someone else carved their names on *our* tree!" Two days ago, Lane + Leni 4ever inside an oversized heart was the only thing marring the bark of the tree where it all began.

I rush over to the tree and Lane follows. Together, we trace the outline of the newly carved names.

"Huh. Looks like we have to share with Stella and Jack now."

"I don't like sharing. You know that."

"You don't like sharing your food, but you never said anything about not wanting to share your good fortune."

"Listen, Mr. Optimistic, I get what you're trying to say, but this is *our* special tree. No one else's. I was hoping you'd ask me to be your wife under it one day. And then we'd bring our kids here once in a while to tell them all about how Mommy and Daddy fell in love over a concussion. And to take the dream even further, they'd continue the Sheffield tradition by bringing their special someone here and carving *their* names in it when the time was right. But now this Stella and Jack went ahead and—I don't know—cheapened it all up."

"Babe, that's all really sweet and I can make every one of those wishes come true, but there is nothing cheap about what we got." Lane wraps his arms around me and presses his sweaty torso against my even sweatier back.

I do have to give it to him there. Cheap is no longer a part of our vocabulary. Ever since Siobhan called on me to be *the* top model for the plus-sized collection that's taking the fashion world by the balls, let's just say . . . life is sweet. Like warm chocolate lava cake topped with rocky road ice cream sweet. Who would've ever imagined my big ass would be my biggest asset? I guess being skinny isn't always how the better half live.

I lean into Lane's embrace and surrender to the calming effect he will forever bewitch me with. Even on days when I feel down on myself for giving up on the weight loss goal that once dictated my every breath, Lane is sure to remind me that we have each other and everything else is an extra helping we weren't banking on.

Pulling me back onto the track by the arm, Lane starts to jog in place. "You have time for one more lap or does Raven need you again today?" I still moonlight at the studio whenever Raven asks because makeup will always and forever be my true passion. Something about giving women the gift of beauty empowers me and I never plan on letting go of that ego boost.

I join Lane in a steady trot past our tree, and tell him my plans for the day. "Nope. No work today. I arranged it that way. After our run, some breakfast, and a nice long shower, I was hoping we could spend some quality time together—tangled in the sheets."

"Oh, that sounds like the perfect way to waste the day away."

"Waste not, want not." I giggle.

"You sound more and more like Confucius every day, Leni. Do I need to hide your Joel Osteen books from you again?"

"Bullshit! You mean, do you need to hoard them for yourself again?"

"What? Can you blame me? The dude knows his shit."

"That he does," I agree. I can't call myself a believer in faith, but I am most certainly a believer in love. "After all, even though I have you, he taught me to love myself and the rest will follow."

"Smart guy, that Joel. If we ever get to meet him, remind me to thank him for knocking some sense into my stubborn girlfriend."

"Babe, you're the stubborn one. Stop giving him all the credit and own it. If it weren't for you I'd still be a mopey, overweight makeup artist, dreaming her life away."

Lane flashes me that look—the glare that silently warns me to shut my trap and accept that to him I'm the *perfect* size. "Madeline Moore, don't make me tell you again."

"Ah, come on. I like hearing you say it."

"You're insufferable, you know that?"

"You bring out the best in me. Now, say it."

"Fine," he huffs, although I know he loves his corny catch phrase as much as I do.

I bite my lower lip at the sight of his dimples, feeling like the luckiest chick on the planet.

Out of breath from the pace, the bright morning sun glistening off the perspiration on his forehead, Lane clears his throat as if he's about to take center stage. Kind of fitting since the moment I laid eyes on him, he took center stage of my heart. "God made you this way so I'd have more of you to love. There. You happy?"

Happy is an understatement, but he already knows that. "Happier than a fat kid with a Twinkie."

# The End

# acknowledgments

I'D LIKE TO START OFF by mentioning that getting this book "right" was by no means a cake walk. I was worried about offending people or coming across as uninformed, but I assure you I understand Leni's struggles as if they were my own. Growing up, I was a geeky, gawky, scrawny kid. A late bloomer, an easy target to poke fun at, a mess of frizzy hair and braces that made it impossible to feel pretty. I'm not telling you this to garner sympathy or pity—I grew up and everything fell into place according to my wildest dreams—*but* I did suffer from self-doubt and allowed my insecurities to bring me down. Hell, I still do! And I want to know what woman *hasn't* been in that position? If it's you, then kudos, because I admire you for loving yourself. But in reality, most women can relate to Leni because of some flaw or lack of confidence they carry within them. This book was written for all of those women. The girls who think they're too fat or too skinny, too blonde or too plain, too flat-chested or too curvy, too nerdy or too flaky, too *anything* you've ever let bother you. *Love yourself and the rest will follow.* It's so much easier said than done, but if you take anything from Leni's story, let it be that. Be proud of who you are and what you want to be. The world is a lot more interesting because we're not shaped from cookie-cutter standards. Own it, baby! I'm learning to live with that motto in mind myself.

As always, I want to thank my family and friends for being an incredible support system. You have no idea how just being a part of my life has been a blessing, book related and otherwise. To my husband and daughters especially (and let's not forget Rocco, the pooch), there aren't sufficient words to tell you how much I love you and what you mean to me. Thank you for putting up with me while I follow a few more of my crazy dreams and for rooting me on along the way.

There's a posse that comes along with every book, and I'm so freaking proud of the entourage I've got in my corner. To my amazing, hardworking betas who helped me create the best balance possible for Leni and Lane—Ella Stewart, Janice Owen, Laura Murphy, Meredith Lynn Patton, Shannon Mummey, Shaye Walker, and Trish Mint—thank you from the bottom of my heart for letting me pick your brain and moan and groan when things weren't working the way I planned. Each of you gave me feedback and encouragement that pushed me to continue even when I wanted to trash the whole darn thing. I don't know how I would have completed this without you. Thank you to my cover artist, Najla Qamber, for helping me get this cover just right. I love the end result and it ties into the story perfectly! To my editor, Brenda Letendre, for fixing my oopsies and still letting my voice shine through. To my proofreader, Shawna Gavas, for being *the* fine tooth comb and for making me laugh while I went through her notes. To my formatter, Christine Borgford, for never letting me down and always cranking out perfection. To Linda Russell, who I couldn't live without for so many different reasons. Throughout the years of books and releases and everything in between, I've come to consider you all friends—every day, chat-it -out, pick-me-up-when-I'm-down, help-me-in-ways-I didn't-even-know-I needed-help friends— thanks for dealing with my ups and downs and for being an extra special part of my team!

To the Gotta Have Faithers, YOU! You guys are nothing short of FANTASTIC! I feel like I'm home when I'm in my group, and that's all because of the loving and friendly environment you've created for me just by being there. Daily shenanigans, complaints about kids and hubbies, Logan tolerating our man crushes and eye candy, manbuns, memes, and so much more. Thank you for making me feel loved. I hope I've given you a place to be yourself and have fun.

I'd also like to give a special shout out to the Indie Chicks Rock gang, the Indie Chicks Rockin' Readers Group, my fellow author friends, and all the bloggers who have supported this book and the others that have come before. You make the book world and the indie community a better place! I've never understood the reason to compete and compare when the world has such varying degrees of talent to share. Here's to keeping things drama free and fun for all!

And lastly, to the readers. Without you, our words would go unread and unloved. Thank you for taking the chance on me and letting my characters into your hearts. We all know what it's like to have an endless TBR pile, so when you choose a Faith Andrews book out of all the others . . . priceless! As an author, it's one thing to create these stories in your head and be happy with getting them down on paper, but to have someone reach out and tell you that those words, or characters touched you in some way . . . that's nothing short of magic. I encourage you to leave reviews for the books you read. Every opinion, reaction, comment, or criticism means something to us.

If you liked Moore to Love, please check out my other books. You'll always find a piece of me in the pages of my stories, so consider each one a way to get to know me better. Happy reading!

# about the author

Faith Andrews lives in New York with her husband, two beautiful daughters, and a furry Yorkie son, Rocco. If she isn't listening to Mumford & Sons or busy being a Dance Mom, her nose is in a book or her laptop. She's a sucker for a happily ever after and believes her characters are out there living one somewhere…

Website:

*www.authorfaithandrews.com*

Email:

*faithandrewsauthor@aol.com*

Facebook:

*www.facebook.com/authorfaithandrews*

Twitter:

*twitter.com/jessicafaith919*

# books by
# faith andrews

DREAMS SERIES
*Man of my Dreams*
*Back to You*
*After the Storm*

GRAYSON SIBLING SERIES
*Keep Me*
*Keep Her*

FATE SERIES
*Feel Again*
*First Came You*
*Freeing Destiny*

Made in the USA
Middletown, DE
07 August 2016